ABOUT THE AUTHOR

When Chris Behrsin isn't out exploring the world, he's behind a keyboard writing tales of dragons and magical lands. Born into the genre through a steady diet of Terry Pratchett, his fiction fuses a love for fantasy and whimsical plots with philosophy and voyages into the worlds of dreams.

You can learn more about his fiction and download two free books at his website, chrisbehrsin.com.

facebook.com/chrisbehrsin

x.com/chrisbehrsin

goodreads.com/cbehrsin

bookbub.com/authors/chris-behrsin

BOOKS BY CHRIS BEHRSIN

DRAGONCAT SERIES

A Cat's Guide to Bonding with Dragons

A Cat's Guide to Meddling with Magic

A Cat's Guide to Saving the Kingdom

A Cat's Guide to Questing for Treasure

A Cat's Guide to Travelling through Portals

A Cat's Guide to Vanquishing Evil

A Cat's Guide to Dreaming of Fairies

A Cat's Guide to Dealing with Destiny

A Cat's Guide to Serving a Warlock (Prequel Novella)

SECICAO BLIGHT SERIES

Sukina's Story (Prequel Novel)

Dragonseer

Dragonseers and Bloodlines

Dragonseers and Automatons

Dragonseers and Evolution

More works available at: https://chrisbehrsin.com

A CAT'S GUIDE TO QUESTING FOR TREASURE

CHRIS BEHRSIN

Copyediting by Wayne M. Scace
Proofreading by Carol Brandon
Cover Design Layout by Chris Behrsin

ISBN: 978-1-915886-03-3 (paperback)
ISBN: 978-1-915866-09-5 (hardcover)
ISBN: 978-1-915886-15-6 (e-book)

Published by Worldwalkers Publishing Ltd

To Mr Crawford, the teacher who first inspired my development as a writer.

PROLOGUE

Once, I would have stated without question that cats aren't made for flying. I wouldn't have thought cats were meant for casting magic spells either, or for saving a kingdom from imminent destruction. Such ideas would have never crossed my mind. But an irascible dragon, a destiny foretold by a crystal and its gift of magic, and the Kingdom of Illumine proved me wrong.

Mind you, when I was teleported across time and space from my cosy life in South Wales into another dimension and the clutches of the evil warlock, Astravar, it was clear things were going to be different. After becoming a dragon rider, defeating a demon dragon and a demon Maine Coon, I managed to thwart that evil warlock and send him back to where he belonged. I've already told that story once, and I haven't got the energy for telling it all over again.

After all that, we lived in a time of what the humans call "peace" with the remaining six warlocks – a concept rather strange to us cats who never tended to go to war in the first place. I definitely preferred peace to war. There was more tasty food to eat, more places to explore, more ways for a cat to be a cat.

I went out for plenty of flights on my dragon Salanraja's back. She demanded this of me, so the bond didn't weaken between us. If there's one thing I've learned in this new world that I've had to adapt to, it's that you don't want to ignore a dragon's demands.

But though I had a staff capable of producing the most powerful magic in all the seven dimensions, I had no idea how to use it.

To elaborate, I knew only one trick with it, and that was how to produce the red beam of light that I'd used to vanquish Astravar. This beam, it turned out, only worked on warlocks or magical beings created through dark magic. I couldn't, for example, use it to send a noisy dog to sleep or magic up food out of thin air. Now, given that there were no warlocks to defeat, no golems, Manipulators, bone dragons, or those ugly bat-buzzard *aeriosaur* creatures from the Fifth Dimension to fight, my newfound abilities were utterly useless.

In the meantime, other dragon riders had magic in their staffs that could light fires, make it rain, make trees grow, soothe nightmares, or cool down a scalding hot meal. Stuff that's useful for times of peace...

I had none of their skills, and I wasn't one of them. So, what could I do, but go back to being a cat?

Not to say that there's anything wrong with being a cat. Especially when you're a Bengal, a descendant of the great Asian leopard cat. Three months of peace, in fact, and I think the humans, and perhaps even my dragon, Salanraja, were starting to forget what a mighty cat I was.

Then again, perhaps I was starting to forget who exactly I was. It's on that note which this story starts...

THE GREAT BARRIER

It was to be our final day of 'peace' when I sat nestled between Salanraja's spikes, silken clouds streaming by below us. Two rows of these spikes formed a corridor that looked a little like the inverted rib cage of an elephant protruding out from between the red scales on her back. The air smelled of the rain deposited by the thick raincloud that we chased towards the horizon. The sun shone through the airborne droplets, casting a rich double rainbow.

Especially on the longer flights, I couldn't get over the nausea and the excruciating stiffness in my legs. Not to mention the burning hunger. There wasn't anything to eat up on my dragon's back, despite my demands that my dragon rider kin should install a snack bowl with food fit for a mighty Bengal cat. A few crunchy bites might have helped settle my stomach somewhat.

This time, we weren't alone. In fact, we were on a 'field trip'. A special event for the humans, it seemed. In other words, a pointless moment in their lives that meant nothing to cats like me.

The Great Driars Yila, Lonamm, Brigel – the three elder dragon riders who ran Dragonsbond Academy – led the way. From here, I could hear the swishing of their dragons' wings, ever so exaggerated, as if they wanted to communicate to the other dragons exactly who was in charge. Our old mentor, Driar Aleam, flew on his massive white dragon, Olan, directly behind them.

A good hundred students on their dragons followed in their wake. It was only the first-year students, mind. The second years, including High Prefect Lars, Prefect Asinda, and Prefect Calin were back at the academy studying for their pre-graduation exams.

We'd been flying for a good two hours from Dragonsbond Academy, without any dangers. Since I'd defeated Astravar a few months ago, life had been quiet. The remaining six warlocks had signed a treaty at Cimlean Palace, promising that they'd keep their magical creatures at home in the Darklands and not cause any more trouble. Just to be sure, King Garmin had summoned his White Mages on their unicorns to create a massive magical barrier between Illumine Kingdom and the Wastelands.

Only the warlocks could pass through, as the treaty still allowed them to gather magical crystals from the Versta Caverns in the Crystal Mountains, which they needed for their work. But King Garmin's Dragon Corps always accompanied the warlocks on such journeys, and ensured they never gathered more than they needed.

"*There it is,*" Salanraja said, rudely interrupting me from my daydream. "*Isn't it beautiful, Bengie?*"

I growled back at her. "*I thought we agreed you were to start calling me Ben...*"

"*I'm sorry... Old habits die hard.*"

"*Well, Salamander, you're going to have to break them.*"

Salanraja whipped her head back to glare at me. "*How many times have I told you I hate being compared to a tiny lizard.*"

"*Salamanders aren't lizards... Lizards don't swim in ponds.*" In all honesty, I'd never seen a lizard, but the two Savannah cats back home had told me plenty about them.

"I don't care what they are. Stop calling me one."

"No," I said. *"Not until you learn your lesson."*

"Or maybe I'll eat you first," Salanraja said. *"Come to think of it, I've never tried cat before..."*

"You do that, and our bond will be broken, and it will be ever so terrible for you, remember."

"I'm not sure what can be more terrible than your incessant whining. Anyway, your negativity is spoiling the view..."

She turned her head back towards the barrier. I looked up to get a glimpse at what Salanraja seemed so impressed by. It was nothing special. Just the sky seemed a bit darker above the horizon, and streaks of white light occasionally flickered across it. The Great Barrier emitted a low and annoying humming sound, that reminded me of those loud and noisy electrical fans that my master and mistress liked to use during hot summers back in South Wales.

The Great Barrier was exactly what we were flying to see today... "To remind you," Driar Yila had said in our last assembly, "what exactly you are all training for. Times of peace don't last forever, you know, and this is our first line of defence if the warlocks ever decide to break the treaty. Because every adult in Illumine Kingdom knows that one day they will."

As often happens with endeavours that humans like to get all excited about, I failed to see the point. Still, Salanraja seemed to be looking forward to it. She'd told me that this work of magic was the greatest thing the King's White Mages had ever created, and we should be proud of what those funny men in their white cloaks on their unicorns had magicked up.

It wasn't that I didn't trust the White Mages, but I certainly didn't trust the unicorns. Humans seemed to think they were so pure and so innocent, but I saw them for what they were – overglorified horses.

We cats had a creed, you see. Never trust a horse. If you got in front of one, they might trample, or bite you, and if you got behind them, they might kick you in the face. The old Savannah cats in my neighbourhood told me this applied to zebras as well, and – I would tell them when I finally saw them again – unicorns too.

"We've come here to see this?" I asked.

"What's wrong with it?"

"It's not that there's anything wrong with it. There's just not anything particularly special about it."

Plumes of smoke rose from Salanraja's nostrils in front of me. *"Do you know how many White Mages it takes to keep this going?"*

"I..." I tried to recall the figure from Driar Lonamm's lessons, but I think I might have been asleep when she stated it.

"One-thousand and fifty-three," Salanraja said. *"Posted at strategic intervals along the length of the barrier."*

I growled. Numbers didn't impress me much. I never had the head for them. *"Do you know how many salmon are in the Atlantic Ocean?"*

"I don't..."

"More than enough to feed all the cats in the Fourth Dimension. I also hear they leap up waterfalls. Now that would be something I'd love to see. As long as someone caught some to roast on a campfire later."

"Do you always have to make this about you and your stomach, Bengie? Can't you just appreciate the view?"

"Ben," I said, and both Salanraja and I said no more.

Rather she lifted her head slightly and wheeled down towards some smoke coming out from a copse of birch trees below. All the dragons around us had started to descend, almost leaving Salanraja behind.

We could see the Great Barrier much closer now. It almost looked solid, like a sheet of blue glass that someone had stretched across the horizon. It reached so high that it seemed to vanish into the haze. It kept the dark magic out from the Wastelands beyond and, apparently, kept us all safe.

I peered over the edge of Salanraja's back to see what we were descending towards. That's when I saw him. They'd warned us that he would be leading this field trip. Prince Arran, the king's nephew and pompous leader of the King's Dragon Corps stood warming his hands by the fire.

He didn't hold my attention for long, though, because there was something even more alarming down there.

My gaze shot over to another figure sitting not far away from the fire, beating its tail against the ground, its long tongue hanging out of its mouth. Its wide eyes seemed to portray innocence. They made it look as if it was offering its loyalty to every human and dragon about to land. No doubt that 'loyalty' extended to Prince Arran too.

But I knew such creatures were even worse than horses. Every cat's mother taught that to her litter, and mine had repeated it every day so we wouldn't forget it.

"If there's just one creature you never trust," she'd said. "Make sure it's a dog."

BOMBS AWAY

The worst thing about dogs is how they absolutely stink. I could smell this one before we landed, and now its stench was invading my space.

It didn't look like the dogs we had in our neighbourhood back in South Wales. Instead, it had long droopy ears, and a squat body with legs so short I wondered how it could walk on them. Its shaggy fur cascaded down from its back like polluted water. It was the colour of the chicken liver that the master and mistress back in South Wales used to put out in a bowl for me when they felt I deserved a treat.

Hissing, my back arched, and hackles raised, I watched the dog run around the students, fawning for attention as each one dismounted their dragons.

The young woman I trusted the most, Initiate Ange – standing beside her Sapphire dragon, Quarl – laughed and bent down to pat him on the head, much to my annoyance. She had short brown hair, and slightly buck teeth, although she was pretty despite this. Other than Driar Aleam, she was the first human in the First Dimension to treat me as cats should be treated.

Her innate kindness, I guess, was why the crystals had chosen her as a leaf mage. She was also incredibly hard working. During our library sessions at Dragonsbond Academy I don't think I'd ever been able to tear her attention away from her book, no matter how much I meowed, rubbed my nose against her hand, and jumped on the table to tell her that I was much more important than the words on the page. She would simply pull the book away and turn away from me, until the owl-like librarian noticed me on the table, hissed at me so loudly that she sounded like a swan with a megaphone, and waved her arms frantically until I retreated to my place on the chair.

The lad I wanted to be her boyfriend, but who hadn't quite sealed the deal yet, Initiate Rine, stood a good several paces away from Ange, his hair blowing gently in the warm summer breeze. He whistled to the dog, who snapped its head around, then bounded over to make another new 'friend'.

Rine crouched to let the dog lift its front paws onto his shoulders. In response, the dog licked his face. I'd never seen Rine as particularly handsome, but human girls seemed to, and Rine revelled in this. He'd grown his mouse-brown hair just as long as Ange's now, coming down to his shoulders in loose waves.

I'd thought after he'd dumped his ex-girlfriend Bellari and I'd defeated Astravar, when I'd seen him holding Ange's hand, that they'd become a couple. Instead, Rine had decided he wanted to be single for a while. Which didn't seem to mean being single at all, but instead having a different girlfriend every week.

The dog then padded over to Seramina – the youngest human in our party and a dark mage just like me and Aleam. Seramina also knew mind and destiny magic, though she practiced the latter less and less, saying it was better not to know the future. She had flowing platinum blonde hair, that she never seemed to want to cut.

She wore perfume that smelled like snowdrops, and sometimes when she was angry, you could see fire blazing behind her eyes.

Seramina was Astravar's daughter and hence a warlock by birth, though she'd only discovered these facts recently. A vision in the ghost realm had also foretold that she might destroy the world during a battle with the remaining six warlocks, by using her staff to rend the ground apart. No one who had seen this vision – namely, me, Ange, Rine, and Seramina herself – had mentioned this to anyone. Besides, visions don't necessarily come true. There are many possible futures and what we saw was only one possibility.

Seramina didn't seem to want to give the dog as much attention as Rine and Ange. She simply looked down at it with her grey eyes and gave it a dreamy smile as it tried to nuzzle its nose between her legs. At least Seramina had it right. This was exactly how dogs should be treated. They needed to learn how to be independent, just like cats.

"*I still don't understand why you hate dogs so much,*" Salanraja said as she lowered her tail and raised her shoulders to try and coax me off her back.

I growled and scrambled up slightly. "*I don't want to go anywhere near that thing. Let's wait until it gets called back, shall we? Prince Arran surely won't let it misbehave for so long.*"

But the pompous Prince Arran didn't seem to care what the dog did. Rather he was focused on calling the students towards the campfire and organizing them into neat rows. It would be a while until they noticed I wasn't there, and so I had plenty of time to wait this one out.

The dog had lost interest. Or rather, its attention seemed to have shifted to the only dragon that hadn't yet deposited a rider. In other words, Salanraja.

It padded softly and slowly over to my dragon's tail, as if stalking through long grass to hunt a bird. Salanraja looked back at it and gave it a menacing look with one of her yellow eyes that seemed to say she didn't seem to trust it either.

The dog spotted me sitting on Salanaraja's back. It barked at me, wagging its tail violently. Having the gift of being able to understand all languages, I knew exactly what it was saying. From its tone of voice, I could also recognise that it was a male.

"Look, cat! Danger, cat! Scratch me not! Curse me not!"

I blinked at him and yawned. "I can understand you, you know? I speak every single language in all the Seven Dimensions, including your ugly dog one. I'll have you know, cats can do a lot more than scratch, and we are not witches." Witches, after all, knew lots of magical spells, while I only knew one. Well technically two – I could turn into a chimera without even needing the staff, but I hadn't done that for an awfully long time.

The dog completely froze in his tracks and whimpered as he backed away from me slightly. At the same time the students and Driars on the ground spun around to look at me, clearly attempting to identify the second source of barking, or howling, or whatever noise I was making.

I relished the attention, and I sauntered down Salanraja's tail towards the dog. I continued to speak in his language as I approached him. I really wanted to show my fellow classmates which was the superior species here.

"No doubt you've heard of me... My name is Ben, the Dragoncat, descendant of the great Asian leopard cat and also the mighty George."

I called on my staff bearer – a giant, currently invisible hand – to reveal itself. It appeared suddenly in thin air, floating next to me, holding my staff with the crystal glowing purple.

"It was this cat that vanquished Astravar, the warlock who wanted to annihilate this and every other dimension. It is because of me that this barrier exists. Now, if you will excuse me, I must join my fellow dragon riders."

The dog shifted his weight onto his hind legs, his front paws stretched out in front of him. He stared at me with those wide eyes, beating his tail against the ground. I could smell his fear, and I was proud of it. I kept my gaze on him for one moment, then I turned towards the students.

"Come on, come on!" Prince Arran shouted out from behind the crowd. "Join rank and get into your lines. Animals will always be animals, and there is no need to pay them any heed. And cat, I order you to put that staff away. You know the law... Dark magic is not permitted in this realm unless necessary to preserve human life."

I growled at him as my staff bearer vanished into thin air. The law wasn't particularly fair, as it didn't state that you could use dark magic to preserve a cat's life as well as a human's.

The students had lost interest in me, and had their heads turned towards the barrier and Prince Arran, who stood in front of it. I took a few steps towards them, before the dog said more softly. "I know who you are. Word has it amongst dogs that you behave far too high above your station, Dragoncat. You're just like the rest of your species. You don't know how to behave as part of a team."

I froze and stalked back around towards the dog. I was probably the first and only cat ever able to talk to a dog. Now, I didn't just have to stand up for myself, but every single cat across every single dimension.

"Better to be independent than always in the hand of a human," I said. "You dogs rely on your masters too much. Unlike dogs, we cats have perfected the art of not having to work for food or shelter."

"Is that true? Because I've heard that cats are employed in this dimension solely to chase rats and mice."

"That's because they're less advanced than cats like myself from the Fourth Dimension. One day, I shall liberate the cats here and free them from their catteries. They shall learn how cats are meant to be treated. We weren't made to do 'human work'."

"What we do is not work," the dog replied. "Not if we enjoy it. We like to hunt, just like you do. Besides, a bond between a dog and its master is more valuable than anything in this world, including ties to other dogs."

At that I heard Salanraja laughing in my mind. She could hear the dog's voice as it reproduced itself inside my head. *"I should have chosen a dog as a rider,"* she said. *"Sounds like they respect bonds much better than you ever would."*

I turned back and glared at Salanraja. I really didn't need to take insults on two fronts. *"You couldn't say anything more insulting, Salamander. I'll deal with you later."*

I turned back to the dog. "What are you, anyway?"

The dog let out a couple of barks, literally translating to, "Yes, yes."

This is one thing I've never understood about dogs. I mean if you wanted to make a point, there was no need to shout it. But they seemed to get either excited or agitated about everything, and this dog was no exception.

"My name is Max," he continued, "and I'm a Sussex Spaniel, which means I'm from Sussex, the capital of the world."

I blinked twice, as I let the words wash over me. When I'd acquired the gift of all languages, I'd also acquired knowledge of geography, and place names in particular. There was no Sussex anywhere but the Fourth Dimension – or in other words, the dimension which I'd been summoned from.

"You're from where?"

"I'm from Sussex, the capital of the world."

This was just ridiculous. Everyone knew that the capital of the world I once inhabited was the Alhambra Palace. The bravest of cats went on pilgrimages to the Alhambra, although this was rare. The old Ragamuffin back in South Wales said he'd been there once, when his master lived in the dry lands of Spain. He'd met lots of other interesting cats there who told him lots of interesting stories. That's how he'd become so wise.

But the capital of the world wasn't important at this moment, because the dog claimed he was from the Fourth Dimension, which meant someone had brought him here... And he belonged to Prince Arran...

Before I had a chance to question him about it, a high-pitched scream came from one of the students. The air had developed a sudden chill to it, caused by a sudden breeze rushing away from the Great Barrier towards a point in the distance. I turned to see a student standing, her finger outstretched towards that point. I followed this to see a line of flames stretching across the eastern horizon, concealed at its base by a thin line of purple mist.

Driar Yila was the first to react. She called out to us. "Fire golems at nine o'clock. Shield mages, form protective barriers. Now!"

Wind gusted all around me from a hundred dragons lifting into the air. They wouldn't be much good against fire golems, but they needed to scout the terrain to see if there were any other threats.

The only dragon that didn't lift up was Corralsa – jet-black and belonging to the prince. Arran rushed over to her, wrapping his cloak around him to shield him from the wind. I watched him move for a moment, wondering where the whiskers he was going. Fleeing the battle, no doubt, because he'd probably created these fire golems, just as he'd brought Max over from the Fourth Dimension.

Without further pause, I willed my staff bearer towards me, ready for a fight, just as Corralsa took off with Arran on her back.

FIRE GOLEM FIGHT

My staff bearer placed the staff in my mouth, and the crystal on it started glowing purple. But I once again had no idea what to do with it.

If I saw a line of fire golems in the wilderness when out exploring, I'd probably dash for my life rather than fight them. I guess my magical beam could have brought them down if I hit their hearts, or in other words the central crystals that powered them. That was if I had enough time to react, and enough experience to know exactly where to strike a fire golem, but I didn't.

A volley of fireballs took off from the horizon. Fire golems didn't hurl projectiles, as such, but rather they were the projectile. They were designed for only one purpose – to destroy, by launching themselves from their location and exploding on impact, covering the landscape in flame.

The stupid dog, Max, stood next to me barking at the approaching fireballs, as if that would do anything. One fireball was heading straight towards me and him, wide enough to engulf the both of us. A loud humming sound emanated from my left, as the shield mages – all twenty of them that had come on this trip – raised their staffs. The white crystals affixed to these staffs glowed, and white bubbles pulsed out of them, expanding into a lattice of shields that sheltered the students from the oncoming onslaught.

The fire golem roared closer, as others erupted into flames around Max and I, sending up waves of heat. From inside the nearest shield, Rine beckoned me over, with an alarmed expression on his face. He held his staff in his other hand, the crystal at the top, blue but not glowing. I pushed back on my hind legs and readied myself to sprint out of the way, but then I noticed Max, still barking, frozen on the spot, staring at the approaching projectile as if mesmerised by it.

If I didn't do anything then within seconds he'd be dead.

"Move, you stupid mutt," I said, and I batted him on the nose with a clawless paw to break him out of his trance. I sent out a red beam from the staff in my mouth that landed just by his tail to help spur him into action.

He turned towards me, but I didn't see his face because I was already sprinting away as fast as my legs could carry me. The closest shield mage let down the barrier just long enough for me to enter, timing it perfectly as the flames washed over the roof of the shield. I looked back to check on the dog, who sprinted towards us, flames erupting behind him.

"Open the shield!" I shouted to the shield mage.

The student gave the dog a wide-eyed look, and a lump of air travelled down his throat. A blast of heat came just as the shield opened up to let Max through. The flames came so close that they singed the hairs on the dog's tail. The shield turned back on, cutting the flames off.

Inside the barrier, it was the temperature of a desert in the midday sun. The shield mage had opened the shield too long, creating a furnace for us to bake inside.

Rine knew immediately what to do. He clutched his staff tightly and a large cube of ice formed around the crystal. This melted quickly, cooling the air inside to a normal temperature. Max lowered himself down on his haunches, flattened his ears, and whimpered.

I didn't have time to scold him yet. We were still under attack.

The surrounding flames had set the dry grass alight all around us. We couldn't hear anything outside of our shield, but everyone's eyes were on the Council of Three at the centre of our formation. Driar Lonamm held her staff with its blue crystal raised high in the air. She swung it downwards and made a sideways sweeping motion, instructing the students what to do next.

The shield mage called out something, and the shield flickered off. Rine swept his staff around just like Driar Lonamm had, and the other ice mages did the same. The flames roared up towards us, before a ring of ice spread out from our location. It extinguished the flames and caused the burnt grass underneath it to crumble to ash. The stench of burned vegetation mixed with rotten vegetable juice hung in the air. Around us, red crystals that had once been the fire golems lay, lazily strewn across the ground.

"All right, it worked," Rine said, a big grin on his young, hard-lined face. "And we saved both the cat and the dog..."

I growled at him, not liking his implication. I hadn't needed saving – I was the mighty Dragoncat who vanquished warlocks. If anything, it was I, who had saved the dog. If I hadn't batted him on the nose and snapped him out of his trance with magic, he'd be a hotdog by now.

It wasn't over yet. The purple mist still remained in the distance, with a second line of fire golems shining brightly. Whatever or whoever was commanding those things had had the foresight to keep enough fire golems in reserve for another volley. The tell-tale flicker of them launching came from the horizon.

Fortunately, we now knew they were there, and the Initiates and

Driars had time to work the tactics that had been drilled into them through months of training. These tactics didn't involve me, of course. How to use dark magic against your enemies hadn't been on the Dragonsbond Academy syllabus, and I didn't think they'd put it in anytime soon. If it was, maybe I'd stay awake for those lessons, because using this magic I could summon the food I wanted whenever I wanted it.

Driar Yila now held her staff high. "Fire strangles fire!" she called out. "Fire mages, take aim! Shield mages, hold position! Everyone else, crouch!"

Rine and a whole load of other mages, including Driar Brigel and Driar Lonamm ducked down to the ground. I didn't need to, of course – I was already smaller than them. With most of the students crouched, I had a clear view of Bellari, her golden hair whipping behind her as she summoned the fire to her staff. Her free hand was flat against the small of the shield mage's, Initiate Tempuri's, back.

A beam of fire shot out of her staff, heading straight towards one of the approaching fireballs. The whites of her knuckles showed and her face went bright red as she closed her eyes. She concentrated the beam on a point just in front of the fireball, sending out a brilliant explosion.

I'd actually been awake in the lesson when Driar Yila had explained this tactic. The explosion when the beam met the fireball would be so wide that it would starve any fire golems caught within its radius of available oxygen. Both fireballs winked out, and the crystal that had powered the golem dropped from a plume of swirling smoke. Around it, other crystals also fell from the sky.

A little further away from us, a few fire golems got awfully close but the shield mages were ready. Within seconds, the shield arrangement sprung up around us again, and the fire golems bounced off our shields. There was little fresh foliage left to burn, and so the flames extinguished as soon as they hit the ground.

The shields went out, and a cheer erupted from the students.

"Don't celebrate yet," the bald-headed giant, Driar Brigel called out. "We must regrow what has been lost. Leaf mages, it's your turn. Shield mages, stay standing. Everyone else, duck."

The students did as they were told. Ange stood a few metres away from me, the crystal on her staff casting soft green highlights over her short dark hair. She looked down at Rine, whose gaze was focused on a pretty girl just opposite us, and she shook her head.

"On my call," Driar Brigel called. "Give it plenty of water, so the ground around us can't burn again. Go!"

Ange jerked her head to focus on a spot in front of her. The crystal on her staff, held high above her head, glowed green, and strands of light floated out of it like tendrils that touched points on the ground all around her. Where they touched, grass sprung out of the cracked ground, freshening the soil, and creating a smell more like spring than summer. The other twenty leaf mages worked in a similar fashion.

"Now step outwards slowly," Driar Brigel said, "and be ready to retreat on the first sign of danger."

The leaf mages fanned out, sprinkling life around them as they went. They soon rearranged themselves into a line in front of us, Driar Brigel at their centre. A short while later, they changed their stance, each of them focusing a green beam of energy at a combined point several metres in front of them. A ball of green energy gathered at that point. This created a rich humming that sounded like a swarm of a thousand bees and caused Max to start looking about him in alarm.

Driar Brigel raised his hand and counted down from three on his fingers, as he called out the numbers. He closed his fist, and together the students pulled back on their staffs. They sent the green energy ball spinning towards the purple mist still gathered on the horizon. It landed there, casting a prismatic explosion of life energy.

When this faded, the purple mist had gone, leaving only a faint barrier of smoke that soon dissipated.

Still, the work wasn't done. Driar Aleam now stood at the centre of the formation, his yellow staff held high in his wrinkled hand. "Now lightning mages, it is time for us to call a storm," he said.

Technically Aleam wasn't a lightning mage, but a dark magic user. In fact, he used to be a warlock, but his white dragon, Olan, prevented him from being corrupted by the dark magic. So instead, his crystal had granted him the gift of lightning magic, which allowed him to fit in as an elder of Dragonsbond Academy. Only five of the students were also lightning mages, and they joined him with their staffs raised to the sky, the yellow crystals at the top of them glowing.

Aleam's wrinkled brows furrowed as he and the other young lightning mages summoned a blanket of thunderclouds overhead, darkening the scene. They thrust their staffs forward, and the clouds pushed out towards where the smoke had been. A thunderclap crashed from the sky, so loud it caused me to jump to high alert.

The clouds continued to build, and soon rain poured out of the clouds above us. It drenched us and the ground and caused the grass to reach upwards. Any fire golems left would no doubt be destroyed by this, and even if they survived, they wouldn't be able to burn freshly grown and watered grass.

For a moment, silence enshrouded us, as if everyone needed a moment to contemplate what might have happened if the shield mages had put up their barriers a second later. It wasn't just that. It was just as Driar Yila had said...

Our times of peace with the warlocks were over.

4

A GOOD SCOLDING

An uproar followed the relative silence. It started with a murmur, then grew into a loud chatter, continuing to grow until it became too loud for my sensitive ears. Students whooped, and hands punched the sky, using the elation from victory to quell the fear that we might soon get attacked again. Others spoke in alarm about the dangers of the impending war, their voices competing to be heard over the racket.

Usually, the Great Driars wouldn't tolerate such unruliness – particularly Driar Yila, who seemed almost as sensitive to loud noises as I was – but they surprisingly allowed the students a moment to share their experiences with their friends.

The Council of Three and Aleam probably also needed a little time to work out amongst themselves who the whiskers had just attacked us. Because we'd been told time and time again that there was no way that the warlocks could get golems past the Great Barrier without King Garmin knowing. Prince Arran and his trusted Dragon Corps were meant to have it all under control.

I looked for a place I could retreat to, darting between legs, trying to find the end of the crowd. As I weaved my way through, searching at least for a quieter spot, I heard students asking what had happened to Arran. Clearly, I wasn't the only one who was suspicious of him.

"He's a dark magic user," I heard one boy saying. "He must have called in those fire golems to attack us. Who else could have done this?" I saw the boy was Initiate Tempuri – the wiry lad with dark hair and a top-knot ponytail who Rine's ex-girlfriend, Bellari, was currently going out with. Or so I'd thought.

"Don't be stupid," a girl said back to him. It didn't take me long to realise that the voice had the same whininess of Bellari herself. "Prince Arran leads the king's Dragon Corps, and nobly, I might add. He's the last person who would betray us. Didn't you see how he fought in the battle against Astravar? He's a hero..."

"Of course I did. I also saw how he suddenly revealed himself to be a dark magic user right before the battle. We all did. Just think about it. If he'd kept a secret like that from even his closest friends all these years, how do you know he doesn't have other secrets?"

Bellari turned up her nose and looked down it at Tempuri. Her face had gone so red that I thought she was going to scream like she had at Rine that time in the forest when he'd dumped her. Instead, her voice remained remarkably level – by her standards, anyway. "You know, you could be thrown in prison for saying such things publicly. It's called treason."

"So we don't have free speech?" the boy asked. "Surely I should be allowed to say what I like to my girlfriend?"

"I am not your girlfriend..." Bellari folded her arms. "I would have thought you'd have realised that by now... You boys are all the same..."

The boy paused. "What do you mean?" he asked in a lower tone.

"Oh, for demon's sake! This conversation is over. You know, I thought you might be something, but you're just as cowardly as the rest of them. Nothing like... Never mind. If only there was a man like Prince Arran at Dragonsbond Academy..."

She stormed off, almost kicking me as she went. If she'd seen me there, I had no doubt she probably would have. Or started her exaggerated sneezing charade, since she was apparently "allergic" to me. Initiate Tempuri watched her go for a moment, his shoulders hanging low.

I wanted to tell him that he hadn't done anything wrong, and then share with him exactly what Max had shared with me. How Arran had yanked another being from the Fourth Dimension just like Astravar had, and so Tempuri had a right to be suspicious of him. But the boy had already walked off somewhere else, and I hadn't even taken the opportunity to study his scent.

The cool breeze had faded, and the warmth from the slowly waning summer sun again permeated the air. The students continued to chatter loudly away, and I eventually managed to find my way out of the tangle of legs into a clearing. I emerged in the spot where I'd just saved Max from being fried, evident from the wide char mark stretched across the ground.

The dragons hadn't yet returned. They were circling over the distant terrain where the fire golems had launched from. Fiery dragon breath couldn't cause explosions like the fire mages could, and so they couldn't extinguish the golems as easily. But they could scan for traces of a warlock hiding nearby.

"*I see you made it through unscathed,*" Salanraja said to me. "*You shouldn't have stuck your neck out for that dog, you know? But you did. You acted like a hero, even though you don't like him. You've certainly changed, Ben, despite how stubborn you can be sometimes.*"

Ironically, now that I had done something that Salanraja liked, she had decided to call me by my proper name. "*Oh, he's got a good talking to coming. Believe me.*"

"*I'm sure he has. Anyway, I'm glad you're safe.*"

"Yeah, but I didn't have a chance to use my magic. All this power I've got in the staff, and I don't know what to do with it."

Salanraja paused for a long moment, and I couldn't tell if it was because she was secretly laughing at me, or carefully considering what to say next. *"Hallinar tells me that Seramina feels the same. But don't worry. Your time will come. All we need is another vision from the crystal. It will tell us what to do."*

"You mean a new destiny? I mean..." I shuddered. *"Does that mean we'll end up going to the Ghost Realm again?"*

"Chances are, no... We'll find and arrest the perpetrator who summoned these fire golems, then you'll probably end up doing something like herding sheep or helping me contain a forest fire. You know, the safe stuff."

It all sounded awfully boring to me. *"I wish I could work out how to conjure up those salmon like I did in the Third Dimension that time. I could have used them to put out the fire golems' flames, and they'd cook at the same time. Just think how delicious it would be. A battle, then a feast for everyone. That would have given this field trip some purpose."*

Salanraja laughed. *"In all my training, I've never heard of an army of golems being destroyed by a school of fish."*

"Then maybe one day I'll change history for a second time."

"Yes, maybe one day you will..." Salanraja seemed a little different towards me than before. As if me almost getting roasted by the flames had made her consider how devastating it would be for her if she lost me. *"Anyway, better focus. Corralsa is barking orders at us, and she's just told us we don't have time to communicate with our riders. She seems in an awful hurry..."*

"She sounds worse than Arran, that one."

"She's much worse, believe me. Arran doesn't have sharp teeth."

"Salmon do..." I said. *"The old Ragamuffin in my former neighbourhood told me that he'd seen a salmon that hadn't been cooked on*

his travels, and its teeth were very sharp…" I paused. I was going off on a tangent again, and I had more important issues to address. *"Salanraja, did you hear what Max said about where he came from?"*

"I said, not now, Bengie. Corralsa will know…"

"But—"

"Really, I'll block you out of my mind if I have to."

I mewled softly. *"Fine,"* I said. Maybe I could find Driar Aleam and tell him, then he could tell the Council of Three, and we could arrest Arran as soon as he returned.

One character had alienated himself from the other students. This was Max, who had crouched as low as he could, whimpering within the freshly grown grass. He no longer wanted to socialise with the students, it seemed, instead now thinking it better to hide.

I said that I would scold him, and that's exactly what I did. I made my way through the soft grass, purring as it rubbed against me. The way it felt reminded me of back home where it used to always rain in summer. The grass here, recently, had been dry and horribly scratchy. There wasn't much rain in Illumine Kingdom this time of year.

Max watched me approach with narrowed eyes, sinking further into the grass as if he thought I couldn't see him, but the grass wasn't that long. Besides, I could smell him a mile away.

"What were you thinking?" I asked him as I approached. "You just stood there barking at an approaching fireball, just waiting for it to hit you. Do you want to get yourself killed?"

"I'm not here," he said. "Just leave me alone…"

"No. You can't hide from a cat, particularly a highly skilled Bengal like me. And you can't hide from The Council of Three either. If you annoy them, trust me, you don't want to know how they will punish you…"

Max looked over at the dragons in the distance and he sniffed the air. "I've... I've never seen anything like this before... How can fire launch from the sky like that?"

"It's called magic. You've been around Prince Arran long enough. Surely, you've seen him cast plenty of spells. I bet he uses his dark magic in private quarters, even though he discourages everyone else from using it."

"No..." Max said. "He's never done that..."

"Then what about the dragons? Haven't you seen them at least breathe fire?"

"I've only known dragons the last couple of weeks. I was scared of them at first. But not anymore. They're just big horses with wings, at the end of the day. Can they really breathe fire?" Something about his voice sounded faked. As if he was putting on an act about something.

I chuckled under my breath. "Don't let Salanraja hear you comparing a dragon to horses... Or zebras, or unicorns for that matter."

Max paused. "I don't know about you, but until recently, I had never seen one that could—Well, I'd seen them jump over hedges, but I'd honestly never thought horses could fly."

It wasn't the dog's utter ignorance that caused me to twitch my whiskers in disbelief, but the fact that he clearly hadn't been in the First Dimension long at all.

"How long have you been here, exactly?"

Max pulled his paws through some loose dirt, unearthing an earthworm who had come up for some air. "My master only just brought me here a few weeks ago. And I love him, because he brings me food and tells his servants to take me for walks and lets me swim in the canals."

I looked at him, incredulously. "And just to get this straight... You came here from Sussex, the Fourth Dimension..."

"Yes," Max said. "I'm from Sussex, the capital of the world. But I don't know anything about any Fourth Dimension..."

"And who exactly removed you from your home in Sussex?"

"The good Prince Arran brought me here. His hands lifted me through this great white light, and then I was in this beautiful world."

The hackles rose up on my back as I remembered how Astravar had yanked me from my breakfast of milk and salmon trimmings. Despite the variety of food I'd eaten from the Dragonsbond Academy kitchens, I'd never since eaten anything so appetising as what was in my bowl that morning.

"How can you describe Prince Arran as good? I'm guessing you didn't ask him to yank you across dimensions."

"My last owners before Arran..." Max was whining now. "They weren't good. They threw me out onto the streets, and I had to eat scraps from the dustbins for days. But my new master took pity on me and lifted me through this huge shining light with warm and gentle hands. It was raining and cold when he found me, and he brought me into the warmth. Oh, and I was also about to get into a fight with a huge Alsatian for stepping on his turf. My mother told me never to mess with Alsatians – the kings of all dogs – but, you know, I was desperate."

"I think you would find they're called German Shepherds," I pointed out.

Max cocked his head. "What?"

"They're not Alsatians, they're German Shepherds"

"But how can a shepherd become the king of dogs?"

"Oh, never mind..." This dog seemed to be the kind to ask a lot of questions. "Anyway, how would you know that Arran took pity on you? How would you know what his intentions were? Have you ever spoken to him and tried to find out the exact reason he brought you here?"

"I don't speak the human language," Max said. "But I can smell when someone loves me, and I know when they bring me good food."

My ears had flattened against my head. Something was wrong here – very wrong. What would Prince Arran want with a Sussex Spaniel from the Fourth Dimension, when he could have just had a regular dog from the First? I doubted very much that Prince Arran had simply taken pity on Max. To do that, Arran would have had to know about Max first, which meant that the pompous prince would have been studying the Sussex Spaniel across dimensions. Yet why would he take an interest in a street dog?

"And you say you've never seen him casting any magic? You've never, for example seem him playing with crystals?"

Max looked at me as if I was stupid. "Why would anyone want to play with crystals?"

I had more to say, but Driar Yila's harsh voice interrupted me from my train of thoughts. "Silence!" she shouted. "We must complete a register..."

The noise died down to a murmur. Driar Yila clapped her hands loudly, and she raised her staff in the air. The crystal on it glowed red, and the murmur died into silence.

I sniffed to see if I could smell Aleam anywhere nearby. But I only detected Max, and a faint whiff of charred grass and rotten vegetable juice. Even amidst this freshly grown terrain, the scent of the previous battle still lingered as if impossible to push away.

5

THE REGISTER

Unlike before, the silence was haunting. Not even Max dared whimper and not a single student dared stir. Even the sough of the wind through the trees hesitated, and all I could hear was the humming of the Great Barrier, and the distant and rhythmic beating of dragon wings.

The Council of Three now stood on a raised granite outcrop, putting them a few feet higher than the students. "Everyone sit down cross-legged on the ground," Driar Lonamm said, as Driar Brigel handed her a vellum scroll that looked hundreds of years old. "I want to be able to see everyone."

She put her hands to her hips and waited for everyone to obey. Clothes rustled, joints creaked, and the crowd tried to break the silence once again.

"Silence!" Driar Yila called out, and Driar Brigel coughed loudly. Driar Lonamm waited, passing a stern gaze over the students.

The crystal glowed red on Driar Yila's staff. The students quietened down awfully quickly.

"Good..." Driar Lonamm said, once satisfied with the new noise level. "Now, when I call out your name, I want you to stand up and raise your hand. Then stay standing until I tell you to sit. That will give Driar Aleam a short moment to assess you for any obvious injuries. Magical ailments can bury themselves deeper than the skin, and it sometimes takes a skilled healer to recognise them."

I guessed, while Aleam checked for burns or skin damage or whatnot, the Council of Three would also be keeping an eye out for any sign of guilt on the faces of the students. Rumour had it that all three of them were incredibly good at finding culprits.

I doubted anyone could have summoned the fire golems amongst us though. Out of everyone here, only Seramina, Aleam, and I could use dark magic. Arran could as well, of course, but he was somewhere else.

It was still possible, I guess, that someone was working with the warlock who did the deed. Whiskers, I wouldn't be surprised if Bellari had a hand in this, given how she'd behaved towards Initiate Tempuri. But she wasn't stupid enough to be *that* obvious, was she?

The students did exactly as they were told, sitting cross legged on the grass as they craned their heads up at the Council of Three. Aleam hobbled up to the top of the outcrop, using his staff for support. He put his hand to his forehead so he could both peer down at us and shield his eyes from the sun.

"Initiate Aida," Driar Lonamm called.

"Yes, Ma'am..." a female student replied. A hand sprung up, followed by the student who stood in a ramrod posture.

The students leaned away from Initiate Aida, and Aleam squinted down at her. He turned back to Driar Lonamm and nodded. Driar Yila turned her hawk-like gaze on the student, and Driar Brigel watched her out of the corner of her eye. Driar Lonamm nodded to Driar Brigel, then turned back down to the register in her hands.

"Initiate Alopa," Driar Lonamm continued.

"Present and well, Ma'am…"

Though the register was called in alphabetical order, they'd tacked me on to the end as I was late to join Dragonsbond Academy. That put me second to last to Seramina, who had joined after me. At thirteen, she was a few years younger than everyone else in our year except me. They'd snapped her straight out of her previous school when they noticed how brilliant she was at magic.

She was a bit of a child prodigy, in other words. Seramina, Astravar's daughter, who might one day destroy the world…

I started to groom myself, knowing that this would take a while. My fur tasted charred and had been significantly ruffled by the previous battle. I didn't like that at all.

"Ben, there you are," Seramina's soft voice floated over to me, interrupting my grooming. I looked up to see her standing over me. But I couldn't detect her perfume, which normally had the aroma of snowdrops.

"Seramina, are you using a glamour again?" I asked. I let off a little chirp as well to let her know that I could do with her coming over and giving me some affection right now. I didn't care if she might be a world-destroyer sometime in the future. At that moment, I needed a good pet.

"They'll get suspicious of me if I step away," Seramina said. "I've already heard some of the students saying that I might have summoned the fire golems."

"But they don't know you're Astravar's daughter," I said.

"Doesn't matter. With Prefect Asinda back at Dragonsbond Academy, there are only three of us here with the power of dark magic, and no one would ever believe Aleam would have summoned the fire golems."

"So they're saying it's either you or me?"

Seramina raised her hand to her mouth to stifle a giggle. "No… It's either me or Arran. Or another one of the warlocks has managed to slip into the Versta Caverns unaided by the King's Dragon Corps. There are all kinds of possible conspiracy theories, but we have to think about this rationally..."

"Why can't it be me?" I asked, and I probably had a slight hiss in my voice.

Seramina shook her head. "Ben, I've not seen you casting much magic lately. I can't imagine you could have learned all of a sudden how to summon anything – no offence. Besides, you don't have hands to carry the crystal necessary to do the deed."

"I could swallow one like I did that time with the clay golem."

"There's a difference between a crystal that a golem carries, and a crystal used to create golems, Ben. For powerful magic like that, it would be far too big to fit in your mouth."

I growled at Seramina. I didn't like being patronised. Really, I had enough of that treatment from Salanraja.

"Initiate Ange," Driar Lonamm called out from the outcrop. Ange stood up in the crowd, revealing enough of her for me to tell that she was okay. She looked over her shoulder at me and nodded with a faint smile. She'd probably been unable to see me over the crowd until now. But she wouldn't have been able to see Seramina, as her glamour would have been intended only for me.

The caw of a crow came from overhead, and I shuddered as its shadow passed over me. Astravar had once been able to turn into a crow, and the other warlocks could turn into carrion-eating birds as well, some of them – like a condor – large enough to prey on cats. I bowed down and took a mouthful of grass, letting the smooth taste of it soothe my nerves.

Seramina watched me, passively, a soft smile on her face. Often humans, when they saw me do this, would ask why cats eat grass. But I didn't want to let us get distracted, and Seramina didn't seem to care too much, either.

"Well, clearly it's not me that summoned the fire golems, and it's not you or Aleam either," I said. "So it must have been Arran. Because, from what Salanraja has told me, there's no way that any warlock can slip by the Great Barrier undetected."

Apparently, not only did the Great Barrier keep all the warlock's creations out, but it also pinged the White Mages nearby, notifying them whenever and wherever a warlock passed through. Salanraja had said before that lots of White Mages kept station at the border, so they would have known if any of us were about to be attacked.

Seramina put a hand to her chin. "Let's be rational about this, Ben. We shouldn't point a finger at Arran before we've discounted all the other possibilities."

"Like what?"

"I guess it could also have been one of the dark mages who we know inhabit the land. Can't you remember Aleam said that there were others in Cimlean City..."

"But would anyone be powerful enough? They'd have to be training for an awfully long time, and if they got too powerful, wouldn't the White Mages take notice?"

"I don't know. I'm just considering the possibilities. Treating things rationally as I've been taught to do. Keeping cool and under control." Her gaze went distant for a moment. Then, she extended three fingers of her hand. She counted them off one by one as she spoke. "So, we've already considered the dark magic users who were here when the event happened, and we've considered the dark magic users in Illumine Kingdom. That leaves the possibility of travel through the other dimensions."

"What do you mean?"

"Well, none of the six warlocks can cross the Great Barrier in this world without making their presence known. But if they opened up another dimension, and could open a portal back here again, then they could slip by undetected."

Whiskers, I hadn't thought of that. "You mean they could pass through the Faerie Realm, or my world, and then come out the other side?"

"Theoretically, yes. But the only realm they could survive is the Faerie Realm, and they would need a fairy to open the portal on the other side. But no fairy would cut a deal with a warlock."

"Maybe they had a deal with one of the demons to pass through the Seventh Dimension." I'd been inside that blazing hot, sulphurous realm once, but I hadn't stayed there long. Instead, I'd found my crystal, and it had whisked me out before I got scorched to a crisp. It gifted me with the ability to turn into a chimera, then it had sent me back to the First Dimension to help my friends.

Seramina shook her head. "No demon would rightfully make a deal with a warlock that could harm their world, and the warlocks wouldn't survive long enough in that heat to do that anyway."

"But Astravar had told me and the fairies that he'd paid a debt to Ammit in the Seventh Dimension," I said. "He sent me there to pay that debt, apparently."

Seramina nodded. "That debt was probably accrued from all the creatures that he summoned from there. But there's a difference between invoking demons and asking for passage."

"So what you're telling me is there's no way the warlocks could have done anything. Which means that Arran must have called the fire golems, right? We already know he uses dark magic and he's the only one who has the power to do this. You know, there's something not right about him, Seramina..." I growled as I said those words. I'd never liked that pompous prince, and I knew Seramina didn't like him either.

"What do you know, Ben?"

I looked up at her. When I squinted my eyes, I could see faint traces of white light around her glamour. But I had to really focus to notice them. "How do you know I know something?"

"I learned to read others intuitively long before I became a mind-mage Ben. I sensed something in that conversation you had with the dog just before the fire golems attacked, but I didn't have time to ask."

I patted the ground in front of me, making an impression in the freshly grown grass. A fresh scent came out of it. "It's that dog. He told me he also came from the Fourth Dimension. He's from a place called Sussex."

Seramina raised an eyebrow. "Go on…"

"He says Arran brought him here. But the stupid mutt seems to think that the prince did so out of the kindness of his heart."

The mage cocked her head. It looked so odd when she was in her glamour form, since her light hair didn't move as if it was frozen in time. "So what?"

"Well, it would take an evil warlock to steal an animal from another dimension, right? Just look at what happened to me. And the worst thing is that the dog thinks that Arran did him a favour…"

"Maybe he did…"

"But why would Arran even go looking for him in the first place? I wonder what—"

"Initiate Bellari…" Driar Lonamm's call interrupted me from my train of thoughts. I bristled every time I heard that name.

Bellari shot straight up as if she had ants in her pants and thrust her hand upwards. "I'm here, Ma'am."

A roar came from the distance, and Bellari sharply turned her head to the right. A blue dragon was approaching, framed by the sun which was now massive and low in the sky.

"Daddy," she called, and then lowered her head as if she hadn't realised how loud she'd called it. She righted herself, then pointed out at the dragon. "I'm sorry, that's my father. I didn't know he was visiting us."

The Council of Three and Aleam all turned their heads, every one of them looking alarmed. Clearly, Bellari's father wasn't meant to be here, which meant one of two things. Either he had come to bring bad news, or he had been behind the summoning of the fire golems, and he'd brought something with him with the power to finish us all off.

Maybe I hadn't been wrong to suspect that Bellari had been behind this all along.

The crowd started to murmur again, and the noise escalated for a few seconds.

"Silence!" Driar Yila screamed once again. "Stay calm and stay seated!"

Driar Yila's words hung in the air. They faded, and my ears perked up detecting a rustling sound in the distance – thousands of feet padding over loose leaves. Amidst this, very faintly, I heard gnashing and snarling. There came the whiff of dogs on the breeze.

"What is it, Ben?" Seramina asked.

I turned to her and sniffed the air again to make sure.

"Wargs!" I said. "I can smell wargs!"

6

SURPRISE!

I sprinted straight through Seramina's glamour, knowing that an illusion couldn't stop me. A shiver ran down my flexible spine, and I wasn't sure if this was due to the magic or just my imagination. My chest burned, and I could taste bile at the back of my throat. The scent of the wargs seemed to follow me as I ran.

A bark came from behind me. "Where are you going, Dragoncat?" Max called.

I didn't have time to answer him. I needed to get over to the outcrop as fast as possible to warn the Council of Three and Aleam about the wargs.

I tried calling out to them, but the rising chatter from the students cut me off. Bellari still stood in the centre of the crowd, looking a little lost as if she wondered whether to run to her father or sit back down. Whiskers, if she'd had anything to do with the wargs, I'd transform into a chimera and deal with her myself.

I dashed around the students, knowing it would be difficult to weave my way through them. I scrambled up the edge of the outcrop, digging my claws into some rough clumps of grass to gain purchase, and I pulled myself onto level ground.

A scuffling sound came from behind me. Max, somehow, had kept close on my tail, managing an impressive pace against the speed I'd inherited from the great Asian leopard cats, and my father – the mighty George.

"Danger," he called in a loud barking voice. "Danger. Danger. I smell danger!"

"You're not the only one," I barked back at him, and I turned to see that I was about to crash right into Driar Yila's leg. I stopped myself just in time, tumbling over myself clumsily.

She looked down on me, that cruel frown on her gaunt wrinkled face. "Initiate Ben, what is the meaning of this?"

I shook dust off my fur as I stood up. "I heard wargs, Ma'am. They're coming this way. Driar Reslin must have brought them with him."

"That's absurd," Driar Lonamm butted in. "Driar Reslin has been an honoured member of King Garmin's Dragon Corps since he graduated from Dragonsbond Academy. I taught him myself, and he would never—"

"I know what I heard. There's an army of wargs behind him, and it won't be long before they attack us."

I must have been screaming louder than I thought I had, because the word 'wargs' got picked up at the front of the crowd. It bounced around like a fly drunk on late summer fruit. Soon, the crowd was roaring with panic.

"Silence!" This time it was the bald giant, Driar Brigel, who screamed. Or should I say he bellowed so loudly that I almost mistook his voice for thunder. It crashed over the students below, and they all snapped their heads towards him, stunned into silence. "We're trying to focus here for demons' sake. Now everyone stand, draw your staffs, stay quiet, and await our command."

The students stood up as instructed, and they started to chatter amongst themselves again.

"Quietly!" Driar Brigel yelled. "You're respected dragon riders, not chickens in a coop."

The insult seemed enough to get the students to follow orders. Together, they drew their staffs in a practiced motion.

A warm gust of wind swept over us as Driar Reslin's dragon reared in the air, getting ready to land. Max came wheeling around the gentle rise of the outcrop, having been unable to scramble up the side after me.

He was still barking as he stood next to me. "Danger! Danger! Wolves approaching."

"They're not wolves, they're wargs," I said, or rather I barked back.

The dog stopped in his tracks. "Warg what?"

"Wargs. Look, imagine you, and then imagine yourself just much fiercer, like a grizzly bear is to a teddy bear. In other words, something to be very scared of."

Max whimpered. "Danger! Danger! Wargs approaching! Scary, grizzly wargs."

"Would you shut that dog up?" Driar Yila snapped. "I can't hear myself think." She banged her staff on the ground, as if to emphasise her point, and the red crystal on it glowed.

"Max..." I said, this time making sure I didn't bark. "Remember what I said about not annoying these humans? Their magic is something to fear."

"Even more than wargs?" Max wasn't barking anymore.

"Definitely more than wargs."

Max lowered himself back into the grass. This time, he flattened himself so well that he almost became concealed. I could still smell him, though, and I was sure the wargs would be able to, too.

Aleam looked down at the dog a moment, then he glanced at

me. "Initiate Ben, have you any idea how soon the wargs will arrive?"

I perked up my ears and focused them on the distant sounds. I could tell how far away they were, but I had to rack my brain to remember how fast I'd seen them move before, and then translate this all into a human concept of time. It gave me a headache and made me sleepy. I let out a huge yawn.

"Ben?" Aleam said. "Come on, focus."

"What... Oh, thirty minutes... I don't think we'll have longer than that."

"And can you hear anything else? Manipulators, bone dragons, sounds of forests moving in unnatural ways."

"No... Just the wargs."

"Then we'll have time to ask Driar Reslin a few questions," Driar Brigel said. "Don't be so quick to jump to conclusions, Initiate Ben. The man has been loyal to our school for as long as we've all known him."

Aleam drew his staff from his back as he turned to look towards the horizon. "Better to be cautious."

Driar Brigel nodded at him and did the same. Driar Yila and Driar Lonamm looked at each other, and they presently also drew their staffs. All four Driars were watching Reslin's royal blue dragon, Tonnadi, with intent. Each of them had their staffs raised and ready.

Reslin turned the dragon at the last moment, and landed Tonnadi with her flank to us. He saluted the Driars as soon as Tonnadi had touched down. But then he noticed how their hands were clutched on their staffs, as if gearing up for a fight.

"Did I come at a bad time?" he called. Then he shook his head hard. "Oh, forget that. No time. There's wargs coming your way."

"That's exactly what we are concerned about," Driar Brigel said. "Please, Reslin, tell us those wargs have nothing to do with you."

Driar Reslin's jaw went slack. "Of course not... I was part of a meteorology survey team near Aurorest Forest, tracing some strange weather with the White Mages over there, when we spotted a pack of them gathering. We thought they were coming at us at first, but they went straight past us, as if moved by a higher power... Then I heard the grunt of a condor. Really, Tonnadi tried to warn your dragons, but they weren't responding..."

The Great Driars and Aleam all paused for a moment, and they scanned each other's faces. "Lasinta," Aleam said. "She can't have crossed the barrier, can she? Every single White Mage across the perimeter would know."

Reslin shook his head. "None of us saw her. But condors live in high places, Aleam. Not here, on the plains..."

Aleam put his hand to his chin. "Are you sure it was a condor you heard? Not just a hawk, or a red kite?"

Reslin nodded. "I was with meteorologists. They know their birds..."

"And the wargs are what? Thirty minutes away?" Driar Lonamm asked.

Reslin raised his eyebrows. "Good guess. How could you know? Come to think of it, how did you know they were coming in the first place?"

Aleam put away his staff as he cocked his head towards where I stood, Max still concealed in the grass next to me. "We have animals," he said.

"Oh..." Reslin said. "I remember. The cat who talks." Either he didn't see Max, or he deemed the dog as unimportant.

"I do an awful lot more than talk," I said.

"Yes, yes, I remember what you can do..." Reslin had seen what had happened when Astravar had tricked me into summoning those bat-buzzard *aeriosaur* creatures out of the portal to the Fifth Dimension. They'd gone on to attack Dragonsbond Academy during the same battle when I'd knocked Astravar off his demon dragon perch. "I just wanted to make sure my Bellari is safe... And all the rest of the students, of course." Reslin shrugged. "But particularly my Bellari. I'm sure you understand."

He looked at Driar Yila for affirmation. Apparently, she was the only member of the Council of Three who had ever had children of their own. Driar Yila nodded, then turned back to the students and addressed them.

"Listen, students. The worst thing that you can do is panic. Wargs are coming, and so we need to abandon this field trip. If we can summon our dragons back, and move in an orderly fashion, we can make a quick escape." She paused as if in thought.

Driar Lonamm sucked in a breath. "Our dragons," she said, her voice sounding a little airy. She spoke slowly as if not quite with it. "Can any of you reach your dragons? I can't find Flue anywhere." She let off a yawn.

My dragon... I yawned again. I wasn't just sleepy, I felt as if the earth wanted to drag me down into it. That was when I noticed. I hadn't the usual sense of Salanraja in my head. She was there, but she wasn't there consciously. Rather, when I listened, I heard strange, unintelligible murmurings, as if from a distant dream.

"Salanraja?" I asked. *"Salanraja, are you there?"*

No response. This was magic at work – some spell that cut me off from my dragon without me noticing. Without any of us noticing, it seemed. My body felt light. I felt as if I could simply float off into nothingness.

Something was happening. Something bad...

Driar Yila shook her head. "I can see the dragons... They're landing over there." Her hand floated upwards to point towards the horizon. "Drifting on the breeze... I can't see Farago... All I hear in my head is nonsense." Her voice also sounded light and airy. Very unlike the stern Driar Yila that I'd come to know.

Aleam pulled at the wattle under his chin. "It's more than just mind magic... Something is sending the dragons to sleep. I can hear Olan but she's fading, and she's not making any sense."

"The same with Plishk," Driar Brigel said, rubbing at his eyes. "But what could be doing this? Who could be doing this?"

I knew exactly who... I clenched my jaw. "Arran..."

Driar Yila looked down at me with narrowed eyes. I thought for the moment that she was angry, and about to tell me not to accuse someone in such a position of power. Disbelief then washed over her face. That expression quickly transformed into one of abject shock.

She wasn't looking at me anymore, but at a figure scrambling through the crowd. Seramina was pushing her way toward the front, her staff held out in front of her. The white crystal on top of it glowed brightly.

Yila wasn't fast enough to react, but Driar Brigel shouted out, "Watch out!" A green beam of light shot out of his staff that became a tangle of vines that started to wrap around the thirteen-year-old student.

But even Brigel hadn't been fast enough to stop Seramina's spell. The beam that shot out of her staff wasn't aimed at any of the Council of Three, but up into the sky.

"Stop, Brigel," Aleam said. He was squinting up at the point where the white beam hit the sky, erupting into a floating globe of light. "She's breaking a glamour, not attacking."

Driar Brigel looked at Aleam. The green light faded from his staff, and the vines loosened around Seramina, who shrugged them off.

At the same time, Aleam reached behind his back towards his staff, but he froze as he stared up at a massive shape that was materialising above us. A great black dragon appeared. It was Corralsa with the amber glow of the low sun reflecting off her scales, Prince Arran sitting in her saddle. She had her claws outstretched, though she moved rigidly as if she didn't quite want to follow Arran's commands.

The dragon was heading straight for Aleam, and she scooped the old man up in her claws. Corralsa lifted Aleam away, but Aleam's body wasn't stiff. Rather, he folded loosely in the dragon's claws, as if in ultimate surrender.

"Gracious demons!" Yila shouted. "The traitor."

She had her staff raised and a red beam shot out after Corralsa. It hit the dragon on the tail, causing her to roar out in pain. But she was already too far away for Driar Yila's magic to do much damage.

"I'll go after him," Driar Reslin said, and he stepped towards Tonnadi.

"No," Driar Brigel put out a hand to stop him. His voice sounded broken. "We don't know what's waiting for him, and we might need your dragon to deal with the approaching wargs."

"But he'll get away."

"And you could end up getting ambushed by Lasinta..." Driar Brigel said. "Remember the condor... Please, Reslin. We mustn't act irrationally..."

Reslin looked down at Bellari, who was staring up at him with almost pleading eyes.

Suddenly, something whinnied in the distance. I raised my ears and latched onto the sound of a rapid galloping of hooves. Three objects glistened on the horizon, and as they got closer, I saw them to be unicorn horns.

"The White Mages," Driar Reslin said. "And now of all times... What could they possibly want?"

✵   7   ✵

UNICORNS

At Dragonsbond Academy, I'd learned much about what the students considered the fastest land creature in the realm. "A unicorn could outrun a warg by miles," Rine had told me over dinner once, "and even the fittest of chimeras would have a hard time keeping up."

I often wondered how that compared to animals back home in the Fourth Dimension. We didn't have many fast animals in South Wales, admittedly, other than arrogant horses and wolf spiders. But the two Savannah Cats in my neighbourhood had told me about all kinds of speedy beasts of their ancestral land. "You would never win a race against an ostrich," they had said, "and an ostrich would never win a race against a cheetah."

Legend had it that when the old Ragamuffin heard that story and quizzed the Savannah Cats about the stamina of the cheetahs, the elder pointed out that surely the ostrich would win the race in the end. After all, nothing could keep sprinting at a cheetah's pace for long. But the Savannah Cats responded that the cheetah would eat the ostrich before it had a chance to go anywhere.

✧ 45 ✧

The unicorns that sprinted at full gallop towards us, were certainly running faster than any land animal I'd ever seen.

"They're strange looking horses," Max said to me from our perch at the top of the outcrop, watching the unicorns kick up a cloud of dust behind them.

The air had developed a certain staleness to it, and the encroaching night had started to sap it of its latent warmth. The falling sun cast a fiery hue over the land, one that might have inspired those who had hands and could stand the smell of paint to paint a picture. Once, I used to like sunsets, because they tended to signal the time that the mistress back in South Wales would call me in for dinner. Now, they just made me homesick.

Driar Yila waited with us, looking out at the unicorns galloping at full speed towards us. Driar Brigel and Driar Lonamm were on the ground below us, getting the students into formation, ready to fight. The wargs were only about five minutes away by that point.

I turned to Max. "They're not horses... In fact, they'd be rather offended if you compared them to a horse, just as a dragon would."

"But they move like horses, and they sound like horses, and—" Max sniffed the air – "they smell like horses. What else could they be?"

"Unicorns," I said. I reminded myself patiently that he'd not been listening in the human language to hear the announcement of their imminent arrival. "Surely you must have been around Arran long enough to encounter at least one of them."

"Why do they have horns on their heads, and why do they glow?" Max asked.

"In all honesty, I don't know... All I know is that it's part of their magic."

"There's that word again... I have no idea what this 'magic' is."

"It's anything that's not nature and not science."

"And what's science?"

"It's the practice of asking too many questions, which you seem to be particularly good at."

Three unicorns had come in total, with three White Mages riding them bareback, wearing white flowing cloaks that seemed not just to reflect but also to emit white light.

Two of the White Mages were women, I saw, one a man, all of them around Driar Reslin's age. The unicorns reared at the last moment, scuffing up clods of damp soil that I barely managed to dodge.

Each White Mage carried a staff in their hand, but unlike dragon riders and warlocks, none of these staffs had crystals at the top of them, and they weren't straight. Rather, they look like wood fashioned out of the branch of a gnarly oak, with smaller transparent crystals arranged in the whorls, knots, and features in the wood, as if their creators wanted to make art out of nature.

One of the women turned her unicorn to face Driar Yila. She had a gaunt face and eyes with massive bags under them, as if she hadn't slept for years. Her red hair curled inside the hood of her cloak, pushing it out a little. The deep frown on her face caused her bushy eyebrows to nearly meet at the centre.

Max had somehow buried himself even further into the grass, and he was looking with wide eyes at this woman's unicorn and its massive sky-blue eyes. The unicorn seemed to be focused on Max, as if it could see right through the grass. Whiskers, from what I'd heard about unicorns, it probably could.

I considered trying to strike up a conversation with it. But I had no idea how to start. Who knows what goes on in a horse's mind, particularly the type of horse that thinks itself special because of a glowing protrusion on its head.

"Great Driar Yila. I am Captain Alliander of the King's White

Guard," the White Mage on top of the unicorn said. "We have come under order of King Garmin to arrest Prince Arran for plans of insurrection and trying to overthrow Illumine Kingdom."

Driar Yila was tapping her foot. "Well that explains a lot. Now we know why Arran was in such a hurry. I'm guessing he was working for the warlocks all along."

Captain Alliander furrowed her eyebrows. "In a hurry to do what?"

"Arran took Aleam." Yila put her hand to her mouth to cover a yawn. "And he also somehow put our dragons to sleep. Meanwhile, we have an army of wargs approaching, and we could do with your help."

Alliander looked back in the direction from which she'd come. Cimlean City was in that direction. "As much as we wish to help, we were tasked by edict of King Garmin himself with the mission of stopping Arran and bringing him back to stand trial at Cimlean Palace. Now, in which direction did Arran go?"

Driar Yila took a deep breath and hesitated. From below us, beneath the outcrop, came a humming sound and the faint whiff of ozone. Under Driar Lonamm's and Driar Brigel's command, the students had set up the shields. Those who weren't shield mages had arranged themselves with the ice mages at the front, the fire mages in the centre, and the leaf mages and lightning mages at the rear.

The students kept yawning. But if one student would even close their eyes, the Driars would yell at them, making sleep impossible. Driar Reslin flew Tonnadi over the shield formation and supervised the scene from above.

Reslin would be high enough to see the wargs now. I still couldn't see them from where I stood. But I could hear them gnashing and gnarling, and their stench drifted ever closer on the breeze.

"If you please, Great Driar Yila," Captain Alliander said. "I can see that you're well equipped to deal with those wargs. But if we let Arran get away, there might be no stopping him."

Driar Yila shook her head and looked back at the captain with her stern gaze. The average human would wriggle beneath that gaze, trying to escape it. But this Captain Alliander was no average woman. She didn't blink, and her face remained as still as bowl-water.

"Driar Yila, I won't ask again," she said.

Driar Yila took a deep breath, then pointed with her staff to the northwest. The captain didn't hesitate. She saluted Yila, and she turned her unicorn and beckoned the other two White Mages onwards. The unicorns neighed, before turning on their hoofs under the White Mages' commands. They galloped off into the distance, kicking up heavy clods of dirt behind them.

A heavy sigh escaped Driar Yila's lips as she watched them go. There was history there, and for a moment I considered quizzing Driar Yila on it. Perhaps it would endear her a little more to me, because I'd always found her a tough nut to crack.

I'd like to say that the air smelled better now that the unicorns had gone, but I could still smell Max next to me, as well as a thousand approaching wargs.

"Ben, I need to ask a favour..." I turned to see Seramina standing next to me. Again, I couldn't detect her perfume. "Don't say anything, please. Just meow to say yes and growl to say no."

I growled at her as I already knew in my gut that whatever she suggested would be a bad idea.

"There's no need to be like that, Ben... This will help us both. I need you to turn into a chimera and carry me over to Hallinar. You'll be much faster than me."

I looked up at Driar Yila, who was watching the unicorns disappear behind the horizon. Clearly, she didn't have a clue that Seramina was there talking to me. I turned back to Seramina and growled again.

"Just listen, Ben. I've managed to work some magic to wake Hallinar up. He's out in the field, waiting for me, though there's still something in the air that's dragging him back to sleep again. If you can take me over there, then we can go and stop Arran. We can stop him and save Aleam, Ben... If we work together..."

Fire burned at the back of her eyes. When that happened, her magic seemed to be the most powerful. But, in my experience, this also meant she wasn't fully in control of her capabilities.

I growled one more time. Seems like my gut feeling had been right – this was a really bad idea.

"Please, Ben. Aleam, to me, is like the father I never had. We can stop Arran before this gets any worse. I know we can..."

I hesitated, but I didn't growl or meow. She had a fair point, I guessed. If I stayed there with the students, I'd be absolutely useless. But maybe I could fight Arran like I'd fought Astravar.

I looked up again at Driar Yila. The scowl on her face told me that if I even started to move in the wrong direction, she'd cast some magic on me to scorch my tail or something.

"Don't worry," Seramina said. "I'll cast an illusion so that no one knows that you've gone."

I meowed. I needed an adventure anyway. It felt so strange not having Salanraja in my mind anymore. What had Arran done to knock all the dragons out so quickly? There must have been some powerful magic behind it.

"Thank you, Ben," Seramina said. "We must be quick, though... See that light over there? Only you can see it." She pointed at a glowing sphere in the exact spot where Salanraja had been sitting before the fire golems attacked. "Meet me there. Don't turn into a chimera until you get there." She paused. "Trust me – you won't be seen."

"Okay," I said, and Seramina's glamoured form vanished.

I took a deep breath, then I sprinted towards the white light, releasing the pent-up energy I'd gathered by sitting around for too long.

⚜ 8 ⚜

CHASING ARRAN

Seramina had promised that I wouldn't be seen, but the first thing I heard was Max panting away as he chased after me. He probably hadn't seen me but smelled me. He used his squat form to stay completely concealed in the grass.

"Where are you going, Dragoncat?" he asked. "What scheme are you hatching up?" He was howling now... loudly... and the hum of the shields and Great Barrier didn't seem to drown out his voice. "Stay behind," I growled back at him, as softly as I could without being noticed.

Behind Max, who continued to howl questions, Driar Yila scoured the territory, looking for the source of the noise. Seramina's staff probably still showed me and Max sitting in the tufts of grass next to her. Which meant she now would have thought another dog had entered our proximity.

"Will you be quiet?" I asked.

"Only if you tell me what you're up to."

"I'm on a mission. We're going after your master, who has kidnapped one of ours."

"You mean I'm going to see Arran again? You're returning me to my master?" he sounded excited. I don't think he'd quite worked out that 'his master' was the bad guy here.

"I've still not worked out exactly what Arran wants with you, but if you don't shut up, we'll never return you to him."

Max lowered himself into the grass. "What must I do?"

"You must stay very silent and follow me. Imagine we're hunting."

"Okay," Max said, now only panting.

He stayed remarkably silent as he followed me towards the light. I could see now why people would want to use Max as a hunting dog. His shortness and soft paws helped him navigate the terrain well. Perhaps the reason that Arran had wanted him here was the simplest one – he just couldn't find a better dog for catching game.

But I just knew in my gut that there had to be more to it than that.

"Ben, you came," Seramina said as we arrived at the light. "I tried to wake up Salanraja too, but my magic only worked on Halli-nar. He's ready to fly. I just need to get over there as quickly as possible."

"So why don't you just get him to come here?" I asked.

"Because I can't cast a glamour spell that far. If anyone sees him take off or fly overhead, they're going to be awfully suspicious. The last thing I want is that Driar Reslin chasing after us."

While Seramina was speaking, Max was looking up at her, wagging his tail. "Ben, who is this?" he asked.

Seramina turned her gaze downwards, evidently surprised to see Max sitting there in the long grass. "You brought the dog?"

"It's Arran's dog, and I have a feeling he's part of the puzzle here. He brought him into this dimension for a reason and then abandoned him. Maybe if we take him with us, we can find out exactly what Arran was planning."

Seramina shook her head. "The thing about dogs, is they're always loyal to their masters. He might attack us as soon as we turn our staffs on Arran."

"Trust me, I'm working on convincing him that Arran is the bad guy."

"And how's he going to react when he sees you turn into a chimera?"

"Hopefully, he'll be very scared of me, and will decide that he better do exactly what I tell him to do."

"Good luck," Seramina said. She didn't look particularly convinced.

"You sure no one can see me?" I asked.

"The glamour is tight. But the longer you delay, the further Arran escapes."

I didn't hesitate. I focused on my muscles and willed them to strain and tear. I said I hadn't cast dark magic for a while, but it was even longer since I'd turned into a chimera.

The pain overtook me so much, that I wanted to roar. But I bit my heavy lion tongue to stop myself. Max, as he watched me, started barking. "Danger! Danger! Dragoncat is a grizzly warg!"

"I thought you said you'd shut up," I roared back, and then I rammed the back of my lion's head with my goat head to shut me up. I'd already revealed my disguise. Driar Yila jumped off the rise above us, surprisingly spry given her age.

I spoke softer as I watched Driar Yila move slowly towards us. "This is magic, and I'm not a warg. But right now, I'm your best chance of surviving the wargs." I switched to the human language. "Seramina, you can get on now..."

Seramina approached me, and she gently stroked my mane. She clambered onto my back, seeming to weigh absolutely nothing – but then I was ten times as strong as a chimera than I was as a cat, and Seramina was slight, to say the least.

Max growled at me, and I turned my snake head to him and hissed back at him. "Get on Max... We've not got much time."

I noticed he was still wagging his tail, backing away, barking.

"You probably want to stop hissing at him," Seramina said.

"Oh right..." I willed my tail, namely the snake head, to coil up, and through my goat head I let out a soft bleat. It was always strange being able to see through three heads at once – I don't think I'd ever get used to it.

Max took a step towards me. "How do I know I can trust you?"

I cocked my lion's head over at Driar Yila who was now sweeping her staff through the long grass, in an attempt to break through the glamour and discover our location. "It's either you trust me, or you trust her. And when she finds you, she'll be very angry."

"But I didn't do anything wrong," Max whined.

"Just get on my back, will you? We're going to see your master."

Max turned his head a couple of times between me and Driar Yila, and then seemed to decide that I was his best option. He sprinted clumsily onto my back. He slipped over it to settle onto Seramina's lap.

"You know, he's kinda cute," Seramina said as she secured Max in place using one arm as the other clutched the staff that she'd used to cast the glamour. "I never thought I liked dogs. But he's like a very big cat, with a... long tongue. Yeuch, stop licking me!"

I was seething inside as I heard Seramina speak those words. The last thing I wanted was for her to become a dog person.

"What's his name by the way?" Seramina asked.

"It's Max..." It really didn't seem worth the effort making up a nickname.

"Initiate Ben," Driar Yila called. "Now is not the time to be turning into a chimera, and Initiate Seramina, I know you're with him. The longer you hide from me, the more severe the repercussions are going to be."

"They're so quick to distrust," Seramina said, and she tightened her thighs to spur me into action, as one might a horse.

"Let's get out of here," I said. "Direct me, Seramina."

"Very well, just follow the light." She thrust her staff forward. The crystal on it lit up, and a set of glowing cat footprints appeared before us, leading through the grass. On paws and hooves, I galloped off along her magical path, leaving the seething Driar Yila and all the students behind.

FLIGHT OF THE CHIMERA

The wind picked up as we went, and I could taste the stench of wargs on it. I still couldn't see them, but a dust cloud kicked up by their charge now filled the horizon. Fortunately, there was no trace of rotten vegetable juice in the air suggesting magical conjurations of warlocks. My comrades, I hoped, would only have to deal with the wargs.

Seramina kept her arms wrapped around my goat neck as the wet grass brushed against my paws and hoofs. We were veering away from the approaching army. Part of me wanted to swerve back towards the wargs and fight them head on. But having three heads and the strength, speed, and venom of legends didn't make me invincible.

Besides, we had to get to Hallinar as quickly as we could.

Max continued to bark away. "This is fun! This is fun!" he repeated.

Fortunately, it didn't matter anymore how much noise he made. I doubt the Driars back at the formation could hear us over the hum of their shields. Even if they could, they weren't going to come chasing after us when they needed to save their own skins.

Seramina's paws of light led me further away from the wargs, and we eventually found the dragons. I noticed Quarl first – Ange's sapphire blue dragon, lying peacefully, his wings outstretched, and his head resting against a clump of dirt. His scales and the skin underneath it remained unscratched and unbruised, as if he had just glided down to the ground as he surrendered himself to sleep.

I charged past him, then past Ishtkar – Rine's emerald dragon. Bellari's citrine dragon, Pinacole, was there too. In the distance, Olan – Aleam's gigantic white dragon – was sprawled over a boulder that jutted out of the terrain. Underneath the giant majestic dragon lay Salanraja. It made me feel empty to see her so vulnerable like that.

"Salanraja... Salanraja, are you there?"

No reply.

I wanted to reach out and tell her that my bond with her did mean something. It meant as much to me as Ta'ra, the former Cat Sidhe who would be waiting for me in Aleam's quarters, the scent of mackerel and milk on her breath.

As I went, my legs became sluggish, and my eyes heavy. Max had stopped barking and was instead making soft whining sounds. There was a sweet smell in the air, one which made me happy to be alive and part of this world. The sun had almost sunk behind the western horizon, making the shadows long.

A green glowing haze rose from the earth, and I bristled when I realised what it was. It was coming from mushrooms... Lots of them scattered across the terrain, their heads wide with red and white polka-dots.

"Gracious demons," Seramina said, and she said it through a yawn. "*Somnambulis* mushrooms. I might have known."

"Somna..." I didn't even have the will to repeat what she said.

"They're those mushrooms that grow in the Aurorest Forest. You know the ones that send you to sleep? Arran must have planted them here. Hang on, I'll cast a different spell."

A moment later, something warm and wet touched the back of my lion's head. It gave my muscles enough strength to move again, and a little clarity returned to my mind. Max also woke up, making a heavy panting sound as his tail slowly and gently patted my back. But still, I felt sluggish.

"Need more power," Seramina said, again holding her voice through a yawn. "This won't last for long... Ben, it'll be easier if you're smaller. We can take the rest on foot."

I guessed I was far too large for her magic to be effective. Maybe, Seramina wasn't actually as strong as I thought.

I lowered my back, and Max sprung off me, followed by Seramina. The dog gazed up at her as if begging for food, or at least fawning for attention. She looked down at him and shook her head.

It hurt much less to turn back into a cat than it had to turn into a chimera in the first place. The skin now felt less bloated, and just shrank back to wrap around its natural form. Soon, I was once again a Bengal – a descendant of the great Asian leopard cat and the mighty George.

Shortly after, a white light had appeared on the crystal at the top of Seramina's staff, and from it a white glowing bubble pulsed out. This was different to the protective spells that shield mages like High Prefect Lars could cast. Instead, it had the ability to push the green spores produced by the *somnambulis* mushrooms away and freshen the air somewhat.

A sense of cleanliness washed over me, as if I'd just stepped out of a waterfall without getting soaked. I yawned, then I noticed I didn't feel tired anymore.

Max started barking again. "What happened? What happened? I was asleep. Now I'm awake. What happened?" He seemed to want to eat the air as he spoke, and his tail waved violently above his rump.

"He's an anxious little thing, isn't he," Seramina said.

Max looked up at her and continued barking in his gruff voice as if he wanted to scare her. But when Seramina looked back at him, with those burning fires in her eyes, Max seemed to get scared himself and backed down.

Seramina turned away, then started walking, the protective barrier following her. Her voice sounded airy as she spoke. "This way... Stay close..."

The mushrooms parted away from her as she walked, and even the grass seemed to bend away from her spell. The spore clouds also seemed to eddy away from the protective bubble, creating what looked like a vacuum on the spell's outer wall.

Max and I padded after Seramina.

"Is this magic?" Max asked as we went. "Or am I dreaming? Because I could swear I just went to sleep."

"No," I said. "This is magic... Seramina is doing this to protect us from your master, Arran..."

"But how do I know I'm not sleeping? This is the kind of thing I see in dreams."

Every so often, Max surprised me. This time, he made me wonder what kind of dreams he'd had that involved things like magic. Because I'd always dreamt about bowls of milk and food and chasing butterflies, not about casting spells.

"What?" Max barked, when he noticed me studying him.

"You're a strange creature," I said.

"No, you're wrong. It's you cats who are strange; you always have been. Dogs are sociable, and cats are obtuse..."

"I'm not obtuse," I said. I had my back arched, my claws digging into the ground ready to strike. I spoke not in dog but in cat, hissing away. "I'm a Bengal, descendant of the great Asian leopard cat – the mightiest breed of cat ever."

Actually, I'd discovered in the Ghost Realm that they weren't that mighty after all. But I had no reason to tell anyone that. I was, after all, the only living creature in this dimension who had met an Asian leopard cat.

"Will you two stop fighting?" Seramina said. "Because if you keep slowing me down, I'm going to leave you here."

We had already fallen a little behind, and almost passed the threshold of Seramina's protective spell. I strode over to her, and Max followed in close step. We couldn't see far beyond the sphere of white light, but she seemed to know where she was going.

It wasn't long before we saw the head of a charcoal dragon resting on a mossy boulder, covered in lichen at its base. Hallinar had his eyes open. They gazed straight past us, the inky pupils almost filling his yellow eyes.

"Hallinar," Seramina said. "Okay, Ben, Max, don't fall asleep. Make sure you tell him Ben, because I know he doesn't understand me."

I relayed the command to the dog, speaking as fast as I could, without barking. Then I turned back to Seramina. "Why, exactly?"

She didn't answer the question, for she had already turned her staff towards Hallinar. The bubble around us shrank into a beam of white light, that Seramina directed towards the furrow between Hallinar's grey, scaly brows.

The dragon's pupils suddenly became narrow, vertical slits, his eyes glowing as they reflected the ambient green light. His tail thumped the ground, and he tossed his head upwards. A roar followed a fast jet of amber fire from his mouth, landing just next to us. Max barked at the dragon.

"Dragons breathe fire," he said. "Dangerous! Dangerous!"

"I told you they did," I barked back. "Now shut up, or it will eat you."

Max buried his head in his paws. "I want to go back to Arran," he whined. "I want good food and a good master again. This place isn't right..."

Seramina had almost finished mounting Hallinar, using one hand to pull herself up, whilst the other remained focused on casting the spell against the back of the dragon's head. She beckoned us up with vigour.

That sweet smell had filled the air again, and tendrils of gas slowly crept in towards us, questing inwards as if it had discovered we were once again unprotected.

"Come on, you two," Seramina said. "If I break this spell, Hallinar will fall asleep."

Max was still barking at Hallinar, and I didn't think we had a chance of getting him up on Hallinar's back. I had half a mind to leave him there, but something told me that we needed him. So I turned towards him. "Remember how you mounted me when I was a big scary monster?"

"Yes," Max said, his eyes wide as he watched the glowing gas seep ever closer. A tendril coiled through the air towards him and touched the rim of his nose.

"Trust me, this dragon is nowhere near as scary. But this gas that's trying to send you to sleep is."

"Why, what will it do?" Max said.

"Just follow me," I said, and I scurried up Hallinar's tail, taking my place behind Seramina.

Max stayed on the ground, staring up at us. At its edges, the gas cloud seemed to take on the shape of several glowing cloaked figures, ready to wrap Max in their embrace.

"Is he coming or what?" Seramina said. "We need to take off now."

"He'll come," I said.

"I'm giving it three…"

Max lowered his back to the ground.

"Two…"

Max sniffed at the air, then he sneezed.

"One…"

Seramina's thighs tightened around Hallinar's saddle, and the dragon spread out his wings, wafting the gas away from Max, temporarily. At that moment, the dog remembered himself, and he launched onto Hallinar's tail. He clambered up it, just as the dragon took off.

Hallinar lifted quickly into the sky. As we went higher, the glow got fainter, and I could see how helpless the dragons looked inside the sleepy, polka dotted field. Even higher, and I could see the shield barrier and the army of wargs about to hit it.

We flew over them just as the first magic spell launched from our ranks. My comrades would be able to handle themselves against these wargs, but I had no idea what other tricks Prince Arran had up his sleeves.

We had to stop him before it was too late.

10

TRAITOR

We weren't long in the air before the grunt of a condor came from afar, clearly defined over the fading growls, barks, and gnashes of the wargs. We flew towards a low grey cloud, dark streaks from it touching the horizon. I could feel the humidity from the approaching storm.

The sun had just vanished from the sky, and dusk was fading towards twilight. I sat at the back of Hallinar's saddle, remembering how Salanraja had once told me what a crime it was for a dragon rider to ride another's dragon. But I hoped, given the circumstances, she'd understand.

Seramina sat in front of me, and I leant to the side so I could see the terrain unfold before us. Max sat again on Seramina's lap, panting happily. Despite us being I don't know how high in the sky, he remained remarkably silent.

While I'd found my first flights on a dragon terrifying, the Sussex Spaniel seemed to quite enjoy flying. Mind you, I hadn't actually asked how many times he'd ridden Corralsa before this. I guessed he must have done so at least once, so as to meet us at the Great Barrier in the first place.

The condor grunted once again, and I twisted my head to see its massive blurry form pass through the grey cloud. Not as large as a dragon, I guess, but still bigger than any bird I'd ever seen in South Wales.

There, we had some pretty big red kites, and my mother had taught me as a kitten to hide from them whenever we noticed one soar overhead. Even when fully grown, I still darted for the nearest hedge whenever I saw one, preferring any thorns I might encounter to falling under a kite's watchful gaze. You never knew when they'd spear down from the sky and strike you unawares.

I did exactly the same when I saw the condor. I clambered over the back of the saddle and hid behind the cantle. Seramina didn't seem to notice.

"An eagle?" she asked. "What's it doing all the way over here?"

"It's a condor," I said. "I don't know if you heard when Reslin told the Driars, but he heard one when they spotted the wargs. They think it's a warlock."

"Lasinta..." Seramina said, distaste evident in her voice. "If Arran's working with her... This is a lot bigger than I thought."

"Wait, I've heard of Lasinta..." Driar Yila had mentioned her in our 'A Modern History of Magic' lessons. Of course, I'd been asleep during most of them, not caring about any type of history that didn't involve good food. "She's one of the six, right?"

"They say she's the oldest of them all. Their leader..."

I emerged from my hiding spot and rubbed my head against Seramina's waist, at least appreciative for the warmth coming from her hip, against the bitter cold wind. I might have even been purring, but perhaps that was more to soothe anxiety of what lay ahead, rather than contentment.

"Lasinta's also incredibly powerful, I hear," Seramina said, stroking me. "At least that's what I've read about her in the library."

"More powerful than Astravar?"

"In ways. Astravar had greater magical abilities, but Lasinta has charm, and she has influence. That's why I didn't want to be so quick to discount the possibility of an accomplice before. Despite the treaty, I'm sure she'll have people working for her inside Cimlean City. Now it seems, she even had an ally in King Garmin's palace."

"So Arran is her accomplice?"

"I don't know yet... But I'm sure we're soon about to find out."

A distant roar of thunder came from the clouds, followed several seconds later by a flash of lightning. I growled – I liked thunderstorms almost as much as I liked fireworks. Why, when things went wrong in life, did they always seem to want to do so in thunder and rain?

Another flash of lightning came, and all of a sudden, time seemed to distort.

The wind seemed distant, and a white light tore through the clouds on the horizon, seeming to rip space and time in two. The freshness in the air became lost, and I caught a whiff of rotten vegetable juice.

I suddenly remembered that time I'd been standing in the kitchen of South Wales, eating a nice breakfast of milk and salmon trimmings. There had come a flash of white light, and a great gaping hole had opened up in front of me. Then two hands yanked me into this world. The rest, as they say, is history...

"What in the seventh dimension?" Seramina asked. "They're using the lightning to open a portal..."

"Aleam's lightning... Is he casting the spell?"

Seramina hesitated. "No, impossible... Aleam would never..."

"Could they possibly be controlling Aleam?"

Though I couldn't see Seramina's face, I could all but imagine the tightness in her features. She spoke through clenched teeth. "We have to get down there fast…"

The air ahead seemed to shimmer, then the portal opened to display a bright blue sky and a verdant terrain. "That's the Fairy Rea—"

I got cut off when Hallinar suddenly dived towards the ground. I screeched as I dug my claws into his scales to keep purchase. Max had started barking again, but this time, it wasn't a bark of warning.

"Such fun! Such fun!" he screamed. "More! More! More! More!"

"Shut up, Max," I barked back at him. "Don't announce our arrival."

Hallinar lifted his claws as he approached the ground. I heard galloping hooves, and I peered over the edge to see three unicorns storming towards the warlocks. They had their staffs raised high in the sky.

"Is that Captain Alliander?" I asked.

"Who?" Seramina called back.

"The captain of the White Mages who we met before. Whiskers, those unicorns are fast."

"At least that means we're not going in alone…" Seramina's voice trailed off as she focused on the crystal on her staff which started to glow white once more. I thought I saw something pulse out of the crystal for a moment, but I only had to blink and it wasn't glowing at all.

Another flash of lightning came out from the cloud, glinting momentarily off Corralsa's scales which had been previously camouflaged against the rocky terrain. Pillars of stone towered around her.

I spotted Arran just next to the portal, his staff glowing purple. A beam coming out of this fed a larger crystal. The crystal refracted this into a larger white beam that fed the portal. Arran no longer wore his red cloak, instead being completely clad in black cloth.

Aleam still wore his normal brown cloak. He had his back to us, his thin grey hair billowing behind him in the wind. He also had his staff raised. This time, his crystal glowed yellow, and another flash of lightning streaked down and tore the portal open even further. The condor let out a hissing wheeze and it descended towards three neatly stacked shallow boulders. It perched itself on a segment of the rock that jutted out at a sharp angle from the second boulder.

"I've already cast a glamour over us," Seramina said. "They shouldn't be able to see us."

"But they can see the White Mages."

"Once the White Mages realise that there's more to worry about than Arran, I'm sure they'll retreat. I just hope it's only the three of them, Ben... We must stay hidden. Tell Max that too."

I told Max exactly what she had told me.

"But Arran... You said that I was going to see my master."

"Max, I don't know how to tell you this. But Arran is not the man you think he is. If he sees you, he'll end your life, and then he'll end mine, Seramina's, and her dragon's too."

"My Arran wouldn't do that..."

"Oh, believe me, he would. Do you see that big bird over there? It likes to eat dogs like you for breakfast."

11

PLOY

Hallinar touched down on the ground, his feet remarkably silent as they pressed into the soft forest floor. I guess this was also an effect of Seramina's glamour – perhaps it could partly mask sound as well as sight. The speed gained by Hallinar's descent had caused us to overtake the unicorns, but we hadn't gained much on them.

Soon, twelve mighty hooves stormed past us. The light from the unicorn's horns seemed to cut a path ahead of them, as if their magic could push away the swirling purple mist. Thunder boomed, and cold rain poured from above. Luckily, I was of a breed that didn't mind water so much, because this storm would have sent most cats scarpering for the nearest bush.

The White Mages pulled their hoods further over their heads as they dismounted their unicorns. They held their staffs in front of them and trudged through the swirling puddles towards Arran.

The unicorns padded after their riders, their hooves virtually silent against the water. Each took a position beside their White

Mage, and the air between the horns and the staffs seemed to shimmer, almost as if one was feeding the other with magic.

"Can you hear what they're saying, Ben?" Seramina asked. "Because I can cast a spell to amplify their voices, but it might draw some power from the glamour."

"I can... Let me listen, and I'll report later." I perked up my ears and focused on the sounds. This, I didn't want to miss.

"Prince Arran of Castigate," Captain Alliander said. "The White Guard hereby arrests you for plans of treason and—" Her eyes fell upon Aleam – "What in the Seventh Dimension? So this is where he disappeared to. Drop your hold on Driar Aleam and surrender yourself or feel the wrath of his majesty and your liege, King Garmin."

Arran guffawed, throwing his head back like a chicken. "I've never heard such insolence... You know I am the right hand of King Garmin and the head of his Dragon Corps. You should answer to me."

"That position has been rescinded. The king has ordered your immediate arrest and return to the palace for detainment. Your schemes have been uncovered, Prince Arran, and you will serve as a spy to the warlocks no more."

"A spy?" Arran looked up towards the condor. "Do you hear that? I told you that they were starting to work things out. But now, once the key arrives, then we can force the knowledge that we need out of Driar Aleam and dispose of him. I'm afraid the plans are already in motion, Captain—er what was your name again?"

"Don't play games with me, brother," Alliander said.

Arran scuffed his foot against the ground. "Step-brother, I think you'll find. In other words, I don't consider you related at all."

He raised his staff, and Captain Alliander shouted out, "Now!" to her comrades.

Three beams of light emerged from the space between the horns of the unicorns and the staffs of the mages. These wove outwards to create an intricate web of light in the sky.

All three White Mages shouted out in unison as they pointed their staffs at Arran. But he responded with a spell of his own – a tiny purple globe that he didn't direct at the mages or the web, but rather the condor.

I only needed to blink, and the condor had somehow vanished and reappeared behind the unicorns, a cloud of smelly purple dust rising up around it. The cloud dissipated and Lasinta stepped out from within it.

She was a wraith-like woman – older looking even than Aleam, and so wrinkled that the skin seemed to want to slide off her bones. She had her purple-crystal staff in one hand, and in the other another fist-sized purple crystal that also emitted a faint blue light. She threw this at the ground in front of the unicorns, and it exploded into a thin mist that enveloped them.

At the same time, the White Mages had their web wrapped around Arran. He was trapped, but so were the White Mages, underneath Lasinta's paralysing mist. The unicorns stopped making their whinnying sounds, and both the horses and the humans had become as still as stone.

Lasinta made a grunting sound, and she walked right past her frozen enemies. She stopped for a moment, and put her hand on Captain Alliander's unicorn's horn, then she repeated the action with the other two. The glow left the horns, and the web wrapped around Arran dissipated.

"Grandmother," Arran said, his hands on his hips as he watched. "I told you they were on to me."

"Grandmother..." I repeated. Seramina looked down at me, her eyebrows high. "It sounds like Arran and Lasinta are actually related."

"Doesn't surprise me," Seramina replied.

In the distance, Lasinta wrapped her arms around Arran and pulled him into an embrace. She whispered something in his ear, too quiet for me to hear. Then she walked over to examine Aleam. The old man was now facing us, and I could see an unnatural white glow in his eyes. I'd seen a similar look in Seramina's eyes when Astravar had possessed her in the past. It had happened twice in fact.

I just couldn't believe what I was seeing. Somehow, I'd always thought Aleam to be invincible.

Arran wasn't watching Lasinta, but instead had his gaze affixed on Captain Alliander. "We should dispose of them. Leave no tracks, so they can't report the details back to King Garmin."

Lasinta jerked her gaze towards Arran. She spoke in an acerbic tone. "Have you not been warned before about manipulating destiny? The crystals have shown us it's not time to kill them now."

"But surely there must be one possible future in which she dies. I've always held that the future cannot be set in stone."

"That's because you are a fool, Arran. As much as you are my blood, you still haven't learned the wisdom in magic. Some visions can be bent, and others can't. If we kill her now, our fates will be much, much worse. We need to give them a fair chance to survive."

"Then we should send them somewhere. A portal to the Seventh Dimension—"

"Will surely kill them," Lasinta snapped. "The demons there will devour the unicorns first and leave the White Mages for dessert."

Arran put his hand to his chin. The sour scowl on his face told me he didn't like the way his grandmother was speaking to him. "Then we can send them to the Ghost Realm," he said.

Lasinta shook her head slowly. "It was Astravar's undoing to send the magic-wielding cat and his companions there. Can you remember how the denizens of the Ghost Realm aided them? We won't let that happen again." She looked in our direction, and I wondered for a moment if she'd noticed us. But she just shook her head and turned back to Arran.

"Send them to the Fourth Dimension, where the crystals are so far buried underground that they won't ever be able to cast the magic they need to return here. That way, at least we'll know your stepsister is still alive."

Arran let out a soft chuckle. "I know just the place. Aleam, do you know of that place the textbooks call the Great Desert? The one that's larger than even the Calimar Desert here in the First Dimension."

He turned his staff towards Aleam as he spoke, and from out of it shot a white light that hit him right on the forehead.

Aleam's words came out dry and slow, almost as if they've been rehearsed by an incredibly poor actor. "I know of the Great Desert of the Fourth Dimension, where the sun blasts the sand at day and the stars twinkle over cold nights."

"That's what your textbooks say," Arran said. "So let this desert be their undoing. Is that satisfactory, grandmother? They can't, after all, cast magic in the Fourth Dimension."

"Do it..." Lasinta said, and she turned to Aleam. "Open a portal to the Great Desert of the Fourth Dimension. After that, we will go about finding your so-called key to the Sixth, which you appear to have misplaced."

"It is the dog," Arran said. "He is the key to the Sixth Dimension. He will come. I cast a spell... Although it seems to be late working." He shrugged.

"What?" I said, and I looked up at Seramina, my whiskers twitching.

"What is it, Ben?" she asked.

"Arran just told Lasinta that Max is a key."

"A key to what?"

"The Sixth Dimension..."

I looked over at the Sussex Spaniel, whose tongue was hanging low. I had no idea how a dog could be a key. The notion sounded ridiculous. But I guessed we would soon discover the answer to that mystery. We just had to work out how to save Aleam and the White Mages first.

12

DESERT PORTAL

Max was whining under his breath as he watched a large bee leave a tulip and buzz its way towards us. I listened to it for a moment, then focused again on what was happening in the distance. Aleam cast another flash of lightning that ripped open a second portal to a sandy landscape.

From where I stood, I could see one of those animals that the humans called a camel, chewing on the spiny rind of a cactus. It turned and stared back through the white halo that rimmed the portal, probably wondering where the whiskers the First Dimension had appeared from. I knew exactly how that felt.

"Very good," Arran said, and he turned towards the crystal. This crystal now had two beams coming out from it, each feeding one of the portals, as well as the one that Arran fed into it.

Lasinta also had her staff drawn. From it, she cast another beam towards the holding spell that surrounded the White Mages. The cloud dispersed where the beam hit it, transforming into a loosely shaped bubble with incredibly soft edges. Lasinta had her nose turned up to the air, sniffing it like a dog.

"Wait," she called. "Arran, there's someone else here... A powerful presence. Could it be?"

Arran turned to his grandmother. "Who?"

Keeping her staff pointed towards the White Mages, Lasinta strode towards us.

"Are you the one they call Seramina, I wonder? I've read in the crystals that you shall one day be a powerful warlock..."

Before we could react, Lasinta whipped her staff around and shot out a great purple fireball. It came towards us so fast, that if I'd have blinked, I would have missed it. Within its light, I caught sight of a glowing smiling skull, rimmed with fire.

The spell exploded just before us, but it didn't produce any heat. Rather, it washed over the glamour bubble that Seramina had cast, revealing what looked like a warped sheet of glass. This shattered into a thousand pieces, which in turn crumbled into dust. The stench of rotten vegetable juice assaulted me even harder. The same paralysing mist that surrounded the White Mages also hugged us tightly.

Fear washed over my body, as my muscles gave out. I couldn't even extend my claws, though the magic gave enough room for my heart to pound in my chest, my lungs to breathe, and my eyes to look out the corner of their sockets to see Seramina paralysed on the spot next to me. Her dragon was also completely rigid, looking like a gigantic, reconstructed dinosaur.

Arran, with his hands on his hips, took a few steps forward. "Pathetic," he said, looking at Seramina. Then he turned his gaze down upon me. "I see you brought the cat, and an entire dragon too... And the dog. I told you that my magic would bring him to me, Grandmother."

Max stepped in front of us and started barking. "My last master bad! My current master bad! I trust no masters!" he shouted.

Lasinta screwed up her eyes as she looked down at the dog. "It actually appears your magic did not work. Impossible, yet so fascinating... Let's try that again." She turned her staff downwards, and a beam of purple light hit the Sussex Spaniel right between the eyes. But it seemed to do nothing to him.

"Your magic doesn't work either, grandmother," Arran said, his head cocked. "How can this be?"

"Your 'Key to the Sixth Dimension' must be a lot more than just a dog."

Max now growled and he had his hind legs tucked back, ready to pounce. He went straight for Lasinta's legs. But she was faster than him, and swirled her staff around her feet, creating a cloud of purple gas that she could float upon, cross-legged. Arran did the same, both levitating over the gnashing teeth of the dog, whom the cloud didn't seem to affect one bit.

"Most interesting indeed," Lasinta said. "Let us get rid of our evidence, then we shall summon a suitable golem to restrain him. Arran, you handle the White Mages, and I'll handle the young warlock and the cat."

Arran nodded, then he spun around on his cloud, and he focused his beam on the crystal once again. The purple mist glowed around the unicorns and the White Mages. Under Arran's control, they lifted off the ground, and floated like lilies on water over to the portal that Arran had opened to the Fourth Dimension, taking the mist with it.

Another beam came out of Lasinta's staff, again aimed in the direction of the larger crystal. I felt nothing as Seramina, Hallinar, and I lifted off the ground except a slight stinging sensation in my eyes and a lightening of my breath.

The paralysing gas seemed to follow us as we floated towards the portal, and I felt as if I was in a dream. As we went, Max continued to gnash and bark at Arran above him, all the while snapping his head around to see what was happening to us.

"Master is using magic! Magic is bad. Bad master is using bad magic!"

I wanted to scream for him to shut up, or at least do something to try and free Aleam from this spell. Or even better, try and topple the massive crystal that kept these two portals open. Then maybe we would have a fighting chance.

Time seemed to slow as we passed the threshold to the Fourth Dimension and the portal started to close under Arran and Lasinta's command.

That was when, on the other side of our portal, I saw a blue wisp floating out of the first portal – the one that Arran had opened to the Faerie Realm. It was a fairy, but what was it doing here? The blue wisp spiralled down to the ground and materialised into human form. My breath caught in my throat when I recognised the man behind the glamour.

Ta'lon. The name echoed around my head. Ta'ra's former betrothed. The man who I knew Ta'ra still loved at the bottom of her heart, but she never admitted it to me. He turned to look at us, but his eyes glowed white just like Aleam's. Was he also under the warlocks' control?

Still on Arran and Lasinta's side of the portal, Max had stopped barking, and instead ran around in a circle, as if he couldn't decide whether to help us, help Aleam, try to attack this new fairy, or keep barking at Lasinta and Arran. Eventually, his gaze settled on us, and he ran towards us.

Beside us, I could see the Three White Mages and their unicorns, still floating in the purple cloud just as we were. From our viewpoint hovering above the sands of the Fourth Dimension, the portal was now a thin slit, and it had almost closed completely.

Max came bounding through just as the portal winked out of existence. He hit the ground and tumbled over it in a clumsy roly-poly fashion. At the same time, the paralysing clouds dissipated, dropping Seramina, Hallinar, the three White Mages, the three unicorns, and I to the scorching desert floor.

13

SCORCHING SANDS

I'd like to say my landing was the most graceful out of all of ours. But somehow, Hallinar extended his wings at the last moment, and used them to glide down for the last metre or so. Seramina also had her staff out, and she was quick to cast a sheet of white light underneath her. On top of the sheet, she floated down on her side like a feather. As soon as she touched the sand, Hallinar outstretched his wing to cover her with his shadow.

Despite being a cat and being made for hot conditions, the sand was far too scorching for the exposed skin on my paws. I scurried over and took refuge under Hallinar's wing. Seramina's magic had now seeped into the sand and cooled it enough to handle. Max wasn't far behind me, and he lay down in the shade, muttering unintelligible whimpers.

"I can't cast any more magic here" Seramina said as she examined her staff. "What's blocking me?"

"The warlocks said that we cannot cast here," I pointed out.

Seramina nodded. "I read something about that in a book from the library. A people of your kind called the Egyptians overused the magic for their own gain, and so the crystals found a way to bury themselves beneath the sands."

I tried to imagine the crystals buried under all the dunes that I saw stretched out before me. I guessed it would take a lot of digging to bring them back up again.

I didn't see how the White Mages landed. But I did hear Captain Alliander giving her commands to the other two White Mages. "Mount your unicorns immediately," she instructed them. "We need to find some kind of shade."

She looked around at the rolling landscape of dunes, but I wasn't sure what she expected to find. She and her two companions had completely bunched themselves up in their white cloaks to protect them from the sun. Captain Alliander was already sitting on her unicorn, and the other two mounted without asking any questions.

The horns weren't glowing on the unicorns anymore. Now, they just looked like white horses with props on their heads. Honestly, I'd seen a seashell in my master and mistress' place back in South Wales that looked just like their horns.

Once the three White Mages had regrouped, they wheeled around and started to trot over to us. Seramina addressed them before they even stopped to hail us. "You can come and shelter here, if you want," she called out. "We are not your foes…"

As if understanding Seramina's offer, Hallinar outstretched his other charcoal wing, casting a long shadow.

Captain Alliander stopped in front of us, still in the sun. "First… White Mage's duty. Have you any injuries that need attending to?"

"Your magic won't work here," I said. I tried to summon my staff bearer to confirm this, and I couldn't feel it anywhere nearby. "We're in the Fourth Dimension, and apparently the crystals are buried far underground."

Alliander looked down at the gnarled oak staff she carried in her right hand. She shook it a little bit, and then sighed. She raised her eyebrows and turned to her right to look at the female White Mage.

"Carmista?" Alliander asked. "Any luck?"

Alliander's companion looked only just a bit older than the students of Dragonsbond Academy. She hid incredibly straight raven hair underneath her hood, and her flat face only just poked out from this.

Carmista nodded back at Alliander. "I tried to cast a cooling spell as soon as I hit the sand. It didn't work."

She turned her head towards her other companion. This one didn't seem to have any hair beneath his cloak. He looked a thinner and smaller version of Driar Brigel – in other words normal human size. "How about you, Larmend?"

"I've had no luck either," Larmend said. "I tried to hold the portal a little longer, but my magic got sapped away as it closed."

"Then we should get out of this sun as fast as we can."

"What about the unicorns, Ma'am?" Carmista asked. "Siliana seems quite distressed." She reached down and stroked her unicorn's head, who whickered back in response.

"Follow," Alliander said, and she led her unicorn over to the shelter provided by Hallinar's right wing. For a moment, I could watch them all through the gap beneath Hallinar's underbelly. But Seramina put a hand on her dragon's flank, and he lowered himself to the ground, as if to give them some privacy.

I thought of Salanraja then. Every time I'd crossed dimensions in the past, my link to her had been severed. I couldn't even hear her muttering away in her dreams anymore. Each time my bond was cut off from her, I felt even emptier. I guess it's just as she always said that a bond between a rider and a dragon grows with time.

"Can you still hear him?" I asked Seramina, and I looked up at Hallinar who was staring at the camel chewing the cactus several metres away from us.

Seramina nodded. "I guess not all magic fails here. I'm sorry, Ben. We'll find a way to get out of here and get Salanraja back on her feet again. I know it's tough."

I sighed in a very human way. Sometimes, I found myself using their simple mannerisms. "I never thought I'd say that I missed her. But it's strange how we change."

Seramina had a wide grin on her face. "Well, I guess you're home Ben. You always wanted to return here, right?"

"Not to the desert," I said, and I wondered in fact which desert we were in. When the crystal had given me the gift to speak all languages, I had acquired the names of all the geographical features known to every creature. So I had an entire almanac of desert names at my disposal.

If this was the Sahara Desert, that would mean that I wasn't far from the ancestral grasslands of the two Savannah Cats back home. That's where hippopotamuses lived – the scariest and most dangerous creatures on Earth.

"So how far is it to your home, I wonder?" Seramina asked.

"A long way, I think." I hesitated as I remembered something. Ta'lon's face as he changed from his golden wispy form into a human-fairy one. It made me miss Ta'ra as well. The pain of knowing that I might never see her, or Salanraja again was too much to bear.

"Seramina," I said. "Did you see the fairy that came out of the other portal? The one to the Second Dimension."

"To the Faery Realm... No, I didn't."

"I did, and I recognised him. It was Ta'lon... We've met him before."

Seramina sucked in a breath. "He and Ta'ra were meant to get married, right?"

I growled. I never really liked that fairy-man. He had abandoned Ta'ra too many times in her life. Then, since she'd become a full cat, he'd never visited her – something that Ta'ra had complained a lot about.

All the better for me, I guess, as it meant there was no competition for Ta'ra. I don't know what I would have done if he'd suddenly appeared with some fairy magic and turned her back into a fairy again.

Despite the fact I didn't like Ta'lon, I still thought it better to tell Seramina the truth. "Ta'lon was possessed just like Aleam was."

"Well, that would explain how the warlocks crossed the Great Barrier. They were using the fairies. It's so obvious when we think about it."

"But no one can open the Second Dimension from the First. Someone has to open it on the other side, right?"

Seramina shook her head. "I don't know... Maybe there are other ways that we don't know about. We'll think about it later. But let's rest first. It's so nice and warm here."

I wanted to say something else, but the stench of something nasty assaulted me. Somehow, I'd managed to get used to the smell of Max, despite him never grooming himself. But now he'd done the worst thing of all. He'd dropped his waste in our presence and left it lying in the sand. To make matters worse, the shade had shifted away from it, and it had started to bake in the sun.

I left Seramina and strode up to Max. "What the whiskers are you thinking, Max?" I growled in dog language.

He lay now in the shade, well away from the offending waste. "What do you mean?" he asked. "I'm lying down because it's been a long day and a master of mine, once again, proved to be a bad man."

I pointed a paw over at the smelly stuff. "Before you do anything, clean it up!"

He looked over at his waste casually, his ears virtually touching the ground. "Why? It's not as if there's anywhere else I can do my business here."

"For one, it absolutely stinks, and believe me as a Bengal, descendant of the great Asian leopard cat, I've got super sensitive smell. But also, it will leave us open to predators. I'm sure there are very dangerous beasts nearby that might latch on to this stench and come looking for new prey."

Max turned his nose up to the air. "You want me to bury my own waste? That's disgusting..."

"It's disgusting to leave it out in the open like that. Look, just imagine its treasure. Like a bone or something? That's what you dogs do right? Bury your treasure so no one can find it?"

"It's not treasure... It's the remains of my previous meal."

"Just do as I say," I was getting really angry now. "Or I'll turn into a three-headed lion-goat-snake beast again." I said it that way, because dogs didn't have a word for chimera in their language.

"A warg?"

"It's not a warg... A warg is something completely different. And you're not doing what I say, so I'm going to transform now." It was a complete bluff, of course. I didn't have any magic, or connection to any crystals to do so. In all honesty, I was surprised I could still speak the languages, but I guess that ability was now embedded in my brain.

Max barked at me defiantly, but I just stared at him and hissed with my back arched. Eventually, he conceded, and went over to bury his waste in the sand. I returned to Seramina, and I kept one eye on Max, making sure he didn't miss a speck.

He was efficient when he went at it, and soon enough, the air had regained the smells of aloe vera, cacti, and agave. Seramina seemed amused as she watched him.

"You're like a mother to him," she said.

"A what? I'm nothing of the sort. I'm a male, a tom cat if you like, and a proud descendant of the great mighty George."

"Not the great Asian leopard cat?"

"Them too, but many of them are female, and I wanted to make my point."

From the other side of Hallinar, I could hear the White Mages speaking in muted tones. I didn't bother even trying to listen to them though. I doubted somewhat that these unicorn riders would have any clue how to survive in my own world. Besides, deserts weren't made for horses, which is why nature developed camels.

Speaking of which, that one-humped giant nearby was still happily munching on its cactus. It had paid us no heed since we'd fallen out of the portal, as if either it thought we were meant to be here or just didn't care.

Max came sauntering back from his task, though he approached us cautiously. He retook his position lying in the shade, but this time he kept his front paws as far away from his body as he could as if he were ashamed of them. He closed his eyes and went to sleep.

Seramina had sat down cross-legged on the sand. Like Max, she now had her eyes closed, and I have to admit a nap was awfully tempting. Particularly after the ordeal we'd just been through – I was in no hurry to return to the First Dimension.

But then I realised that, despite not really wanting to stay here, I still really wanted to see my master and mistress again. Maybe I could actually tell them a few stories. My tummy was also rumbling. Come to think of it, I hadn't had anything to eat since we'd left Dragonsbond Academy.

So, I walked over to the camel to ask the most important question of all...

14

A CONVERSATION WITH A CAMEL

I had the words formed in my head, and I knew exactly what I wanted to ask.

"Excuse me," I said, then I realised that the camel language was like no other language I'd spoken before. My paws were burning against the sand, and so I positioned myself inside the camel's long shadow.

"Yes?" he (I checked) replied, looking down at me.

What I wanted to ask was, *Do you know where I can find some salmon around here?* But as soon as I tried to translate the question in the camel's language, I realised he had no word for salmon.

"Come on boy," the camel said. "Out with it. It's only a short time until sunset, and I need to go and refill my hump."

I glanced at the sun – not long enough to blind myself, but enough to see where it was. "The sun is still high."

"It sets fast here," the camel said. "Now, is there a point to this conversation? Because camels aren't libraries, you know?"

I decided I didn't need salmon after all. I just needed something to eat. "Where's the closest source of fish?"

The camel let out a rasping whinnying sound, which I presumed to be his version of a sigh. His nostrils flared when he did this, much as Salanraja's would when she was angry. Except this camel wasn't angry, or at least he didn't seem to be.

Strangely, the question didn't seem to occur to him as to why I spoke camel. As if he thought it was the most natural thing in the world. *Stupid creature,* I thought.

The camel cocked his head in the direction leading away from the sun. "It's ten days trot to the big river that way," he said. "But there's crocodiles in there, so you might not find fish before they find you, if you know what I mean..."

I looked at him, blinking heavily and saying nothing. Crocodiles, apparently, didn't live far from hippopotamuses, so I certainly didn't want to go fishing there.

"Anyway," the camel said. "If you want to go the other way, and have enough water stored in whatever you use to store water, you might want to try the sea. It's fifteen days trot, though I'd watch the horned sliders on the desert floor as you move."

"Horned sliders?" I asked.

"They hiss, and they strike with venomous fangs. Be careful, because you're only small and you won't see them coming. So small, in fact, that I doubt you'll be able to withstand their venom."

"I've got pretty good hearing, I'll have you know," I said, feeling slightly offended at the camel's implication that I couldn't look after myself. I also didn't particularly like being called small. These things are relative, after all.

"Ah, but the sliders are silent when they move. They can trick even the sharpest mice."

It was obvious that these horned sliders were actually snakes. I considered telling him that my chimera form was part snake. But he didn't seem to like snakes and if camels were anything like horses, I didn't want to anger him. He probably wouldn't believe me anyway.

The camel didn't seem to appreciate me hesitating. Now that we were in conversation, he seemed to want to fill any empty space with small talk. "Say, what are you anyway? I haven't seen a creature like you around here before. You're a little too large to be a desert rat..."

I told him exactly what I was, and I said it in such a mighty tone that I made sure he wouldn't forget it.

"I see you're very proud of your heritage..." The camel stopped as if to think a moment. "And I'm very proud of my one hump. Those who have two, I don't know why they think they're anything special. Why would you grow more than you need, I say?" He spat out a dry bundle of thorns that went tumbling across the sand. "Anyway, that's all the information I can give you, little one. If you excuse me, I have a very important digestion routine to return to."

"Wait..." I still hadn't got anything useful out of this camel. "At least tell me what I can eat around here. Because it sounds like going fishing would be far too impractical."

The camel ripped off another chunk of cactus in its mouth and chewed as it talked. "This is quite tasty, you know. Full of nutrients, if you can stand the thorns."

I looked at the cactus, then I pushed my nose to it to sniff it. It didn't smell particularly edible and, to add insult to injury, it pricked me in the nostril with one of its little spines.

"Not to your taste, I guess," the camel said. "Though I find it hard to fathom why."

"Because I eat meat. And so does our dragon, and the dog over there..."

"Then you should go to the sea we talked about, and catch yourself some fish. Or perhaps on the way to the sea, you might find a mountain goat in one of the desert hills." The camel blinked with its heavy eyelids, then it looked at Hallinar as if seeing the dragon for the first time. "Humps and bruises, please don't tell me you're planning to eat me. I don't know what that thing is you have over there, but I don't want to have to fight it. I have a very dangerous thorn spitting ability, you know?"

I let out a friendly chirp. "Don't worry. I really don't fancy camel today. Besides, you don't look particularly appetising."

"Thank you. I'll... er... take that as a compliment."

I turned back to my party to see that Seramina was rummaging through Hallinar's panniers. Captain Alliander had brought the unicorns and other White Mages around to stand in the shadow of Hallinar's left wing. Both unicorns and mages were now sitting on the sand.

"Is that all?" the camel asked. "Because we are minutes away from sunset now, and I don't want to stay here with the horned sliders when the night falls."

Alas, so far I'd learned nothing useful. It's not as if I was ready to trek for days looking for food – not when we had a dragon that could fly. But there was still one thing I hadn't discovered yet.

"Where exactly are we, anyway?" I asked.

The camel made its horrible bleating sound again. I didn't need to speak his language to know that he was laughing at me. "What dune have you been buried under all these years? This is the Great Desert, of course..."

"I know it's the 'Great Desert', but which great desert?"

"There's only one Great Desert," the camel said. "My brethren with two humps don't appreciate that."

It occurred to me that just as this camel didn't have a word for salmon, he also didn't have a name for his desert. The camel language didn't seem to have words for lots of things, in fact. But they didn't, after all, seem particularly sociable creatures.

There came a blast of hot air from the west that whipped up the sand in a loose eddy. Above us, a vulture wheeled past the sun, and screeched as it did so. The camel let out a bleating sigh.

"There's always a death before sunset. I wonder who's been out hunting today ..."

"Predators?" I asked, and the fur shot up on my back. I looked around at the dunes. "I can't see anything other than cactuses and sand."

"Oh, there's foxes, desert crocodiles, scorpions, horned sliders, wild dogs, and worst of all," he bent down to speak softly as close to my ear as he'd dare get. "I hear also that a cheetah has entered our domain."

"A cheetah? I thought cheetahs lived in the Savannah?"

"The Savannah?" the camel asked. "Oh, you mean the grasslands. Yes, well its rare, but sometimes they live in the desert too. I'd be careful, little one. They often eat rodents like you."

"I'm not a rodent," I said. I really wanted to swipe at his face, but I saw how thorny and nasty that pile of thorns he'd spat out of his mouth looked. "Anyway, I thought cheetahs ate ostriches."

Now the camel made a slightly different sound a bit like a bear having an asthma attack. I guess it was just another way of laughing at me. "You are a strange creature. Do you know how big the great ostriches are here? Do you know how dangerous they are? Have you seen their sharp, long claws, or felt the weight of one of their mighty kicks?"

"No," I said, "I'm not from around here."

"Well, it would take a good several cheetahs to bring down one of those fierce birds. Don't get near it if you see one in the desert, little one. Particularly if you see it guarding a nest."

"I don't intend to. All I want is to find something to eat." The thought occurred to me all of a sudden. "What do desert cheetahs eat, anyway?"

The camel didn't seem to hear me, or perhaps he didn't even care. Rather he craned his neck and turned his head as if listening out for something. "Yes, I better join the others tonight. Safety in numbers, you know. Be careful, little one, the cheetah hunts at night..."

He turned away from his feeding ground, leaving the shells of half-eaten cacti surrounding him on the ground. His silhouette faded to blackness against a rapidly descending sun. The heat was quickly getting sapped out of the air, and I knew from what I'd heard of deserts that I'd better return to my friends before it got dark.

It wasn't just to keep warm, but I thought I could smell another cat in the air. The last thing I wanted, was for that desert cheetah to pick me off before I'd had a chance to have a good meal.

15

A FEAST FIT FOR A UNICORN

I'd only taken a few steps away from the camel when I caught the smell of mutton sausages starting to roast on a fire. Logs now lay in a pile, with a spit balanced over some poles. The three White Mages sat around this, next to Max, and the unicorns. Seramina stood a little away from them, cupped her hands over her lips, and called out to me.

"Ben, supper's on the fire!"

Once I had caught a whiff of the deliciously smoky scent, I couldn't let it go. Maybe I was the desert cheetah myself for a moment, bounding on my four legs towards my prey. I stopped at Seramina's feet and stared up at her, keeping my eyes as wide as possible.

"I'm so hungry," I said. "I thought that we'd have to eat cactuses."

Seramina laughed. "Aleam gave me a bundle of sausages to put in Hallinar's panniers, just in case we had to camp overnight somewhere. I know we need to work out what to do next, and I've already had a chat with the White Mages about how to get back to the First Dimension and rescue Aleam. But first, we need to eat."

I could hear Max panting happily next to the campfire, and I went over and sat next to him. "You don't get any, until I've eaten," I said to him.

"Why not?" Max said. "I saw it first."

"Because I'm a cat and you're a dog, and you must know the natural order of things."

"Dogs eat before cats," he said.

"No, they don't."

"Yes, they do."

"Not when you're a super intelligent cat that can talk to the humans and use magic. If you're not careful, I'll tell them not to give you anything at all."

Except for giving an impudent whimper, that seemed to shut him up. Still, it didn't stop him staring up at the mutton sausages which Captain Alliander turned above the fire. The White Mage looked down at him and swooned when she saw his wide eyes.

"Aww, does the doggy want some sausage?" she asked.

Max barked yes.

"I said cats eat first," I reiterated with a growl. Max ignored me.

Seramina sat down next to me by the fire. "I saw you talking to that strange beast, Ben." Then she laughed. "You know, it was so funny, I never thought I'd hear you making such weird noises. What is that thing anyway?"

"That's called a camel," I pointed out, "and the one-humped variety is called a dromedary camel. Don't you have them in the First Dimension?" In all honesty, I had never seen a camel before I visited this desert, and I knew that Seramina didn't have them in her world. But I had the gift of all languages, and I wanted to sound smart.

Seramina shook her head. "It looks like a cross between a horse and a cow..." She glanced over at the White Mages. "No offence to your unicorns, of course."

The male White Mage, Larmend, looked up at his unicorn, who had trotted over to nuzzle against his chest. "Patinsil says no offence taken. Unicorns don't particularly consider themselves horses, anyway."

"But that's what they are," I said. "How could you think them any different?"

Alliander shook her head. "That chimera I hear you can turn into, Dragoncat. Is it a lion, a goat, or a snake? Surely you don't think of yourself as any three of them individually, but rather an entirely different creature as a whole?"

Honestly, I didn't get her point. "A chimera is a combination of those three creatures," I said. "So it can't be any one of them individually. But a unicorn is just a horse with a glowing horn."

The White Mage captain sharply turned her head away. Larmend also covered his face with his hand for a moment, as if he didn't want to look at me. Out of the three mages, only Carmista didn't seem offended, but she spoke in a patronising tone, just like Driar Yila might when lecturing in class.

"If you've known unicorns long enough, you'll discover they're completely unique creatures. You've probably learned plenty about your dragon to know it's much more than just a giant lizard with wings."

I growled, not so much because I knew she was right, but she'd reminded me of how much I missed Salanraja. It just didn't feel natural anymore to be separated from her for so long.

Captain Alliander had returned her attention to roasting the sausages on the spit. She examined the one closest to her with a fork, which looked pretty good for eating. She lifted it delicately away from the fire.

My legs took over from my brain, and I was sprinting towards her, giving the cutest chirp I could muster to endear her to me. I sat underneath her, mesmerised by how the fat sizzled and hissed on the surface of the sausage as it let out a soft, smoky scent.

But I had competition, because Max was next to me, his pink tongue hanging out of his mouth, his ears flattened against the side of his boxy head, and his bushy tail wagging high above his rump. Next thing I knew, he was standing on his hind legs, and he tucked his forelegs into his body and raised himself to beg.

"What are you doing?" I hissed at him for extra effect.

"I'm showing respect for the food," Max replied, this time his words coming out in pants. "If I do this, the humans are more likely to feed me. It's an old dog trick, handed down through generations."

"Not if I convince them to give me the food. I have the gift of all languages." I changed to the human tongue, and I spoke fast, because I could already see that 'oh isn't he cute' expression on Captain Alliander's face. I couldn't let this long-snouted creature who didn't even know how to bury his own waste to get first choosings.

"Captain Alliander, it wouldn't be proper to give food to a dog before a respected celebrity of Illumine Kingdom. Might I remind you that it was I who saved the kingdom from Astravar. Surely, I deserve a little respect."

All I got from Captain Alliander was a derisive snort as she tossed the sausage down to Max. I already had buried my weight into my hind paws and was ready to spring forward and claim that sausage as my own. But Max was too fast in snapping up the sausage in his snout and moving to the exact spot where he'd buried his waste.

He dropped it on the ground, and then barked out, "I win!" He was right, because there was no way I would eat that sausage after it had touched that spot.

I looked up at Captain Alliander and growled. "I better get the next sausage," I said.

She shook her head, a smirk tracing the corners of her lips. "No, the next three go to the unicorns, then maybe you can have the one after that if you stop moaning." She was enjoying this.

"Unicorns don't eat meat!"

"No," Larmend said. "Horses don't eat meat. Unicorns eat whatever they want to eat, and today that just so happens to be mutton sausages."

"Fine, I said. The *unicorns*, then me."

That was exactly how it went. The unicorns had a sausage each, then I got one, then Alliander tossed another ten over for Hallinar, and by the time all of us had eaten, there were exactly four sausages left roasting over the fire. I decided to eat mine slowly, as something told me that I wasn't going to get anymore.

As I ate, Seramina was standing over the fire, watching the remaining sausages turn. "Such a strange custom," she commented, "where the animals eat first."

"That is the way of the White Mage," Captain Alliander said. "We rely on our animals, and so it's only proper that we give them the best of the meal. The dog needed to eat more than anyone else here, and that's why I gave him first pickings. The decision wasn't just made by me, but also our unicorns." She reached out and patted hers on the flank. "It was Tanni here who gave us the final approval." And that's exactly why I say you can never trust a horse...

Captain Alliander finally handed Seramina some food, along with a slice of bread. She gave the same to her two companions, and the captain was the last to eat of any of them.

"So," I said looking up from my food. "Seramina tells me you have a plan to get back to the First Dimension."

Captain Alliander raised an eyebrow at me. "Do you want to go back?" she asked. "Because rumour had it that you always wanted to return to this land."

I decided conveniently to ignore that question. Instead, I turned my head towards the horizon and took in a breath of fresh desert air.

Finally, the last vestiges of daylight had left the sky. I huddled closer to the fire so the bitter breeze didn't freeze me to the marrow. There came a chirping sound from somewhere in the distance, in the direction where the sun had set. It sounded a little familiar, but I didn't pay it much heed.

Rather, I was immensely enjoying the warm juices of the mutton sausage washing over my tongue. It tasted better than anything I'd eaten had tasted for years – maybe there was something about the dryness of the air here that augmented the taste, or maybe I was just so thirsty that I appreciated the moisture more.

"Ben," Alliander said after a long pause. "I asked you a question..."

"What?" I looked up at her.

"Do you want to stay here? Because we can arrange that, I'm sure. I can explain to King Garmin and the Council of Three the exact reason for it. Though once we get out of here, you will have to arrange your own passage home."

"Of course he wants to go back to the First Dimension... Don't you Ben?" Seramina said, and she reached out to tickle me under the chin. She was smart that young woman – she knew exactly where to stroke to make me feel comfortable.

"Please, let the cat answer," the captain said. "Don't put the thoughts into his head. What do you want, Dragoncat?"

"I..." I thought about my nice comfortable life in South Wales. All the delicious meals of salmon, and milk, and how I'd never had to work a day in my life. But then I thought about Salanraja. There was no salmon in her world, but she could cook for me virtually any other meat I wanted just by breathing on it. Then I thought of

Ta'ra, my companion who would be waiting for me back in Aleam's study, wondering where the whiskers I was.

"I'm nobody in this world," I said. "But in your world, I'm Dragoncat, vanquisher of Astravar, and you need me..."

Captain Alliander cocked her head. "Do we?"

I looked back at Max who had almost finished his sausage, and I knew that if I didn't finish eating soon, he'd be trying to steal mine as well. "I belong in the First Dimension," I said, and I never thought I'd hear those words come out from between my lips. "I may not have a destiny anymore, but Rine, and Ange, and Seramina, and Ta'ra as well... They need me."

Seramina chuckled, and I didn't know if it was because she agreed, or if she was just humouring me.

"Then you shall return to your academy," Alliander said. "Though I hope you don't learn to misuse that dark magic of yours, because none of us want another warlock to fight."

She gave Seramina a cursory glance, making me wonder if her words were meant more for the young teenager than for me?

"How do you plan to return home, anyway?" I asked.

Captain Alliander's lips curled upwards, and she reached into the pocket of her robe. She held a disc shaped object in the palm of her hand. I sniffed her fingers, then the object. It had three tiny slits on it, and a word I couldn't read – since I could only *speak* every language known to every creature. But I knew it wasn't written in any human language of the First Dimension. The disc smelled of that plastic material common in the Fourth Dimension, but that I'd never encountered in the First.

"King Garmin equipped all three of us with one of these, as he knew there was a risk we'd get sent here. Apparently, his crystal had forecast this eventuality. Using this device, our envoys in this world will know of our location, and the king will send someone to retrieve us..."

Seramina raised an eyebrow. "You communicate with people in this world?"

Carmista coughed, and Alliander looked at her. Then she turned back to me. "Tell nobody. You're not meant to learn about this until you graduate, if then. Our interdimensional network must be kept top secret. If our magic was to enter this world, it would destroy it. The same would be true if their magic entered ours." By magic, I assumed she meant technology.

Seramina reached out to touch the device. "What does it do?"

Alliander shook her head. "I'm not sure how the magic of the Fourth Dimension works, exactly. But this mystical device allows our envoys in this dimension to track us. Someone on this side of the world will discover where we are and tell someone in the First Dimension to open a portal for us."

"So we wait, in the cold?" I asked.

"We do..." Alliander said. "But we have enough firewood to at least get us through a night."

A strange and familiar birdsong came from the distance, followed by the screech of threatened prey. It sent a shiver down my spine, as I returned to my food. Max brought the sausage closer to the fire pit, as if also frightened by whatever was out there. Perhaps it was that vulture I'd spotted before.

But then I remembered what the camel had told me about that desert cheetah. It was out there somewhere, and it hunted at night. I wolfed down the rest of my meal, knowing that I might need the energy to flee from our enemy – if indeed I had a chance. Whiskers, the fire would make us more visible, and the cheetah would smell the sausage upon the breeze.

I gulped down my fears. Surely there were enough of us here, with staffs that we could use to defend ourselves. But if the cheetah was as fast as I'd heard, what was to stop it picking us off one at a time?

The sound came a third time. Now, I recognised it not as a bird sound at all, but as the same kind of chirp that the Savannah Cats and I would utter, except with more menace and bite to it.

I smelled rotten meat before I saw the desert cheetah's lithe and shadowy form stalk through the cloak of twilight. It stopped right before us, and I could smell the putrid menace on its breath.

It snarled out its next words, probably not realising that any of us could understand it.

"I am a Saharan Cheetah," it said. "Queen of the Great Desert. You are now in my dominion, and you must pay tribute. One of you is to be my next meal."

WHO SHOULD I EAT?

As if he thought he could defend us, Max pushed forward and barked at the cheetah. "Danger! Danger! Danger! Brave Max will protect you."

I glanced back at him and yawned. The cheetah also didn't seem particularly threatened by Max. Naturally, of course.

"That one smells vile," she said, and I could tell she was a she from the tone of her voice. She moved over to the unicorns and raised her nose to the air, still keeping her distance. "But if I can bring down one of these fine beasts, I won't go hungry for days."

A chill wind gusted from behind the cheetah, whipping up sand that hit me in the face and stung my eyes.

"What's it saying?" Seramina asked. "Ben, do you understand it?"

"The cheetah wants to eat one of us," I said.

"Well, that's not good..."

I turned to Captain Alliander, who had her hand clutched on her staff and was eyeing the beast. "She wants one of the unicorns."

The unicorns all whinnied as if they'd understood what I'd said.

Carmista and Larmend both gasped together, and Alliander's face twisted into a sour expression as she glared down at me through narrowed eyes. She had her staff gripped tightly in her fingers, and her knuckles were turned towards the cheetah as if she thought she could fight that thing.

"You don't understand how special unicorns are," she said. "Each one of us would rather sacrifice our own lives than let our unicorns die. I would have thought you would be the same with the dragons. Yet judging from your behaviour, Dragoncat, I'm not so sure."

I growled back at Alliander for jumping to conclusions. "I didn't say I thought it was a good idea."

The cheetah came a few steps closer, and she kept pacing along our perimeter, watching us from her flank.

"We should be able to outrun it on our unicorns," Alliander said. "Or fight it. Strength in numbers and all that."

"Do you know what that creature is?" I asked Alliander, and I didn't wait for an answer. "It's a cheetah, and it's the fastest creature on land."

Larmend snorted. "It can't possibly be faster than a unicorn."

"Of course not," Carmista said. "We could just escape, while you mount your dragon, and toast the thing. That will teach it to be so cocky."

I glanced over my shoulder at Hallinar, who was unfortunately fast asleep. Seramina put her hand on the dragon's outstretched wing. "You've forgotten something... You had to light the fire with a flint box, remember? Hallinar has no fire in him. So, he has nothing in his belly to keep warm. That's why he's doing what most lizards do during cold desert nights... Sleeping." She folded her arms.

"You're not going to outrun her anyway," I said. "It can reach speeds of seventy-five miles an hour."

Alliander laughed, and I knew what was coming next because

the old Ragamuffin had said exactly the same thing about the ostrich. "Nothing can keep up that speed for long. Look at that thing… It's not even half the size of a unicorn, and I can't believe it's a quarter of the weight."

What they were saying made a lot of sense. But this cheetah was so gaunt and ravenous looking, I felt she might be desperate enough to risk attacking us despite the costs. Whiskers, being the smallest here, she might even decide to snap me up in her jaws and run off with me.

"Let me try to reason with her," I said. "Will you shut up, Max?"

"Danger! Danger!" Max turned to me. "What?"

"I need to talk to this cheetah."

"Speedy cheetah is danger! Speedy grizzly warg!"

"Max, shut up!"

This time, I roared at him like a lion would. My sudden outcry stunned him into silence. It also caused the cheetah to snap her head towards me.

"Who are you to use the mighty roar?" she asked. She took a few further steps forward, and Alliander swung her staff at the cheetah's head. But the cheetah simply ducked out of the way, ripped the staff out of Alliander's hands, and tossed it casually aside.

Behind Alliander, her unicorn reared and made a furious neighing sound.

"Delightful," the cheetah said, and she lowered herself onto her hind legs, ready to pounce. At first, I thought she might be going for the unicorn, but then I saw her eyes were focused on Alliander.

A creature would have to be mad or incredibly hungry to attack all of us like this. I guessed this creature was.

The other two White Mages pushed around Alliander and her unicorn, their staffs held tightly in their hands. Seramina also clutched her staff in both hands, but she seemed to understand her limits and she safely kept her distance.

Max had a little more bravado and was now both barking and growling at the beast. Yet, despite his apparent courage, he didn't get close enough for the big cat to swipe at him. I didn't doubt with her powerful legs that the cheetah could pancake the dog to the desert floor.

I took a deep breath and let out a lion's roar again. The wind picked up as I did so, and for a moment, I imagined I saw the shapes of my ancestors – the great Asian leopard cats – in the patterns of eddying sand. The cheetah pushed her face so close to me that I could taste her rancid breath at the back of my tongue.

"Once," she said, "I can forgive. But twice, I take as a challenge. You don't have much meat. Still, you'll be enough to satisfy the hunger pangs for a day, whatever you are."

I spoke back to her in her own language for the first time. "I'm a descendant of the great Asian leopard cat. A Bengal – one of the most powerful domestic cats in the world."

"Domestic..." The cheetah almost purred, not at all seeming surprised that I could talk to her. "So, in other words, you're partly human..."

"I'm more than that. I'm a vanquisher of warlocks, and I can transform into a beast of nightmares." Of course, I couldn't perform magic in this realm. But I hoped that the cheetah wouldn't call my bluff, and would instead flee in fear of my threats.

"You said you're descended from a puny wildcat..." The cheetah pulled her claws through the sand. "And you're actually proud of that? This is going to be fun. Come then, let us see what you're made of."

She turned and stalked over to an exposed and flattened area of sand.

"What's she doing, Ben?" Seramina asked.

"I, erm... Seramina, I think she's just challenged me to a cat fight. A duel, if you may. Or maybe I just challenged her, I don't know." I stood up.

"You can't possibly be considering it can you, Ben?"

But I was only half listening, because another female voice emerged in my mind. It was incredibly familiar – smooth with a lilting accent that sounded almost Welsh.

"*Dragoncat,*" it said. It was the voice of my crystal that always seemed to turn up during moments like these. "*There you are... I've been waiting for you to show yourself on these sandy plains.*"

Time suddenly ground to a halt. The flames no longer danced on the fire. Max and the unicorns looked like taxidermies. All four humans looked like wax sculptures, their eyes affixed on the cheetah who crouched frozen on the dark and cold sand. Even the air was devoid of all the things that air should smell of, like pollen, and sand, and the dryness of the desert terrain.

"*Now, this has to be a dream,*" I said in my mind. "*Or maybe someone put some mushrooms in my sausages. Because we've already established that all crystals have been destroyed in this realm.*"

"*Believe me, this is very real, Dragoncat. Magic can still be contained in us crystals, even when we are splintered into a billion pieces.*"

I looked out at the empty sand, and the cheetah frozen in time, a snarl plastered upon her tapered face as it would be on a statue. "*Is this the moment of clarity I get before death?*" I asked my crystal – or at least the voice I thought was my crystal. "*Am I going to go to cat heaven soon, where I can eat all the smoked salmon and tuna that I want? All the sausages are gone now, and I think the food will be better up there than down here. Desert food smells awful...*"

"*No, it is not your time yet to die,*" my crystal replied. "*Not until you live the life that has been destined for you...*"

"*I thought I fulfilled my destiny when I defeated Astravar in a*" *battle of staffs. But now I'm going up against a mighty cheetah, without my staff bearer to help me. How can I possibly win?"*

"You have your wits, Dragoncat," the crystal said. *"Everything that you've learned over the years. Magicians don't gain their strength through magic, but through the skills they gather when learning to use it."*

I stepped around the frozen cheetah, examining her. Her body was sleek – clearly designed for speed, but when I looked closer, I could see the corded muscles and tightly wound tendons.

"What must I do?" I asked.

"Fight it. But remember you mustn't kill it."

"Why not?"

"Because the Saharan Cheetah is an endangered species. A death of one might result in the death of them all."

"Somehow, I think it's me who is the endangered species." I threw in a snort of derision for effect.

The crystal didn't reply, and I caught a slight whiff of the desert again – the first sign of time beginning to resume its flow.

"What must I do?" I asked the crystal again. *"How can I win this?"*

My crystal's voice came back ever so faintly in my head. *"Just follow the sand, young Dragoncat... The path to victory has already been paved."*

A huge plume of sand bellowed up from behind the cheetah, and for a moment the plume seemed to glow. I saw my crystal in the pattern of falling grains. It seemed to spin on its axis as it had every time that it had gifted me with magic.

Then, the spell was broken. Time sped up again, and the stench of the cheetah's fetid breath washed over me as I stared into her piercing brown eyes.

17

READY! FIGHT!

I'd seen those films on television back in South Wales where two men in strange hats duelled it out with guns at each end of a dusty street. I didn't have to watch them for long to learn how the fights worked. The opponents didn't watch the guns. Instead, they watched the eyes in an attempt to read whether the other intended to strike or flee.

In the end, it wasn't the man who had the fastest hand or the strongest arm that won, but the man who read his enemy the best.

Of course, there were also those duels where the men turned their backs to each other and waited for someone else to give them permission to strike. Those duels were just stupid and couldn't hold my attention for long. It seemed much more fun to watch the birds landing on the feeder outside.

Fights between cats are not much different to the first type of duel. We don't use guns, of course, and I've never understood why humans like to use such weapons in place of claws. But in terms of etiquette, the fight with the cheetah was no different to the ones I'd watched on the telly.

The cheetah spoke no more words, rather she crouched again on her hind legs and studied my eyes. I glared back at her, trying to give nothing away as I circled her in an attempt to get a better angle of attack. She kept steady on her hind legs, as she made slight adjustments on her front legs to keep facing me.

I knew if we pounced against each other, then she would overcome me through sheer size, speed, and strength. But if I could read her strike, and dart around her, and repeat the same motion over and over until I tired her out, perhaps I would stand a chance.

I could be like the proverbial ostrich that won the battle through stamina alone. A very small ostrich, perhaps, but I'm sure I've made my point.

The cold breeze seemed to whistle over the sand, creating a dusty carpet that tickled my paws. I half expected to see the shape of my crystal again in them, but I knew if anything drew my attention from the cheetah's gaze, she would take that opportunity to flatten me to the ground.

"How the whiskers am I meant to follow the sand?" I called out in my mind, hoping for an answer from my crystal. *"What does that even mean?"* But she was conveniently nowhere to be heard.

"You know," the cheetah said, "my mother told me all about you domesticated cats. 'You've lost the laws of the wild,' she said. Honestly, I'd never imagined you to be so foolish. Do you really think you can beat the mightiest hunter you've ever met? One who has trained for life in a land of famine?"

I snarled. "I've beaten bigger enemies before... Multiple times." Though I didn't tell her that most of those times I'd done so with either a magical staff or the strength, speed, and venom of a chimera.

The cheetah let out a high-pitched bark of derision. "That's impossible," she said, hissing out the penultimate syllable. Then she pounced.

I danced out of the way, thinking that she'd made it too easy.

But when I turned back, I saw that she'd been toying with me. Behind her, Seramina approached with her staff raised.

"Leave him alone, you bully!" She swiped down with her weapon, but the cheetah turned at the last moment and grabbed it within her maw.

She threw Seramina down with the staff. The girl who was meant to be all powerful was sent spinning like a tumbleweed against the sand. The cheetah barked out again and raised a sharp set of extended claws over the teenager's head.

"No!" I screamed, and I charged forward and raked a sharp claw down the cheetah's flank. It yowled, then turned back to me and hissed.

The three White Mages approached, holding their staffs high. They parted to make way for the unicorns, who scuffed their front hooves against the ground like bulls. The White Mages spread out sideways, to give the unicorns room to trample the enemy.

The cheetah had one side of her mouth raised in a snarl as she turned her head between me and the unicorns. "Coward," she said. "Are you really going to break the rules of a duel?"

I considered it a moment. Those mighty horses could save my life. Alliander's unicorn, Tanni, lowered his head. His horn looked awfully pointed as he turned it towards the cheetah.

"You mustn't kill it..." The crystal's words echoed in my head once again. They sounded so clear that I wasn't sure if they were real or belonged to a distant fragment of memory.

Tanni kicked up an eddy of sand and charged.

"No!" I shouted. "This is my duel!"

I turned and hissed at the unicorn, who reared, whinnying.

"Dragoncat, are you mad?" Alliander asked.

"We mustn't kill the cheetah."

"Why in the Seventh Dimension not?"

"Because the Saharan cheetah is an endangered species, and

besides this is my fight to fight. This is a cat thing... Trust me, you wouldn't understand."

"I don't," Alliander said, her eyebrows raised.

"Also, I have been given a mission by my crystal. I know there's not meant to be magic here, but it called out to me. It's somewhere in there between the grains of sand, and it told me that it's my destiny to fight."

The cheetah now was completely ignoring me, clearly having decided the three unicorns the greater threat. Instead of having her weight balanced on her hind paws ready to pounce, she had inched herself forward slightly, as if ready to turn and flee.

Alliander studied me, her free hand holding her chin. She lowered her staff, raised her free hand to her temple, then nodded at Tanni. The unicorn let out a whickering sound that almost became a feral growl.

For a second that felt like a minute, I thought Tanni would try charging a second time. But then he turned his head away from the cheetah and folded his front feet underneath his chest as he sat down on the sand. The other two unicorns did the same.

"What in the name of sinking sand and sandstorms..." the cheetah said. "You are the cat that controls horses..."

I hissed at her, my back arched, trying to ignore Max's persistent barks.

"Fight me!" I said. "It is I who challenged you to a duel..."

The cheetah turned back to me slowly and studied me with her piercing hazel eyes. Her voice sounded dreamier than before. "The humans could have saved you and defeated me with their domesticated animals. But you would still fight?"

I repeated what the old Ragamuffin back home always said during council sessions. "Matters of cat should only be settled by cats. That is the first law of our kind..."

"Agreed," the cheetah said, and then she did something

completely unexpected. She lowered herself to the floor and her ears perked up as if listening to a distant sound. "Could it be…"

The wind picked up again, howling as if speaking to us. It sent a sublime shiver through me. It wasn't just because of the cold, but it felt as if the whole landscape, or even nature itself, wanted to remind us of its vastness.

The unicorns tossed their head towards the wind and closed their eyes. Even Max seemed moved, as he stopped barking and instead opened his mouth to taste the wind on his tongue.

"You won't fight me?" I asked.

The cheetah, who had now started grooming the area where I had scratched her, raised her head and said, "No!"

"So it is you then that is the coward."

The cheetah stood up and prowled towards me, and I immediately regretted calling her names.

"You are as cocky as the prophecies say," she said. "But prophecy is prophecy. You speak the language of cheetahs. You bring with you a mighty winged lizard." She glanced across at the dragon, then she let out a sigh… "If you are truly the Dragoncat, then neither of us is meant to die today."

I puffed out my chest, liking the sound of this. "You mean, my tales of heroism have reached even all the way to the Fourth Dimension?"

"I said prophecy, not legend," the cheetah replied with a snarl. "Come, I have something to show you." She cast a derisory look at Max, now lying in the sand, his head rolling about as if tracing the path of a fly. "Bring the mutt and, if you wish to live, no one else shall come."

"Why?" I asked. "What happens if they do?"

The cheetah examined her claws. "Then the prophecy is false, and I'll be free to do with you as I please."

18

THROUGH THE STORM

I worried that Captain Alliander would stubbornly insist on following us and ruin the whole plan. But being a White Mage all her life, she seemed to understand magic and destiny, and didn't object to me preparing to leave.

Max was a little harder to convince, and as soon as I told him he must follow, he barked his disapproval.

"Scary speedy grizzly warg is not our ally," he said. "It wanted to kill us."

"That was until it discovered who we are," I said. "It turned out that I was sacred to it. But then, I am a Bengal, descendant of the great Asian leopard cat and vanquisher of warlocks." I licked my paw and rubbed it over the top of my head.

"But how do you know this cheetah isn't leading us into a deadly trap?"

"Because it wouldn't find you particularly appetising," I pointed out. "I'm sure dog is the worst thing a cheetah could eat."

Max lowered himself onto his hind paws and growled, his tail wagging violently. "I don't believe you..."

"Look, this is magic, Max. I spoke to my crystal. I don't expect you to understand how these things work... You just have to trust me..."

Max's body went from rigid to limp, as if he was melting within his own skin. "Trust you?" he said, his voice much softer.

I felt a sense of pity for him then. Because a sudden understanding came to me of what Max had been through all these years. I can't imagine what it would have been like to have been abandoned and left to fend for himself in the streets of Sussex. Picking scraps out of dustbins, and then sleeping beneath the undercarriage of cars where it's impossible to keep your paws dry when it rains.

The old Ragamuffin had told me of cats who had to live like that. He'd seen many on his travels. "Lost souls," he'd said. "They scratch and bite those who want to help them. Many of them will never feel the connection between cat and human again."

"Max... I'm sorry... It's been a tough life, I know. Though you smell, you're not a bad dog. Perhaps you're the only dog I've met who isn't bad." To show him I meant it, I nuzzled his cheek, and slid my side against his shaggy fur as I brushed past him.

"I smell like a dog," he said. "And you smell like a cat..."

I wanted to argue with him about that. To tell him that cats smelled wonderful because we groomed ourselves regularly, while all dogs did was try to scratch away their fleas. But such words would have been lost on him. Whiskers, it had been hard enough to get him to bury his own waste.

The cheetah waited a good hundred metres away from us, silently grooming her spotted coat. She stood up and called out to us in that high pitched feline barking tone.

"Are you coming? Because my patience is wearing thin... I'm beginning to think this prophecy is false."

"Come on Max," I said. "We need to do this." I took a few steps forward, afraid that Max wouldn't follow and the whole plan would be ruined."

To my pleasant surprise, he bounded along after me. We were soon standing next to the cheetah, who examined Max while circling him. Max had crouched into a ball and looked ready to take the defensive if necessary. He still didn't seem to realise that he wouldn't stand a chance against the great cat.

"It's strange," the cheetah said. "So strange that creatures of prophecy would be such measly beings."

I waved a paw at Max. "This is a Sussex Spaniel, and he comes from Sussex which he considers the capital of the world. He has also learned to fend for himself on the human streets."

"So he comes from the city," the cheetah said with a sneer on her face and disgust in her voice. "I might have known."

"What's wrong with cities?" I wanted to tell her about Dragons-bond Academy, and its six stone towers that vanished into the clouds, and the dragons that lived in chambers within those towers. But though she seemed to believe in prophecies, I don't think she would have quite grasped the idea of seven dimensions.

"Vile places. Still, the dog is part of the prophecy." The cheetah had her head craned out, and her ears perked up. They pointed towards a thin river of sand, blowing in the wind. She stopped to sniff the air for a moment. I did the same, taking in a whiff of cactus and agave, and perhaps a hint of distant catnip floating on the breeze.

"When you grow up in the desert, you learn to read the magic of the desert," the cheetah said. "The wind, the sun, the sand, and the voices that speak from afar. Come... It is this way."

She stepped into the granular river and strolled along it, not seeming to be discomforted by the sand shifting around her paws. *Follow the sand, young Dragoncat...* Now, I could see exactly what my crystal had meant.

Max and I plodded after the cheetah. As we went, the sand seemed to lift higher in the air, and the wind seemed to blow harder. It became more and more difficult to keep my footing. It was night, and so I shivered under the icy blasts that buffeted my fur.

"Do not mind the sandstorm," the cheetah said. "For it will take us where we need to go."

She took off, not quite sprinting, but bounding just about slowly enough for Max and I to keep up. I found it hard to breathe as the texture of the sand thickened around me, making the icy blasts sting even more. It became difficult to see the cheetah. But I could still see the brown silhouette of her lithe form and I could hear Max panting heavily beside me.

My heart was pounding, as the thought occurred to me that maybe Max had been right. Maybe the cheetah was leading us into a trap. Perhaps, she didn't know just how to read the desert, but how to summon sandstorms. Soon, she might use the cover to take us down and eat us.

"I smell your fear," she barked back to me. "Dragoncat, you are meant to be a hero, not a coward who can't even keep himself together in a storm."

She was right, and strangely I couldn't smell any fear coming from Max. If anything, he seemed to be enjoying himself.

"How long must we endure this?" I asked the cheetah.

"As long as destiny dictates," the cheetah replied. "This is the stuff of prophecy, and it requires some sacrifice. Keep running, or you will become buried."

I kept trudging through with Max bounding along beside me. Soon my legs became stiff, and I could feel the weight of the sand bogging me down. I also worried about Seramina, and whiskers forbid, the other three White Mages and their special horses. What if the sandstorm buried them? What if I had left them all to their fate?

My feet were slipping, and the sand seemed to want to tug me underneath it. Each step I took seemed slower and slower, and the silhouette of the cheetah faded further into the haze. After a while, my legs ground to a halt. The sand buffeted against the outside of my ears. I could no longer hear Max panting. But then, my ears were flattened against my head.

Just when I was about to give up, and lie down to be buried by the storm, I heard the cheetah's voice booming from ahead of me. "Dragoncat, where are you? We have already arrived, and the dog has made it further than you…"

Whiskers, I'd never heard anything so damaging to my pride. I willed my legs up again, even though they shook as I moved. I trudged forward, my muscles so numb that I thought each step had to be my last. I heard Max's muffled barking, and I used that to guide me.

I don't know if it was my pride, or the new companionship I'd found with him that pulled me through. Somehow, I managed to step outside of the sandstorm. I looked back in confusion to see that the sand had formed a wall lit now by a silver moon. It towered as high as the Great Barrier and disappeared into a thin layer of cirrus clouds that glowed in the midnight blue.

I shook as much of that horrible sand out of my fur as I could, hating the itchiness of what remained against my skin. Max was still barking, but clearly it was no longer to guide me, if it ever was. Rather, he was focused on the wall of sand, as if it were the most gigantic and dangerous beast he'd ever seen.

"This is it," the cheetah said. "But both you and your friend still smell afraid."

"You brought me to see a storm?" I asked.

"Look closer," the cheetah said. "Trust your senses and the language of the desert."

I studied the raging wall of sand, wondering what exactly I was meant to be looking for. I blinked in disbelief as soon as I saw it. The blowing sand was converging at one point, taking the shape of some gigantic creature. Max also faced towards it, the hackles on his back raised.

It blew towards a lonely sandstone boulder, which gained definition like a sculptor adding layers of clay to his work. Eventually, as the sand in the storm thinned, I could make out some giant paws, a tail, some folded wings, and the body of a cat.

The head came next, except this didn't look like a cat, but a human female, wearing an ornate headdress that hung down at each ear, stopping in two halves on its female chest. The folded wings on each side of the feline body were thin with a line of feathers carved into the back of them. The whole image was shaped by patterns of shifting sand.

"A half human, half flying cat?" I asked. "But it was created by the storm. How is this possible?"

The cheetah bowed down in deference, putting its weight on its front paws as it lowered its head against them. "This is what I've brought you to see, Dragoncat. Meet our master, the sphinx."

The ground beneath my feet rumbled as the sphinx opened its sandy mouth to speak.

19

MEET THE SPHINX

The sphinx's voice sounded like sandpaper rubbing against brushed metal. As its human lips moved, the upper lip seemed to crumble into the lower one. It spoke first in the cheetah's language. "Thank you, Palimali. You have done well on your mission."

In fact, the whole statue seemed to be crumbling, like a sandcastle made of fine sand. The sandstorm had now died down, but an eddy seemed to swirl around the sphinx, replenishing it with any sand that had fallen to the ground and keeping its substance whole.

"Is there anything else you will require of me, Great One?" the cheetah asked.

"You have fulfilled your purpose with this one," the sphinx said, "but you must still await the arrival of the Lady of the Vines."

The cheetah stood up and took one last look at me. Her hot breath brushed against my whiskers. It no longer smelled rancid, but rather as if it belonged to the desert.

"Save the desert, Dragoncat," she said. "Do not let its magic perish to those who wish to abuse it. If you do this, then I shall surely see you again." She turned and slunk off into the night.

The sphinx next spoke in the dog language to Max, who had stopped barking and now looked up at the statue with wide eyes, as if begging for food.

"You are also destined to become great, dog. You are so much more than the Key to the Sixth Dimension, and both your tale and tail shall grow long."

Max let out a whimper of confusion, and then lowered his head silently. The sphinx rolled her eyes towards me. Her pupils were two squares that seemed carved into the sand. Because of the way the sand shifted, the shape of the pupils morphed into a circle, then to a narrow vertical slit – just like a cat's.

"Dragoncat," she said. "Do you not recognise me..."

I squinted, not so much to see her better in the light, but to keep the eddying sand out of my eyes. "I've never seen anything like you before, and I hope never to see anything like you again."

"But you're a cat, and therefore you should listen and smell more than you see. You can feel the vibrations in the ground through your paws, and you must at least sense what I am..."

I drew on the gift of languages that my crystal had gifted me with. Using it, I recalled the definition I needed. "You are a sphinx. You have the head of a human, body of a lion, wings of a falcon. A mythical beast, as fierce as you are great... Though do not vex me with your riddle, because if I can't get it right, you might eat me."

"Very good," the sphinx said to me. "But you are still only seeing the surface. What do you *sense* within?"

I perked up my ears, and listened, slightly afraid that the sand would blow inside them and deafen me for life.

"I'm not going to fight you. I can't turn into a chimera to do so. Even if I could, I'm not sure how I could beat a shifting whirlwind of sand."

"Ben, I am not a sphinx," the voice said, and it was then that I suddenly recognised it. Underneath the scratching and screeching sound was a soft lilt and a slight Welsh accent. "I've merely taken one's appearance to prove a point."

"But it's not possible. I just can't believe it…"

"I think you can, Dragoncat. You just need to see it for yourself…" The sphinx opened its mouth and out shot a white light. It was so bright that I had to turn my head away so it wouldn't blind me. I closed my eyes, and I studied the patterns in the blobs left by the light. In my mind's eye, underneath a coloured glow, I saw my crystal spinning.

"*There you go,*" my crystal said. It was speaking in my mind now. "*Hold that image. See through blindness.*"

I did as she said. I didn't open my eyes. Instead, I waited for her to speak, for I knew there was more to come. Her voice was now softer in my head, since I was no longer seeing sand grinding against sand to produce words, but rather the pulses of light emanating from the crystal in my mind's eye.

"*The crystals of this world indeed were destroyed by the Egyptians,*" the voice of the crystal said. "*An ancient people of this land who knew magic well, and they abused it far too much than nature could allow. Thus, in this dimension, the one you now know as the Fourth, the crystals decided to render ourselves useless. We surrendered ourselves to the will of the desert, and each of us splintered into a billion grains of sand.*

"*Yet, though we are fragmented, we still exist. Within the sand, each of us knows about every single one of our constituent grains. When the need comes for us to be whole, we speak to the desert, and ask it to use its magic to bring us together again.*"

"So," I said, "I guess that's what the cheetah was talking about when she mentioned the desert's magic."

"*The cheetahs have needed guidance recently. This ancient desert breed has become endangered. But if they follow the way of the desert, and they pass its wisdom down through generations, they will one day thrive again."*

Now my eyes were closed, I also felt attuned to the sounds of the desert. I could feel the sand against my feet, and the way that it tickled my fur as it blew against me. Other than the crystal's voice, I could hear the sand trickling from the sphinx's body. I could hear the hiss of those horned sliders the camel had warned me to be wary of. I could smell the scrubs and flowers and fruit that gave the desert life, despite its sparseness.

"So why do you need to speak to me in this form? Why did you need to show yourself as a sphinx?"

"Because you will soon meet the real sphinx, Ben. Not in this world, but back in a realm filled with magic. It will ask you a riddle and you will need to defeat it with your wit and intellect."

"What does it want with my wit and intellect?" In all honesty, no one in Dragonsbond Academy had praised me for either of those two qualities. But then a cat doesn't need to know how to be clever the way humans see it. We just need to know how to hunt, and how to look cute to humans so we can get the food we need. That, in my opinion, is cleverer than all the science and magic that humans claim makes their lives easier.

The sphinx ignored my question, for she had an agenda of her own. *"You must see what is at stake here, Ben, for the seven dimensions are in danger once again."*

"What do you—"

"Shh, little one. Now open your eyes and watch."

I was so immersed in a dreamlike state I had to force my eyelids apart. Light flooded in, and for a moment I thought I'd slept through the night. The light wasn't coming from the sun or the sky, but a glowing whirlwind spinning before me. It sucked the sand from the sphinx, who now looked like a damaged statue. I couldn't make out the shape of its claws anymore, or any of its other details. Soon, the whole statue had eroded into an undefined lump of sand.

As it did, the whirlwind gained shades of brown, so that amidst the glow, I could also see shifting shadows forming shapes. "*Now watch, Dragoncat.*"

I could feel the tug of the whirlwind also trying to pull me into it, and I could see out of the corner of my eye how Max had flattened his paws against the sand to keep him in place.

"Can you see this, Max?" I asked.

"Yes," he said. "What is it?"

The images in the whirlwind now took further shape, and I could see a castle, and five towers with dragons flying around it, a bailey, and an inner courtyard containing the sixth tower – the highest of them all.

"It's magic," I said. "And my crystal is causing it. It's showing us a vision of the future. Now pay attention, because there's something that it needs both of us to learn."

20

A FUTURE IN SAND

The sand had no colour to it other than its natural brown, offset against the ever-brightening glow of the whirlwind. Still, in the images cast within the vista, I could see details. The more Max and I watched, the more intricate these details became.

In the vision, we were floating down from the sky, riding over Dragonsbond Academy's drawbridge, and then the gatehouse. A sandy version of Captain Onus standing guard in his armour and helmet looked up, as if he could see us passing overhead. Then, we were walking over the sandstone cobblestones that paved the bailey, towards Aleam's study.

The single oaken door opened, and the vision in sand took us inside.

Aleam was there, my feline – once Cat Sidhe – friend, Ta'ra, standing below him. The sand somehow hung so well off her body that I could see the brush of her silken fur. But something was wrong...

Ta'ra had her back arched while facing Aleam, hackles raised. Her teeth were bared and, though all I could hear was the roar of the whirlwind, I could only imagine the angry hiss coming out of her mouth.

Aleam held his staff in two hands, streaks of sand representing the magic glowing out of its crystal. On the desk behind him, the alembic that Aleam used to concoct cures and other potions was absent, replaced by shards of glass scattered across the tabletop and floor tiles.

"What is this?" I asked... "Ta'ra? Aleam?"

My crystal spoke out loud again for the benefit of the both of us. I hadn't noticed at the time, but it must have spoken in the dog language.

"What you see upon this image is unfolding in the other world at this present moment. But to understand its significance, we must travel further back in time."

The whirlwind howled, the glow from it pulsating. The image dissolved within to be replaced by another – an ancient pyramid, four faces of it rising into a thin layer of clouds. It towered higher than Dragonsbond Academy – or come to think of it, any man-made structure I'd ever seen. It was offset against a craggy rockface, and the land around the pyramid looked cracked and dangerous.

"We are looking at this pyramid from the Calimar Desert of the First Dimension. The Egyptians in their time in this world could travel the portals, and many of them eventually left here to inhabit a world of dragons and magic. That was after they tried to exhaust the magic of this world, and they would have exhausted the magic of the First Dimension, had the dragons not risen against them."

The view again whirred forward and passed through the heavy-looking sandy door to the pyramid, and for a moment I felt like a ghost passing through a wall. We entered a large chamber – as tall as it was wide. I caught sight of tripwires, spikes, and arrow slits cut into the brickwork. So many traps looking dangerous and nasty.

The vision whizzed onwards to the next room.

This was a smaller chamber, grey and dusty. Twelve statues stood on the side walls – six on each side. They had spears that pointed up towards the slanted ceiling. Their eyes were set dead ahead, and they were so realistic they looked as if they might come to life.

A sarcophagus stood at the back centre of the room. Its face was painted with ornate details; filigreed curlicues ran along each side.

The sarcophagus statue held an Egyptian ankh. The view in the crystal went up close, so I could see this in all its glory. It had gems arranged along its length and the loop on the top. Light filtered down from slits in the ceiling, making the ankh seem to glow.

It wasn't a large thing. Probably small enough for me to hold in my mouth if I needed. But the intricacy and curl of its carvings made it seem to emanate a certain power.

"The key to the Sixth Dimension," the voice of my crystal continued. "The treasure that the warlocks have sought for generations."

The scene again shifted to show a battlefield, this time in a sandy part of the desert. Colourless dragons filled the sky on one side, and on the other stood warlocks with staffs and those fancy headdresses that I saw the sphinx wearing before.

"The warlocks had uncovered the way to open the Sixth Dimension. But the Sixth Dimension opens all, and the key in the wrong hands will cause destruction across the dimensions. This rogue army was commanded by an evil army of Pharaoh warlocks that wanted to harness the power of the Sixth Dimension. They wanted to unite them all, then inhabit the resultant barren world."

I could hear myself growling deep inside my chest. We had signed a peace treaty with the remaining warlocks to stop the threat of war from emerging again. I had wanted to believe that this had meant they were better people than Astravar. It seemed that I had been wrong.

In the vision, the Pharoah warlocks sprayed dark and dangerous magic at the flock of dragons, and the dragons breathed fire upon the army. Great golems surrounded the warlocks – stone golems made of sandstone, fire golems launching fire back into the sky, and a type of golem that I'd not seen before – towering whirlwinds of sand just like the one currently before me.

That's when I noticed, or rather the scene zoomed in on one of the dragons. It was twice the size of the others with much lighter scales. I couldn't see any colours since everything in this vision was made from sand.

The dragon looked just like Olan, Aleam's dragon. She was saddleless like Salanraja, and on her back rode a man with his hair tied in a top knot. He carried a pointy sword in one hand and a staff in another. Unlike the Pharaoh warlocks who were adorned in all kinds of fancy and shining clothing, this man wore a simple tunic.

"Capitut, a brave warrior and the first and last dragon rider for a long time, stopped this happening. Singlehandedly, he commanded the dragons, and defeated the Pharaoh warlocks, before they could rain down destruction across the realms."

Once again, the scene shifted, this time returning to the pyramid offset against the craggy backdrop that I'd seen before. "After Capitut and his dragons had defeated the warlocks, he built this pyramid on the battleground. Within it he sealed the key to the Sixth Dimension. A priceless treasure that he vowed should never be held by human hands again. He laid one thousand traps of death within this pyramid, and he conjured a guardian sphinx before sealing himself inside."

On the left side of the entrance to the pyramid, a sandy sphinx appeared, inlaid with intricate curls of marble. It seemed to stare out from the vision and looked just like the sphinx I'd been staring at moments ago. I suddenly remembered something, and my whiskers twitched.

"I thought Max was the key to the Sixth Dimension," I said. "But now you're saying this ankh is the key. Is he meant to transform into it somehow?"

I looked down at the dog, looking healthy as ever. He couldn't possibly be a shapeshifter, could he? Maybe he wasn't from the Fourth Dimension at all, but from the Ghost Realm. But Max was warm and nothing in the Ghost Realm had either heat or cold.

"In a way," my crystal said. "You could argue the Sussex Spaniel is the key to the Sixth Dimension. Or let's just say he's the key to the pyramid that contains the key to the Sixth Dimension. It's all a matter of perspective."

My whiskers twitched again, and my head hurt as I tried to wrap my head around this concept.

"Legends talk of an animal that will one day ride dragons," my crystal continued. "Not a human, for Capitut always deemed humans too tainted to guard such power. But a purer soul. One, or perhaps two, or even three, who wouldn't be tainted with greed for such an object. That creature is the key to the Sixth Dimension."

I lifted my head and licked some sand off my paw. "Wait, so that must be me... Not Max, me! I'm the key to the Sixth Dimension. I am the non-human who rides dragons."

"I said, *will be* a dragon rider, not *is* a dragon rider," my crystal said. "You have already become a dragon rider, so the prophecy cannot pertain to you. The dog, on the other hand..."

I turned to Max, who looked mightily pleased with himself, sitting with his back straight and head held high. "You've got to be kidding me. You're telling me that a dragon – a mighty creature like Salanraja – will one day choose a dog as its rider?"

"Humans used to say the same thing about cats. Have you not proven that things can be different?"

Max barked in agreement.

"Young Sussex Spaniel," the crystal said, "you will find your crystal soon enough. But to do so, you must complete the task I've set for you."

"Task?" I asked. "I didn't hear you set any task…"

"The task is for me," Max barked again, snapping his jaws as he did.

I sprang backwards, and stared at him, my claws digging into the sand.

"I have told him what the task is to be," my crystal said. "He is to tell no one. Instead, you should be more concerned about an issue of much greater importance…"

The scene in the whirlwind spun back towards Dragonsbond Academy and entered a fast flyby into Aleam's study. It whirred forwards to focus on Ta'ra's face, so close that I could see that her eyes were glazed…

"Ta'ra?" I said. "You mean to tell me that Ta'ra is in danger? Is this what this is all about?"

"I never said there was only one key to the Sixth Dimension. The great dragon Matharon has in fact graduated two dragons from Bestian Academy – the dragon school in the crystal mountains. A brother and sister are on their way to Dragonsbond Academy as I speak. But they are dwarf dragons – far too small to carry a human mount."

"Wait a minute," I barked a laugh – given we were all still talking in the dog language. "Are you meaning to tell me that Ta'ra will be a dragon rider? She's like a kitten in a cat's body. She's only just learned to walk in a straight line and has still to master how to pounce properly."

"Do you mock her, Dragoncat?"

"I'm just saying… She's not ready for such a task…"

"But if you think about it," my crystal said. "She's already versed in using magic. A cat who can draw upon a crystal to channel fairy magic through her staff could be a powerful addition to your academy, indeed. Don't you think a dragon wise enough to graduate from Matharon's academy would choose someone with such proven stature, over a youth who still has to learn her place in the world?"

"Fine," I said, and I watched the image moving in slow motion. It focused on the window behind the bench where Ta'ra and I liked to have long naps. There was something there on the sill. A bird... A condor..."

"Lasinta!" I cried. "She's behind all this." I'd seen enough... "Okay, I get what you're saying. They are planning to use Ta'ra to open the Sixth Dimension, and we need to stop them before it's too late..."

"You are much wiser than you used to be, young Dragoncat," my crystal said. "Although you still have a lot to learn. Now, you must go with the Sussex Spaniel and retrieve the key to the Sixth Dimension from the pyramid in the Calimar Desert. You will find it in the second chamber, guarded by Capitut himself. After its retrieval, you must protect the key with your life, because the cost of losing it is beyond comprehension."

"So it's that simple? We're on a quest for treasure..." A treasure, it seemed, that would save us all.

"Simplicity is an illusion... The plans will unfold how they are meant to unfold."

"But what can I do about it now? I'm stuck in this world with no magic... I can't even call upon my staff bearer."

An icy wind picked up, squalling around the whirlwind of light, and then converging in the direction of the campfire that I could ever so faintly make out in the distance. A river of sand once again formed, and I got some of the stuff in my eyes.

"If you can't trust yourself and can't trust the language of the desert," my crystal said, "then there is no hope for you. Look to where your friends are. What do you see?"

I let the tears wash the sand out of my eyes. Still, it was difficult to see anything with the sandstorm obscuring the view.

But that's when I noticed it. The campfire was bigger than it should have been. Or rather it wasn't just a campfire shining, but a rift in the sky that had opened up. A bright white one.

"A portal," I said.

"A portal?" Max asked, with a bark. "What's a portal?"

"It's your way back to your destined home," the crystal said. "But if you don't hurry, it will close and leave you in a land where you haven't been trained to survive."

"But..." I started. There was something I was missing, and I racked my brain to try and remember. It came to me soon after. "What riddle will the sphinx in the Calimar Desert ask me?"

"Why, the most important riddle of all. The one that has vexed humans for all of time and has just started to vex you."

"What is that?" I barked the words out in the dog language, knowing it to be the most efficient way of getting words out quickly, second to Chinese.

"The riddle is: *who are you*?" the crystal said. "Now go, before it's too late."

The whirlwind jerked to a sudden stop. The light from it winked out, and the sand joined the raging storm. The wind was bitterly cold against and so strong that it stifled my breath.

"We need to go," I said to Max.

Together, we took off at a sprint, blown along by the scratching, cloying wind. It appeared our quest for treasure had started, but I had no idea how it would end.

21

HURRY! HURRY!

We hadn't been running for very long when I felt my connection to Salanraja return.

"*Bengie?*" she asked in my head. "*Bengie, you're back...*"

"*Ben...*" I corrected. I didn't care if she'd been unconscious and we'd been separated across dimensions. She needed to get it right.

"*It doesn't matter, get here fast! Asinda and Seramina can't hold the portal much longer.*"

"*Asinda...*" Come to think of it, I'd never seen her open a portal before.

"*Just hurry.*"

"*That's what I am doing!*"

Salanraja had distracted me so much that Max had now overtaken me. The sandstorm raged thick and dark around me. Whiskers, it was hard to breathe within it, particularly when I needed to catch up.

But I could still see the light from the portal. It was ever so faint, but bright enough to use as a beacon. I couldn't let Max get ahead of me for my pride more than anything else. I sprinted onwards in an effort to overtake him. But then I got a cramp in my right hind leg. Whimpering in pain, I almost ground to a halt.

"*Don't slow down, Ben,*" Salanraja said. "*You can't let a little cramp stop you...*"

"*A little cramp?*" I spat some sand out of my mouth. "*I'd like to see you sprint through a sandstorm, lactic acid burning through your muscles, bereft of water and not having had a nap in hours.*"

"*Just hurry!*"

"*You're not helping...*"

"Ben!" It wasn't Seramina screaming, but another female voice. Ange... Louder than I'd ever heard her speak before. "Ben where are you? I'm on this side of the portal. I won't go through without you."

"Follow that voice," I barked at Max.

"Stop shouting and concentrate!" Max barked back.

"No, it helps me numb the pain!" The cramp had now started to spread into my other legs, but I kept going. A skeleton of some kind of goat materialised in front of me. I tried to pounce over it but ended up tripping instead. I tumbled over the ground and Max vanished from sight, obscured by haze.

"*Ben,*" Salanraja said. "*Pick yourself up, for demons' sake...*"

I tried to lift myself up but my thighs shook like jelly, and I collapsed under my own weight. I fell face first into the sand, tasting salty grit.

"Ben, call out to me," Ange said. "I'll find you. We still have a little time."

I tried mewling out, but my voice was too quiet to carry over the noise of the storm.

"*Speak in the dog language,*" Salanraja said.

She was right, it would be much louder. I barked out... "I'm here! I'm here!"

"I can hear you..." Ange said. "I won't leave without you, Ben."

"Don't go! Don't go! I'll go!" Max's barking voice snapped out over the roar of the sandstorm. I tried to pick myself up again, but my legs were far too weak. "Where are you?" Max barked.

"Here! Over here!"

"You sound like the weakest of dogs." I heard his insult, before I saw his silhouette bounding through the storm completely in the wrong direction.

"Not there! Here! And I'm still a cat."

Max stopped, and he teetered on his legs a moment. I thought the storm would topple him as well, but I guess him being so squat helped him keep his balance. He trudged over me, the wind blowing his shaggy fur backwards and his ears into his eyes.

"Hold on, Ben!"

He picked me up by the scruff of my neck with remarkable strength. I had thought he might bite into me with his smelly canine teeth, but his touch was gentle, like my mother's had been when I was a kitten.

He carried me windwards toward where Ange waited by the portal on our side. Seramina and Asinda stood on the other side of the portal straining to hold their staffs straight as they fed white light into the large purple crystal that fed the portal.

On our side it was night, but on their side, it was day. The two dark mage's white beams were flickering... They didn't seem to have much energy left to hold the portal, and I knew I didn't have long. Rine stood on the other side of the portal, and he had Ange's hand clutched in his where they met at the threshold.

"Come on," Ange said, and she beckoned Max forward. "Seramina and Asinda are exhausted..."

Max yelped out, and he dropped me on the sand, clearly forgetting he'd been holding me. He whimpered and turned to pick me up. By this point, the portal had become a narrow slit.

"Quickly, Max!" I barked, remembering what the crystal had told me. "This might be our only chance."

On my command, he picked up pace, bounding at an amazing speed. His legs were short, but they were also true and strong, and we went sailing through the portal. Max dropped me on the verdant fields outside of Dragonsbond Academy, and I lifted my head to see Rine still standing on the other side of the portal, holding Ange's hand in the way that I had told him to so many times.

"Ange!" he said. "Run for it."

"I can't," her voice came faintly on the other side. "It's too narrow."

"Seramina! Asinda! Hold the portal open."

"The crystal can't hold it..." Asinda said. "You have to let go."

"Never," he said. "Ange, you must push through."

"Let go," Ange said. "Please... I can survive here."

"No... Ange..." I'd never seen Rine cry before, but now his face was covered in desperate tears.

"Let go, Rine," Ange cried, "or it will rip off our hands!"

He didn't have to, because someone stormed out of the shade of the beech trees behind and bashed his hand with a heavy oaken staff. He cried out, and held on, until another bash came, this time forcing Rine to loosen his fingers.

I saw Ange's face then, as the portal closed trapping her in the Great Desert of the Fourth Dimension. At the same time, a great crashing sound came from my side, and the crystal feeding the portal splintered into myriad pieces, sending out shards in all directions. These splintered and splintered again until they became grains of sand lost underneath the long grass.

I turned my head to see Captain Alliander, the two other White Mages and three unicorns. Rine turned to the White Mage captain, rage plastered upon his face.

❦ 22 ❧

AN ARGUMENT

We had emerged from the portal on the plains outside Dragonsbond Academy. The creepy shapes of the Willowed Woods hugged the northern horizon. All our dragons blocked the view of the treeline, including Salanraja.

"You fool!" Rine screamed as he stared down Captain Alliander. He had grown in the last year, and stood taller than her, though his frame was lanky. "I was about to pull her through..."

"No," Captain Alliander said coolly, not seeming even slightly perturbed by Rine's aggression. "You were about to get both you and her killed. Do you know what happens when you get trapped between two portals?"

"I wasn't going to let that happen..." Rine said.

"Yes, you were. And I shall hear no more of this insolence, young man. You are acting far, far above your station."

"So what are you going to do?" Rine said.

"I know your father, Initiate Rine. I should tell him about your aggressive nature... He won't be too happy about that."

Rine glared at the captain of the White Guard for a moment, then he huffed and turned away.

Personally, I had only just started to process everything that had happened. Ange had stayed on the other side to save us, to make sure that Max and I got through. But we were both small enough to fit through such a narrow slit. Ange wasn't...

She'd been stupid. Rine had been stupid. But, after all, could I blame them? Alliander, I felt, was being a little harsh on him. She could at least have shown some compassion.

I stood up, my legs screaming at me to rest longer from the cramp. But I knew from experience that they'd get better as I moved them, and besides I had a bone to pick. I strolled over to Alliander and growled at her. She turned her head down to me slowly...

"What? Don't tell me I've offended the cat too..."

It was then that I remembered something that Arran had said, and I'd been so stuck in the moment, that I'd never even thought to mention it. "You're just as bad as your brother, you know... You're just as pompous as Arran."

She guffawed. "You think Arran is my brother?"

"I have very sensitive ears. I heard everything that Lasinta and Arran said to you before we got sent through the portal to the Fourth Dimension."

"So you were spying on me?" Alliander said, and cast a look at Seramina, who stood feeding Hallinar and watching the scenario unfold, with a distant gaze. "I forgot that you were stuck behind a glamour. The king wouldn't be happy that you tried to interfere with matters of state, just like this boy did here... You're just children. Students of the academy..." This time she cast an appraising glance at Asinda. "What is this world coming to?"

Asinda stepped forward, her thick eyebrows lowered in a glower underneath her fiery red hair. "For demon's sake. My crystal told me to do this. Have you got anyone else who can open a portal?"

"I am sure King Garmin had everything under control." Alliander reached into her pouch, and I remembered the plastic device she had shown us before.

"So where is your rescue party then? Two nights in a desert like that could have killed you. It could have killed my friends."

Alliander put her hands on her hips. "You have a nerve to speak to a captain of the White Guard in such a tone, young lady. You might be a Prefect in your academy. But you're just a bark beetle crawling at the bottom of a great oak in the grand scheme of things. Must I remind you that opening portals is dark magic, and so forbidden in the realm?"

"Why, thank you, Prefect," Asinda said in mock imitation, "for your work in getting us out of the realm where you cannot use your magic to survive. Isn't it true, anyway, that the rulings of a crystal supersede the laws of humans?"

Alliander stamped the butt of her staff against the ground. "After I get back to the palace, I will be launching a full investigation, *Prefect* Asinda, into the verity of the vision you saw in the crystal. Don't think because of your heritage that the law will let you off lightly."

"See what I mean?" I butted in... "Really, *Captain* Alliander, you're just as bad as Arran. Your brother—"

"He is not my brother! And I don't care how much of a hero you are, young Dragoncat, you should be showing respect for authority as well."

I didn't bother trying to remind her that before I even came to the First Dimension, I served no master.

"So you're not related by blood?" I asked. "Isn't that what a brother is? Because I've got lots of brothers and sisters out there, I'm sure. They haven't all been sired by my father, the great mighty George."

"Such matters of family are none of your business..." The toe of Alliander's steel sole tapped heavily on a rocky slab of ground in front of her. "But if you must know, I only knew my younger brother for two years. He was probably too young to remember when my father left his mother, who by the way was also Lasinta's daughter..."

Asinda nodded. "And Driar Yila's sister, if you don't know... my great aunt. I have also never considered myself related to Arran." My head was starting to spin again. I had known that Prefect Asinda was Driar Yila's grandniece, but I had no idea she was part of the royal line.

Rine now had cooled down a bit. "I'm sorry," he said to Captain Alliander. "I shouldn't have screamed at you. I was just angry..."

Captain Alliander nodded but didn't look at Rine. "You ought to watch that anger, young man... But I guess it's understandable, in its own way. Just don't forget your place in the grand scheme of things... If you behaved this way in school, there would be severe repercussions, I'm sure. It should be no different in the real world."

Rine lowered his head.

Personally, I really didn't want to let Rine's apology soften the mood. "And what about Ange? She's trapped in the Great Desert, and it's freezing there. We've got to open another portal."

"We can't," Prefect Asinda said.

"Why the whiskers not? Seramina, can't you do something?"

She shook her head... "I'm sorry, Ben..."

"What? Why?"

"Because we're not powerful warlocks," Asinda said. "I can't tell you how many hours it took me to power up a crystal to open the portal, and even then, I needed Seramina's help to keep it open for more than ten minutes. If she hadn't been there, we would have lost you to the Fourth Dimension too."

"It's my fault," Rine said shaking his head. "I shouldn't have let Ange go through. It should be me stuck on the other side..."

"You can say that again..." I bristled to hear Bellari's voice coming towards us from the direction of Dragonsbond Academy. She strolled over, her blonde hair whipping across her face.

✢ 23 ✢

SURPRISE VISIT

I'd been so focused on the conflict escalating between Captain Alliander and Rine, I hadn't even noticed Bellari standing by the dragons. She had her hands on her hips and cocked her head as a sly grin traced her lips.

"You can never hold on to a girl, can you Rine? Why did you let her through in the first place?"

As Bellari spoke, Max ran over and started barking at her from his place near her ankles... "Bad smell! Bad vibes! Don't like this one!"

Bellari looked down at him. Her face turned red, and she raised her sleeve as if to cover her nose. "Gracious demons... I thought my allergies were bad with the cat around all the time. Now there's this dog?"

"For whiskers sake, Bellari," I said. "Ange could die over there, and all you want to do is insult dogs and make Rine feel bad for his actions. This really isn't the time for your drama. We need to find a way to open—"

A voice in my head interrupted me. A soft, lilting voice with a

Welsh accent. *"The girl can look after herself... She is not destined to die yet. Trust us, Dragoncat."*

I growled, softly. I really found it hard to trust uncertain futures, even if my crystal had never failed me in the past.

"Ben, did your crystal just speak to you?" Seramina asked as she stared out at the Willowed Woods. "Because mine just did, and it said you knew something important. What did you learn in the desert in the Fourth Dimension?"

I clenched my jaw. A crow cawed overhead, and I watched it fly beneath the clouds as I remembered the faux sphinx's vision of the condor on Aleam's windowsill.

"We need to go back to the desert," I said... Alliander shook her head, and I saw that she was about to say something, but I didn't want to get interrupted. "The Calimar Desert... Not the one in the Fourth Dimension... They took Ta'ra, because like Max, she's a key to the Sixth Dimension."

I wondered if I should tell them the part of her being destined to be a dragon rider. But the thought of it sent shivers down my spine. I didn't want Ta'ra to be getting in the type of trouble that I had landed myself in too many times. I'd already seen her almost die once, and I didn't want to have to see that again.

Asinda took a deep breath, and her face went white for a moment.

"What is it?" I asked her...

"I was feeding Ta'ra in Aleam's absence just this morning. Later this afternoon, I went to look for her, but I couldn't find her. I thought she'd run away."

"Then no one saw Aleam enter his study, or a condor?"

"Not that I know of..." Asinda said. "It was just after that that my crystal showed me that Prefect Lars and I must meet you out here."

"We're getting side-tracked," Captain Alliander said. "Dragoncat, tell me... What has the Calimar Desert got to do with all this?"

I blinked sand out of my eyes. "Ta'ra and Max aren't actually keys to the Sixth Dimension. They are the key to the key of the Sixth Dimension. The crystal told me that there is a pyramid in the Calimar Desert that the ancient warlock Capitut built to house the original key. Ta'ra can grant access to the pyramid, and so can Max."

Seramina's eyes went glazed... "Capitut... I know that name..."

I mewed softly and rubbed my side against Seramina's leg. It was nice to have someone in this world who valued my opinion. Despite being a hero of legend, so many of these humans still thought my voice meant nothing.

"The pyramid," I said, "is in a place where the ground is cracked and made of rock and not sand. We must pass a sphinx and the key is in the innermost chamber, guarded by Capitut himself..."

My words trailed off, as I noticed a sudden shift in the air. Behind the scent of fresh willow bark, I detected a faint whiff of rotten vegetable juice. There came a croaking female voice, and purple gas rose between us and the academy.

"Why thank you, Dragoncat," the voice said. An image developed in the purple gas that twisted into the wrinkled and cruel face of Lasinta. "You have told us everything we need to know."

Seramina narrowed her eyes and stepped forward with her staff raised high, the crystal on it glowing purple. Asinda stepped forwards as well...

"This is a battle between warlocks," Asinda said. "Everyone stand back..."

That caused Lasinta's eyes to screw up, and she tossed back her head and cackled with laughter. "Oh, you've got a long way to go before I'll even consider you a warlock, Asinda, and I'm afraid you'll never have a chance to go that far. Finish them off, Aleam."

A white beam shot out of Seramina's staff, heading straight

towards Lasinta's head. It didn't hit anything solid, but it did cause the cloud to dissipate. From behind it, a condor rose into the sky, wheezing... It flew off with heavy sweeps of its wings and disappeared behind the distant clouds.

"Aleam?" I asked. "Where are you, and what did you do with Ta'ra?"

As if in response to my question, a glamour splintered. Between us and Dragonsbond Academy, a sheet shattered as if belonging to an invisible pane of glass. A portal materialised, showing the lush, verdant hills and waterfalls of the Second Dimension.

Purple fairies floated out of this, darting every which way, clearly not themselves. Glowing spectral Manipulators arose from the ground around the portal. They carried white staffs in their wispy hands, which in turn fed energy into bone dragons that took off into the sky.

Next to the portal stood Aleam, his wrinkled skin seeming to want to slink off the bones of his face. He looked like he'd not slept for days. His eyes were white and glowing, and I couldn't see the pupils behind them.

He lifted his staff, signalling for the battle to commence.

A THORNY BATTLEFIELD

The ground shook, as the dragons launched themselves into the sky behind us and collided with the bone dragons above. They bathed the bone dragons in amber fire, and the bone dragons threw back green clouds of acid. I could feel the pain as the horrible stuff seared Salanraja's scales.

"Ben," Rine said to me, as he turned his staff between his enemies, not seeming to know who to attack first. "Ishtkar tells me to tell you that Salanraja says you really need to stop blocking her out."

"Oh," I said... I hadn't even realised I'd done so. It must have been because of the pain of losing Ta'ra.

"*Sorry, Salanraja,*" I said. "*Stay safe up there...*"

I looked up to see her performing a loop the loop, as the bone dragon chased her tail. "*I've not got time to chastise you, Bengie—*"

"*Ben,*" I interrupted.

"*Whatever... Just go after that Manipulator so I can kill this thing...*"

Whiskers, I'd completely forgotten how to handle Manipulators.

I guess I'd not fought one for some time now. I followed the criss-crossing patterns of light in the sky, trying to work out the point on the ground from which the bone dragon chasing Salanraja sourced its energy. I located it and went bounding after the Manipulator as it simultaneously turned towards me.

It swung its staff downward and shot out a spark of white from its spectral staff. An explosion erupted on the ground in front of me. Out of it, in fast forward, grew a plant of nightmares. I hadn't encountered one of these for a long time...

A Mandragora... Its twisting red thorns sprouted out of wiry branches, and its menacing green head which looked like a Venus flytrap was snapping its jaws into the air. It turned towards me and lunged. I barely managed to dodge out of the way. Another explosion of green landed next to me, and another Mandragora sprouted up so close that I thought I was about to get scratched by its paralysing thorns and eaten whole.

At that moment, a ball of ice buzzed past my ear. It hit the first Mandragora head-on, freezing it in place. This was followed by a jet of fire that reduced the Mandragora to freeze-dried ash. The second Mandragora didn't fare much better and crumbled in much the same manner.

"At least we can still fight together," Rine called out.

"In your dreams," Bellari said back, and she pattered towards another target.

Above, Salanraja had managed to turn the situation around completely. She chased the bone dragon that had been previously pursuing her, a jet of flame touching its tail. Other dragons streaked across the sky around her – both natural and bone.

"Ben, I'm still waiting for you to take down that Manipulator," Salanraja said. *"What's taking you so long?"*

I examined the Manipulator – the one that had launched two

Mandragoras at me. Now, it had resumed feeding energy back into the bone dragon, healing any damage Salanraja dealt.

I decided against turning into a chimera. The last thing I wanted in this battle was to become a bigger target. But I did call upon the great white hand – my staff bearer. It plunged forward and placed the staff in between my teeth. I summoned the only spell I knew – the red beam that I'd used to defeat Astravar. I sent it straight out towards the Manipulator's heart.

My beam hit the crystal that powered the Manipulator. The magical creature exploded in a ball of white energy. Salanraja roared out and tucked in her wings to push herself closer to the bone dragon. A fireball left her mouth, blue at the centre, and scorched her skeletal enemy, which crumbled quickly away.

"*There's more of them,*" Salanraja said. "*Find Aleam, Ben…*"

I scanned for him amongst the twisting forms of light on the field, but instead my ears homed on to sounds of barking coming from my right. Five Mandragora's snapped their jaws in the air, Max trapped between them. He was in danger, and the other dragon riders who could save him were otherwise engaged.

"Hang on, Max," I screamed… "I'm coming…"

His barks propelled me forward. "Evil thorny biting wargs!" he shouted. "Danger! Danger! Evil thorny biting wargs!"

Before the nearest Mandragora could lunge at him, I clenched down on the staff in my mouth and summoned another red beam. It hit the plant right in the centre of its snapping jaws but didn't destroy it immediately. The staff burned in my mouth, searing pain shooting to the centre of my tongue. Whiskers, this magic could ruin my sense of taste for days.

But Max needed to be saved. I screwed up my eyes, and clenched down on the staff even tighter, holding the spell for long enough to reduce the Mandragora to ash. The beam carried through into another Mandragora, just behind the first one, and disintegrated it as well.

"Danger! Danger!" Max continued.

"Max!" I screamed out in his language. "Will you shut up and run!"

He whimpered, then turned to see me look at him through the gap I'd created between the thorns. Another Mandragora lunged at him, but he dived out of the way just before the Mandragora ripped a huge clump of soil out of the ground and tossed it upwards. Max reached me, panting. "That was close..."

"Just stay near me," I said. I needed him to open the pyramid and save Ta'ra. I had a mind to fly with him on Salanraja straight over to the Calimar Desert and leave everyone behind. No doubt, Lasinta was on her way there already, and I didn't know how long we had.

I glanced up at my dragon, considering the notion. But three bone dragons were on her tail.

"*They're multiplying,*" she called out to me in my mind. "*Help Seramina and Asinda fight Aleam. He's using crystals to create more...*"

I scanned the terrain, squinting to lessen the glare from light coming from the Manipulators all around me. Faintly, through two sources of light, I could see where the purple mist thickened. Then, I noticed two purple crystals raised up above the backs of Seramina's and Asinda's heads. Their staffs bobbed as the crystals glowed.

"Max, follow me," I said. "I don't want to have to rescue you again."

I was just about to launch myself toward the two young dark mages, when a swathe of Mandragora's emerged right in front of me, cutting off my path. I looked over my shoulder to see a Manipulator, its white staff pointing out from its ghostly form at Max and I.

The staff let out an orb of white light, the magic growing so fast that I knew I couldn't turn quickly enough. But a spiral of ice came in from its side and hit it right at the centre where the crystal was. It had come from Rine's staff. He nodded to me and then sprinted off towards another target.

Another Mandragora sprung up behind me, and it moved its head towards me so fast that I thought I was going to get poisoned. But a shield barrier sprung out around it and pulled its head back. High Prefect Lars had control of the shield, and he shrunk it into a ball so small that it crunched the plant together, reducing it to compost.

I turned back to the line of plants, trying to find a way through them. I could cut a path, but I could see so many Manipulators around that they would just create more.

There came a flash from my left. Then a neigh, and the smell of horse. Alliander, Carmista, and Larmend sat astride their unicorns, who had their heads lowered to the ground and their glowing horns pointed forward.

Alliander cried out something, and the unicorns charged, their brilliant white manes tossing as they went. The three White Mages held their staffs with intent as if they were wielding weapons. It took me a moment to realise why, because each staff had a glowing magical scythe blade protruding out at the top.

The unicorns' horns cut through the Mandragoras, lopping the heads off their stems. The White Mages swung their conjured scythes in sweeping motions as they went, cleaning up the battlefield ahead and creating a path for the both of us to bound through.

"Go, Ben," Alliander screamed. "Stop Aleam!"

I didn't want to lose my opportunity. I crouched, then sprinted onward, wondering if we had any chance of winning this battle at all.

25

BRINGING DOWN THE CRYSTALS

Max followed me close on my tail, again surprising me how swiftly his stubby legs could go when they needed to.

We stopped between Asinda and Seramina, and I thrust out my staff, crossing it at their ankles. Ahead of us, Aleam stood surrounded by a purple sphere of energy, patterns of electrical light pulsing across its surface in fast moving waves. A circle of crystals surrounded this magical barrier, each as tall as a human's calf. Aleam looked tired – his posture sagging as he cast magic out of the barrier, continuing to summon Manipulators and bone dragons.

Asinda and Seramina weren't in fact attacking Aleam directly, but rather focused the beams from their staffs on the crystals surrounding him. The old man seemed to pay them no heed though... Either he seemed to think that the two young women were no threat to him, or he didn't even know who he was attacking. I doubted he was truly conscious behind those white glowing eyes, because the real Aleam wouldn't do anything to harm the two young dark mages.

"Ben," Seramina said. "Help us destroy those crystals..."

"But Aleam..."

"The crystals are feeding the shield, and they seem to be controlling him too..." Seramina's words trailed off as the crystal underneath her beam shattered into shards that then crumbled into sand. "Fifteen left..."

I clenched my jaw. We had to at least talk to Aleam. "Aleam, this isn't you..." I called. "We have to stop this."

"We've tried that," Seramina said, and her voice sounded strained as if she'd indeed been screaming. "He won't be able to hear us underneath the shield. Even if he could, I doubt words alone would snap him out of it."

I groaned. "Taking down all those crystals will take ages."

"We already dispelled the glamour around the crystals," Asinda said. "Once we destroy them, the shield will come down, and Seramina can break the spell."

"But the Manipulators will surely get to us first."

"Our friends will protect us!" Asinda snapped through clenched teeth. "We have to believe that. But we still need to move fast." A crystal shattered underneath her beam, which she directed at the next crystal directly behind. "Fourteen..."

Max was barking at Aleam, but he was speaking so fast I couldn't understand him.

"Max, shut up!" I screamed, as I willed the red light to come out of my staff, my focus on a crystal... But as soon as the magic emerged, I felt a sharp stabbing pain on my nose. I dropped the staff to the ground.

"What in the Seventh Dimension?" I said, having picked up the dialect of the land. It didn't take me long to see the blue wisp floating just in front of my eyes.

"Hello Dragoncat," a male voice said, and the wisp pulsed as it spoke.

I recognised that voice... Ta'lon, Ta'ra's former betrothed. The fairy who had abandoned her more than once. Now that Ta'ra wasn't a fairy anymore but a cat, he seemed to want to have nothing to do with her.

I swiped at the wisp with my right paw, and he dodged out of the way. I took a wider swipe with my left paw, which Ta'lon darted underneath. I studied him, readying myself to leap, then I reached up at him with both paws, trying to trap him.

Still, I wasn't fast enough.

"Come on," Ta'lon said. "Do you really think you can catch a fairy? And if you did, what would you do? Eat me?"

"What are you doing, Ben?" Seramina asked.

"It's Ta'lon... He's here, and he's taunting me."

Seramina shook her head. "Just ignore him. He's under Lasinta's spell, but she cannot command him to use magic against you..." I growled and picked up my staff once more. I caught a glimpse of Max rolling his head around, watching a couple of fairies dance around him.

Now I knew what to look for, I also noticed a couple of fairies dancing around Seramina, and I think three around Asinda. Behind us, fire and ice cut across the terrain, unicorns danced across the battlefield, and Rine, Bellari, Lars, and the White Mages leaped from target to target, using their magic to take down all the Manipulators and bone dragons that Aleam kept summoning.

With all this going on, and particularly the fairies, I had no idea how Asinda and Seramina managed to focus so well. In unison, two crystals shattered under the strain of Asinda's and Seramina's magic. They glanced at each other.

"Thirteen," Asinda said.

"Unlucky number," Seramina said. "Twelve..."

"*Will you tell the ladies to hurry things up down there?*" Salanraja said. "*I've now got four bone dragons chasing me... We're really getting overwhelmed.*"

Well, things would go much quicker if it weren't for the fairies. "Max," I said. "You want to help?"

"Yes!" he barked.

"Then start chasing fairies."

"What?"

"The flying glowing things. Catch them in your mouth."

Max barked again and wagged his tail, then started running around snapping at things in the air. Another crystal shattered.

"Ten," Asinda said. "Almost there."

The energy holding Aleam's barrier together had started to dissipate. A roaring sound came from behind me, and heat seared my fur, coming from a fireball that I guessed Bellari had sent towards a Manipulator. I focused on creating a beam of dark magical energy which I sent shooting out towards the crystal.

Ta'lon, once again, landed on my nose, and the beam cut off.

"Whiskers," I said... I tried swiping at him, but my staff got in the way.

"Fairy! Fairy!" screamed the excited dog. "Max on fairy patrol." He swiped out at my nose with his paw, not close enough to touch it, but close enough it seemed to scare Ta'lon away.

Another crystal shattered in front of me. "Nine," Seramina called. Despite the elation in her voice, I could hear the anxiety beating in her chest, and I could smell the sweat on her skin.

Ta'lon once again buzzed close to me, but I couldn't let myself get distracted. Aleam was doing evil things, and we had to stop him.

This time, I closed my eyes as I let the magic flow. It came out of my lungs in deep and wild breaths. My whole body coursed with rage out of losing Ange to the Great Desert, the horrors that I'd seen Astravar conjure, Salanraja knocked unconscious through somnambulis mushrooms, Ta'ra out there and in jeopardy, and I'd not even had a chance to say goodbye.

"That's it, Dragoncat," I heard my crystal say in my mind. *"This is the source of your power."*

Though my eyes were closed, I could see the purple crystals glowing in front of me. There were five in a neat row from where I stood, and I turned my staff towards them. I imagined the beam shooting out of my staff, bathing their tainted magic in purple fire. My chest seemed to lift as I felt five souls being released from their dark magic prisons, the crystals shattering into specks of infinity as their essence returned to the soil.

I opened my eyes, to see the extent of the damage – five wide scorch marks surrounding Aleam where the crystals had been.

"Four..." Seramina said. "Ben, you're meant to call the number... That was awesome... How did you do that?"

"It doesn't matter," Asinda said. "It's working. Look."

The sphere of light surrounding Aleam was flickering, the stench of rotten vegetable juice now fading. Magic crumbled around me, and the shield surrounding Aleam gave one final flicker before guttering out.

Above, the bone dragons dissipated into flakes of bone. The Mandragoras wilted into deep purple ash. The Manipulators sank into the earth, and the crystals that powered them fell to the ground. Meanwhile, the blue fairies fluttered downwards like lost feathers.

Despite his magical creations crumbling all around him, Aleam continued his practiced motions. Drawing a crystal from his pouch. Pointing to the northwest with his staff and throwing the crystal out in that direction. Reaching up with his staff towards the sky. Spinning around three-sixty. But his pace had slowed, and magic no longer pulsed out from his staff.

Presently, his legs buckled.

"Aleam!" Seramina screamed out, and she rushed forward to catch him. Aleam's limp form folded into her arms.

26

SLEEPING ALEAM

As if to mourn Aleam's fall, a humid mist rolled out of the Willowed Woods. It came fast and light, carried on a chill breeze that had no place in the Illumine Kingdom summers. Perhaps this was nature's way of replacing the rotten magical stench that still hung in the atmosphere because it quickly washed any traces of the battle away.

Aleam had his eyes closed, and he looked deathly sick in Seramina's arms, his face pale and his cheeks gaunt. I went over to sniff at him, trying to detect what signs of life I could. Max, as if detecting the sadness of the moment, went to sit down by Aleam's feet, and gazed off silently at the billowing horizon. The sun still faintly shone through the blanket that hung over us – a bright orange ball suspended in the sky.

"Is he breathing?" Asinda asked Seramina...

Seramina said nothing, and I saw her cheeks were wet with tears.

"Seramina, is he breathing?" Asinda asked. "Check his pulse..."

Seramina sniffled, but she didn't raise her hand to his neck or listen out for breath. "He's in a coma," she said. "I don't need magic to tell that." She lowered him to the ground and knelt beside him.

Asinda walked over and put her hand on her shoulder. "He'll be okay, I'm sure... He just needs plenty of rest."

Seramina shook her head and gently closed her eyes. "It's my fault... It was me who decided to go off on my own mission and try to rescue Aleam. It was me who got us stuck in the Fourth Dimension, and it was me..." She trailed off. "I caused all this."

"That's ridiculous, Seramina," I said as I rubbed my head against her calf. "You went to rescue Aleam because he needed rescuing. You're a hero."

"No... Aleam always warned me about charging off on my own. That's what he's been trying to teach me. Not to act on instinct all the time. If I don't, then what we saw in the Ghost Realm is bound to come true. I'm destined to destroy the worlds..."

I took a deep breath, not wanting to think about how someone so innocent, could become that creature of nightmares that I'd seen in that vision. If anything, I was meant to protect her – to stop it happening. I meowed, and she reached out with her free hand to stroke me. But her action was half-hearted as if she'd lost herself in the void.

"Not Aleam as well..." Rine said as he sauntered over to join us. "Is he going to be okay?"

Asinda gave him a stern look as if to instruct him not to make the situation worse. "He's in a coma, and we'd do well to get him back to his own bed in the academy... We just need our dragons."

Rine shook his head. "We've lost Ange... We've lost Aleam..."

I growled. "Not to mention Ta'ra." I still felt absolutely awful about her. "We can't let them get to the Calimar Desert. We can't let them open the Sixth Dimension. They will unleash a force that will destroy all of the worlds."

"And do you know exactly what force you're dealing with?"

Rine asked. "You tell us we must do this, and we must do that. But do you even know what you're doing, Ben?"

"I want to save Ta'ra... And my crystal... The sphinx in the Fourth Dimension... It gave me a vision."

"But that's what I mean. Let's say they open the Sixth Dimension. What happens next? Meanwhile, who's going to do anything about Ange? What will become of her?"

Rine paused with his fists clenched by his sides, leaving the question hanging. I took a deep breath of wet mist, as I thought about what he'd just said. My crystal had said that Ange could fend for herself, but that didn't mean that she'd find her way back here. We might have lost her forever.

Rine was right. I didn't have a clue where to go in the Calimar Desert, or even how to get there in the first place. I looked in the direction that Lasinta had flown, sniffing the ground and wondering if I could find a feather or something to give me a sign. Perhaps Max and I could somehow follow her scent.

It was a ridiculous idea, I know, but it was all I had...

"*Okay, Ben,*" Salanraja said in my head. "*I guess I need to give you your pep talk. Ishtkar is already getting through to Rine, but he's divided between that and comforting Quarl.*"

I glanced over to see the emerald and sapphire dragons bunched together, their heads pressed side by side. Close to them, stood Bellari's citrine dragon, Pinacole, watching them passively.

"*Aren't you angry with me for blocking you out?*" I asked.

"*Yes, but I can chide you for that later. All I want to say now, is that I'm sure Ta'ra is okay. I know what she means to you. You'll find a way to save her.*"

"*And stop the warlocks opening the gate to the Sixth Dimension?*"

"*Before we do anything about that, we should gather more information...*"

"What information, exactly?" I asked, feeling ever so slightly anxious about it all.

"What I'm saying, is we don't know what the threat is... We don't know exactly what will happen when the gate to the Sixth Dimension opens. Nor do we know how long it's going to take the warlocks to get to their destination. We might be able to get there faster than them. We just need to look for a solution."

"But we know things are going to get bad, right... Right now, all I want to do is save Ta'ra."

"Ben, our crystal is still safe and sound in my chamber at Dragonsbond Academy. I'm sure it will give us more information when the time is ripe."

"But we might not have time..."

"True... But then again, we also might have much more time than you think."

I didn't like this conversation, and I was half tempted to block Salanraja out of my mind again. If there's one thing that living with humans had taken away from me, it was my feline patience.

An all too familiar scent approached – her perfume so thick I swear I was 'allergic' to it. A slender hand lightly grasped Rine's shoulder.

"She'll be okay," Bellari said, and I bristled. Was Bellari trying to get back with Rine?

Rine turned to look at her. "Thank you, Bellari... I appreciate your support... Really."

Bellari opened her arms and took him into a hug. He buried his head in her shoulder, and I watched the ring dance up and down on Bellari's right middle finger, as her hand rubbed his upper back.

High Prefect Lars crouched down next to Aleam and placed a hand to his neck to check his pulse. Seramina looked up at him from where she cradled Aleam's head against her chest.

"You don't need to do that," she said. "He's alive... But I don't know if he'll ever wake up..."

"You have to believe, Seramina," Asinda said. "Maybe your mind magic—"

"No," Seramina said, shaking her head. "Waking him before he is meant to wake might kill him... They used some powerful magic on him."

Prefect Lars looked over at his citrine dragon. "Initiate Rine, if you can help me lift him, Hallinar can carry him back to the academy. Though I'd thought Olan would have flown over by now." He cast Seramina a sympathetic gaze. "She's been moping around her chamber for days, hardly eating, much as we tried to feed her."

Rine nodded, and turned towards the dragons, without saying anything. But I caught a glimpse of a golden wisp rising up from the long grass. A fairy, it seemed, had emerged from the ashes, and I hoped for the sake of all the dimensions that it came in peace.

27

FAIRY AWAKENS

I watched the wisp float upwards, half tempted to try chasing it away. I really wasn't in the mood for fairies, and besides we didn't know if this one was friend or foe. But I thought twice when I remembered the fairies that I'd met. Ta'ra used to be one of their kind, and some of them, like Be'las, Ta'ra's grandfather, and Go'na, Prince Ta'lon's sister, were quite nice.

The wisp darted around a few times, and then a golden mist emerged around it. Just as the warlocks' purple mist had its own distinct scent, this mist smelled faintly of lavender and oleander. The cloud billowed downwards, as if the ground was pulling it. A human shape materialised, and it wasn't long until we were looking at the handsome face of Ta'lon, Ta'ra's former betrothed. He had dark, long hair that fell in waves down to his shoulders. His face was pale, with a thin jaw, and a small roman nose. Really, he looked like one of those men you saw on the television again and again because the humans liked the way he looked. Except he wasn't human. He was a fairy.

He looked around him, and then his gaze fell upon us. He strode over.

"What happened? How did I end up here? Is that Aleam?" He leaned and touched the old man on the cheek with a glowing hand... "He... This is a magical sleep. I can't lift it... What happened to him?"

I snarled at him. "You did this!"

"Me? Alone?"

"Not entirely, but you helped. Aleam created an army of Manipulators and bone dragons, and Mandragoras. Then, while they had us distracted, you came over and tickled me on my nose."

Ta'lon lowered his head. "I can't have possibly had a role in this..."

Asinda raised her head and opened her mouth to speak. But before she managed to do so, Captain Alliander trotted over on her unicorn and dismounted. "Ta'lon is a prince of the Faery Realm, and so this matter requires diplomacy. It's not to be handled by children, cats, and dogs."

Asinda scoffed, but she didn't say anything to stop Alliander. If she was anything like me, she probably didn't want to talk to this fairy brute anyway.

Captain Alliander dismounted her unicorn and strolled over to take Ta'lon's hand and shook it. "Greetings from Captain Alliander of King Garmin's White Guard. It is an honour to meet you."

"Likewise," Ta'lon said. He wasn't quite looking at her though. Rather, his gaze drifted over the scorch marks and burned grass that surrounded us. "Perhaps, Captain, you could illuminate me on what happened?"

Alliander took a step back. "First, tell me, please, why this attack on our forces wasn't an act of war on your kingdom's behalf. Because for centuries Illumine Kingdom and the Faerie Realm have co-existed in peace, have they not?"

"I don't remember anything," Ta'lon said, shaking his head. "Last I knew, I was in the royal palace – the great oak of *Faerini* city. There was a flash of light, and screaming at the royal court, then my head started spinning... And..." He trailed off.

"That is the last you remember?" Alliander asked, her eyebrows raised.

"Yes..."

Alliander placed her hand on her chin and stared off at Dragonsbond Academy in the distance. "Somehow, the warlocks must have found their way into the Second Dimension. You've been used, Prince Ta'lon."

"But the only way in would have been for someone to open a portal on the other side..."

Alliander nodded. "A mystery we still need to solve. How are you going to get back now?"

The fairy looked towards the Willowed Woods, or at least the shadows that were visible of the creepy trees waving behind the mist. "For those who know the protocols, there are openings at certain locations in this world scheduled at designated hours. Judging by the patterns of the light, I have only five minutes."

"Then I shan't keep you past that," Alliander said. "But tell me... Is it possible that the warlocks could have known when and where one of these designated openings occurred?"

"Impossible. The protocols are a closely guarded secret amongst the royal family."

"So perhaps, they followed someone."

"We always glamour ourselves before passing through, and we glamour the portals too... Unless... Ta'ra..." He spoke it with such distaste, as if he had never known her.

"What did you say?" I asked, striding over to Ta'lon.

"I... My father doesn't know, and I wasn't meant to let him know until we married, but Ta'ra knows the protocols."

"She would never betray any information to the warlocks," I said. Whiskers, she hated warlocks even more than I did.

Ta'lon looked taken aback, he turned his feet towards the Willowed Woods.

"Dragoncat," Alliander said. "Diplomacy, please... Leave this matter to the professionals."

Ta'lon looked back where Aleam had stood, then back to the Willowed Woods again. "I must get back to my kin... They could be in trouble."

On that note, a plume of golden gas enveloped him. Sunbeams burst through the mist and sparkled off it. Ta'lon, now in his wisp form, darted off past Larmend and Carmista on their unicorns. Several golden wisps followed him, and it wasn't long until they had vanished into the cooling mist.

"There is more that I have to report to the king," Captain Alliander said, giving me a distasteful look. "I must also take my leave now."

As if she couldn't wait to be rid of us, she was quickly mounted upon her unicorn and galloping off to the northeast towards Cimlean city, her two subordinates following behind.

"What now?" Bellari asked, watching them. "No doubt she will send a royal missive to the palace reprimanding our diplomacy... Ben, why couldn't you just let the White Guard do their jobs? There could be detention for weeks..."

"Well, if there is, we'll need to escape," I said. "Because we need to rescue Ta'ra..."

Max lifted himself on his haunches and barked out at Bellari as if he agreed. Whiskers, for a moment, I wondered if he understood me. Or worse, maybe I'd forgotten myself and started speaking to Bellari in the dog language. If so, she would have deserved it.

"Ben, what did we talk about?" Salanraja said in my head. *"You know that we need to talk to our crystal first..."*

"I know, but Bellari doesn't need to know that. Whiskers, I hope she doesn't insist on coming with us to the Calimar desert... We need to get her away from Rine."

"You're a strange creature, Bengie—"

"Ben..."

"Whatever..."

"Yes, whatever. Anyway, I've been meaning to ask. What's happened since I've been gone? Last time I saw you, I thought you'd be asleep forever. Then, when we were trapped in the Fourth Dimension, I thought I might never see you again."

"I missed you too..." Salanraja said. *"Anyway, from what I've been told, the Initiates and Council of Three defeated the second wave of attacking wargs. Then Driar Brigel took the leaf mages with him to save us. They used their magic to return the somnambulis mushrooms to the earth. After that, we all returned home. Without you and Seramina, of course... I had long conversations with Ishtkar last night, wondering if you'd ever return. Gracious demons, no one even knew where you'd gone until Asinda saw that vision in her crystal..."*

"I'm sorry, Salanraja. Seramina and I shouldn't have run off."

"Well, what's done is done, I guess... And you live and learn."

I took a deep breath and meowed softly. It was good to be home... Good to be connected to Salanraja again.

"Are any of you listening?" Bellari said, with her hands on her hips. "We need to get moving, get Aleam over to Dragonsbond Academy..."

Prefect Lars patted Rine on the back. "Are you ready? We need to be gentle with him."

Saying nothing, Rine stood up, walked over to Aleam and crouched down to take his legs. Prefect Lars moved over to Aleam's head and Seramina moved out of the way to allow him to lift his shoulders.

Together, the two young men carried Aleam over to Lars' citrine dragon, Camillan, who had stepped forward and turned her side to them. I watched them work.

Somehow, I felt responsible. I should at least have tried to stop Seramina rather than letting her chase after Arran. Maybe, if I'd done what I'd been told for once, I would have been able to protect Ta'ra when Lasinta and Arran came for her.

Not wanting to waste any more time, I scooted over to Salanraja, so we could fly over to Dragonsbond Academy and work out what to do next.

28

THE RETURN

Salanraja refused to fly ahead of the others. Rather, she insisted on staying in formation, just in case an ambush awaited us between the battlefield and the academy. Admittedly, we were all afraid that Aleam would wake up and try to overpower us – even if we had confiscated his staff. We had no way of telling if we had completely removed Lasinta's control over him.

This time, Salanraja headed the formation. The charcoals – Asinda on Shadorow and Seramina on Hallinar, flew on one side. Bellari on Pinacole and Rine on Ishtkar, took the other. Quarl remained at the back, and though I couldn't see him, I could only imagine how the sapphire dragon felt to be missing Ange. Right behind us, Lars sat in the saddle on Camillan's back, holding Aleam and leaning back slightly. Lars had secured Aleam to his chest using a length of hemp rope.

Salanraja had long since broken her rule about only allowing me to fly on her back. Now, she carried Max, who had pushed his head between two of Salanraja's dorsal spikes.

"So much fun, so much fun," he barked. I felt sorry for the

dragon that he would bond with, because this behaviour would get annoying for them pretty fast.

Trying to ignore Max, I peered over the edge to see the mist hanging beneath, obscuring any evidence of the battle. The air tasted fresh up here, and the sun shone over us, warming my fur.

We reached the bailey of Dragonsbond Academy within a good ten minutes, where the Council of Three stood waiting. The elder Driars had their staffs clutched in their hands, as if prepared for a fight.

"Great... Are we in trouble?" I asked Salanraja.

"How should I know?" she said.

"Well, haven't their dragons told you anything? Farago, Flue, or Plishk?"

"In all honesty, none of us wants to reach out to them to find out..."

She readied her forelegs and touched down on the cobblestones, and the other dragons landed around us. Lars touched Camillan down last.

Salanraja lowered her tail, and I sprinted down it, glad again to be back on solid ground. I could still feel the sand stuck in my paws, and I tried to lick away some more of the saltiness. I caught sight of a butterfly, resting on a clump of moss between two cobblestones, and I crouched and readied myself to pounce.

But Max came around the other side of Salanraja and chased it out of the way. He tried gnashing out at it, but his mouth only met air. The butterfly was far too fast for him. What did he expect when he hadn't first stunned it with his paw?

"That was my butterfly," I barked at him.

"Why? You can't own all the butterflies..."

"Because I saw it first."

"But I got to it before you," Max said.

"Except you didn't catch it. If you'd just sit and watch, I can show you how to do it."

It was Max's turn to bark. "No, no. You do it wrong. Cats always do it wrong."

I let out a whine, half expressing myself in the cat language, half in the dog one. If Max was like Ta'ra, he would have nodded her head gracefully – like a human does – and then let me teach him how to chase butterflies properly. Whiskers, I missed her.

"Initiate Ben!" Driar Yila called out. "This is no time for animal antics. Behave like a dragon rider and join your peers."

I gave Max a stern look, to tell him not to try anything. Then, I strolled over to where the Prefects and Initiates had gathered, both my head and tail held high.

Two students passed me carrying a table with a thin mattress and sheet on it. I peered upwards to see that Aleam lay on top. My whiskers twitched... I really hoped he was going to be okay. But at the same time, I knew there was nothing we could do for him right now.

The Council of Three did not look happy. Driar Yila scowled, Driar Lonamm tapped her foot loudly, and Driar Brigel's hand was clenched so tightly around his staff, I could see the whites of his knuckles.

I stood on one side of Rine and rubbed my head against him. I wanted to draw him away from Bellari a bit, who seemed to be inching closer to him. I knew what she was up to, and I wasn't going to let her win this game.

"Now that you are all here," Driar Yila said, and glanced at the sundial at the edge of the courtyard. "It appears you owe us an explanation."

I thought it might be prudent to speak first, so I stepped forward. "I—"

Driar Yila held up a hand showing the palm. "I want to hear the story from the Prefects before the Initiates."

On my other side, Prefect Lars squeezed Asinda's hand. It was she who stepped forward and spoke.

"I'm sorry, Driar Yila," she said. "My crystal showed me a vision, and I knew that Prefect Lars and I had to open a portal. It was their only chance to escape from the Fourth Dimension."

Driar Yila nodded, then glanced at our two companions in turn. "And where is Initiate Ange right now?"

Asinda shook her head. "She got trapped in the Fourth Dimension. She stayed to help Initiate Ben and the dog get through. Seramina and I could only hold the portal for so long... Then we got ambushed,"

"I see," Driar Yila said. "And is Initiate Ange safe there?"

She said the words slowly and cruelly, in a way that seemed to imply Asinda and Lars were somehow responsible for what had happened to Ange. In a way, I guess they were... But then so were Seramina and I.

"No, Ma'am," Asinda said. "Unfortunately not... She got trapped in the desert at night."

Next to me, Rine took a deep breath, and his hand clenched into a fist. Bellari reached out and took his other hand in hers. I don't know what Rine was thinking, but he let her. Driar Yila looked at where their hands met, but she didn't say anything about this. She seemed too lost in thought.

Or rather, she was probably lost in conversation with her dragon, as I'm sure the other two Driars were as well. Right now, I'm sure that our dragons were getting grilled by theirs. Probably, our dragons had already stated everything the Great Driars needed to know. But still, the Council of Three needed to interview us, to see if they could detect any holes in our stories. That was how these things worked.

Driar Yila nodded. "This, I'm sure will be in Captain Alliander's report to the king. But we will send a request to the Acting General of the Dragon Corps in Arran and Corralsa's absence..."

"One more thing... My crystal told me that she'd be safe there," I said, just in case Salanraja had failed to report it. "It said that she can look after herself."

Driar Yila nodded. "I've heard all about your visions in the Great Desert of the Fourth Dimension. A worrying development, that we will need to talk about shortly."

"So you know that they have Ta'ra," I said... "Then we must stop talking and get over there."

"We will deal with that in good time," Driar Lonamm said. "But strategies need to be planned carefully. We can't rush these things..."

Driar Lonamm looked at Driar Yila, as if to ask if she had anything she wished to add. Driar Yila gave her nod, and Driar Lonamm looked at each of us in turn.

"Let me just go through this again," Driar Lonamm said, stepping forward. "So far, we've accounted for Initiate Seramina, Initiate Ben, the dog, you, and High Prefect Lars. But what caused the other three to go along with you? Understand that your dragons have already told us, but we still want to hear your version of the tale."

Asinda looked back at Rine and Bellari. Rine let go of Bellari's hand and scratched his head.

"Ange and I both had visions in our crystal as well," he said. "It showed us waiting at the portal, and that Seramina, Hallinar, Ben, and the dog were on the other side. We had no idea that Aleam and Lasinta were behind this."

"And did you know about the potential ambush?" Driar Lonamm asked.

Rine lowered his head. "We did..."

Driar Brigel sucked in a breath through his teeth. "Did you really think that you could take down an army of magical creations all by yourselves?"

Rine shrugged. "There were five of us, and we've done it before, haven't we? We couldn't let our friends come to any harm."

"This doesn't explain how you came to be there, Initiate Bellari," Driar Lonamm said.

Before I heard Bellari's answer, Salanraja let me know what had actually happened.

"She blackmailed them," she said in my mind.

"What?"

"She saw Asinda, Lars, Rine, and Ange plotting something in the bailey, and followed them to Camillan's chamber. When she saw they were off on an adventure, she said that she'd tell the Council of Three immediately, if they didn't let her tag along..."

"Why would she do that?" I asked.

"I don't know... Maybe you're right that she's trying to get back with Rine again..."

I growled under my breath – hopefully too quietly for the Council of Three to hear. *"It's low of her. Particularly now Ange is out of the picture. But I won't let her, I promise."*

Bellari, of course, didn't give the Council of Three this version of events. I was sure she and Pinacole had worked out her story beforehand.

She spun some spiel about agreeing with the others that she'd be a scout. Her dragon, Pinacole, was fast, and she would quickly fly back at the first sign of trouble. Alas, in the battlefield, she'd got cut off by Mandragoras and needed to fight alongside the others for everyone's lives.

After Bellari had given her version of the tale, the three Great Driars stepped away to talk amongst themselves. They spoke in murmurs so quiet that even I couldn't even hear what they were saying.

"This is so boring," Max whined to me. "Ben, how about we go and find something to bury?"

I blinked at him in disbelief. "Max, I haven't got time for your games. Shut up, I'm trying to listen."

But he didn't shut up, and so I didn't catch much of what the Council of Three said. Soon enough, the three of them stepped forward. Driar Yila – whom I'd always seen as the leader of the three – spoke first.

"Your actions were bold, and you showed great courage today. But you should have reported the visions you saw in the crystals to us before taking action. We could have sent someone out with you. Particularly when we knew that Arran, Lasinta, and a mind-controlled version of Aleam were at large."

"I didn't think we had time..." Asinda objected.

"Which exactly is the problem," Driar Yila snapped. "We are once again at war with the warlocks, and wars aren't fought through quick spontaneous actions. Instead, forces mount, and generals strategize. Victors in battle plan thoroughly, and that is what you failed to do."

"But we knew that they were trapped in the desert," Asinda said, "and it was night. They could have frozen if we hadn't done anything."

"They had three White Mages with them," Driar Lonamm said. "A dragon, some firewood in their panniers, and enough supplies to see them through a night. I might expect this kind of behaviour from first year Initiates. But you, High Prefect Lars and Prefect Asinda, are two of the most respected students in this Academy. You have to live to set an example, and not act on a whim..."

Prefect Lars lowered his head. "We're sorry, Driar Yila. We really are..."

They might have been sorry, but I was really starting to have enough. We were just wasting time while Arran and Lasinta could be at Capitut's pyramid by now.

"We need to get going," I pointed out. "We shouldn't be talking about this stuff, until we've stopped Arran and Lasinta. We need to save Ta'ra."

Driar Yila frowned, and she paused for a long agonising moment. "Need to, need to, need to... That is the voice of an anxious mind, Initiate Ben."

I opened my mouth and hissed at her. With that kind of reasoning, we weren't going to get anywhere.

"I know it makes you angry," Driar Yila continued, "but we can't do anything until we know exactly the next best move. Until we give you permission, you are forbidden from leaving Dragonsbond Academy. Our dragons will be keeping vigil, and they will stop any escape attempts with force, if necessary."

The hackles had risen on my back, and I really wanted to argue back some more, even though a deep part of me knew it wouldn't be a good idea. But some heavy footfalls coming from the archway interrupted me.

I turned to see the muscular student, Prefect Calin, storming into the courtyard. He stopped in front of the dais.

"I'm really sorry to interrupt," he said. "But I just checked on Aleam, and he's woken up. He sent for Seramina, Ben, and the Council of Three."

Driar Lonamm took a deep breath, then looked at Driar Yila and Driar Brigel in turn. "We should all go," she said. "Something tells me this is important."

"Including Max?" I asked.

"Yes," Driar Lonamm said. "Including the dog..."

❦ 29 ❧

HE'S AWAKE!

I'd never seen Aleam looking so pale. Admittedly, I couldn't see him from the floor. But no one objected when I jumped onto the soft flannel blanket to examine him from the bottom of the bed. The old man had propped himself up against a nest of pillows.

Max jumped up too, and we competed to stretch out and fill any space that didn't contain Aleam, like two pieces of a tessellating puzzle.

The room smelled of those kinds of strange herbs that humans called 'medicine'. Several glass vials full of potions stood on Aleam's bedside table, all of them uncorked and half-full of thick oily liquids. I could also smell the kind of sweat that belongs to the deathly ill.

I really hoped this wasn't the end for Aleam... I didn't know what I'd do without him.

His skin seemed to hang off the bones, pulling the flesh away from his eyes. But there wasn't any trace of the evil Aleam left in him. Behind his sweat, he smelled like a human again – no traces of rotten vegetable juice or anything like that.

Aleam turned his head slowly from Max to I, and he chuckled. Then he looked up at the Council of Three, huddled right at the foot of his bed, the five other students spilling out around them. When he spoke, he had very little flavour in his voice.

"Thank you for coming... I'm sorry it was such short notice. But I'll be asleep again soon enough."

"That's okay," Driar Brigel said, and he walked around the students to Driar Aleam's side of the bed and held his frail looking hand. "How are you feeling?"

"Like death," Aleam said with an ironic laugh. "But they've not defeated me yet..."

Seramina let out a laugh too. She wiped her eyes with a hand-kerchief.

"We're sorry to see you like this, Aleam," Driar Yila said, not moving from her place by the doorway. "But you must understand that time is thin, and the warlocks are already on the way to the Calimar Desert. What do you remember, Aleam?"

"Everything..." Aleam said. "They didn't erase my memories. What have you learned so far?"

"There's a pyramid," Driar Brigel said. "Where the ancient warrior Capitut sealed the key to the Sixth Dimension."

"But do you know what the Sixth Dimension is? It's hardly common knowledge."

"We do..." Driar Brigel said. "And we know how dangerous it is. But we don't know what the warlocks plan to do when they open it."

Aleam took a deep breath, that turned into a heavy wheeze. He coughed, then reached out for a glass of water. "I'm sorry... It's just... Never mind..." His expression deepened, and his eyes went glazed. "But we are in much more danger than we realised."

"What is it, Aleam?" Driar Brigel asked.

The old man took another sip of water, then his gaze drifted up towards the ceiling.

"Death and destruction... A pact with the Seventh Dimension... After the warlocks locked Ben and Seramina and the White Mages in the Fourth Dimension, we travelled together through the Fairy Realm... I don't know what spell they cast on me. I could see everything happening in my mind but was unable to control even the smallest muscle in my body.

"From the Faerie Realm, under escort of the possessed fairies, Lasinta opened a portal to a stone circle in the Darklands, bypassing the Great Barrier completely. All the warlocks were there, waiting in their bird forms, sitting on the great druidic stones. They had a crystal as large as a chimera set up in the centre, ready to cast a summoning spell. The warlocks landed on the ground and transformed into their human forms. Then, working as one, they opened a portal to the Seventh Dimension, large enough to let out a thousand demons.

"My eyes were blurry then, as if the dark magic rising around me wanted to sap away my consciousness. But I didn't let it. Through the mist, a giant figure emerged from the portal. It was one of the demon lords..."

At least three people in the room gasped. Jaws dropped.

"Getting so tired..." Aleam said. "Must keep going."

"You can do it, Aleam," Brigel said. "Who did they summon exactly?"

Aleam shuddered, and his lips trembled as if he didn't want to speak the word... It came out softly. "The giant snake... Apopis... The overlord of overlords. The greatest of them all..." He was blinking heavily, trying to stay awake. He let out a snore, and then his eyes shot open again.

"What did they want with Apopis?" Driar Yila asked.

"A pact... They'll use the key to raise an army of demon dragons across dimensions.... In exchange, the demons will let the warlocks reign immortal..." His head drooped, and he started to snore softly.

The room had fallen into stunned silence.

"Things are very dire indeed," Driar Brigel said after a moment.

I stood up and stretched. "So that means we need to get the key to the Sixth Dimension as soon as possible. We've got to take our dragons and try and find that pyramid."

"As we have explained, Initiate Ben," Driar Lonamm said... "The Calimar Desert is so vast that it will take us days to find that pyramid."

"But what do we do in the meantime?" I asked, and I looked over at Aleam nodding his head as he slumbered.

"We try to learn as much as we can, and we wait," Driar Brigel said.

A more juvenile version of me would have tried to escape from the Academy without Salanraja. Whiskers, I'd done so before. But that had resulted in me running into a bed of massive magical scorpions called serkets, and I was almost eaten by their giant spider queen overlord for dinner.

That was one event I didn't want to repeat. But waiting was something I wasn't very good at...

30

WAITING

The night was young, and a full moon hung high in the sky. A cool breeze came from the direction of the Willowed Woods, bringing tonnes of fresh air with it.

Salanraja slept soundly on the floor of the chamber, pungent smoke coming out of her nostrils with each soft snore. As I'd predicted, I couldn't sleep, and so I sat grooming myself as I watched my crystal for any signs of where Lasinta and Arran might have taken Ta'ra. Salanraja had already explained numerous times that the Calimar Desert was a massive place, containing thousands of pyramids – mostly burial temples built by the Egyptian clan warlocks who had inhabited the place for almost a thousand years.

The crystal gave none of the signs I was hoping for. It wasn't even glowing. I tried probing out to it in my mind.

"Crystal? Crystal, are you there?"

Perhaps it was just being stubborn because it didn't talk to me.

I yawned, not out of tiredness but out of boredom. I snapped my jaw shut and stretched my legs, my body aching from sprinting through sandstorms the night before. I sneaked past Salanraja and climbed down the spiral staircase of the East Tower, then went towards the bailey.

The cats were out of the cattery, as usual, hunting mice and scouring the grounds for any signs of carrion eating birds. A white Assyrian she-cat, whom I always thought was quite beautiful, and might have danced with under the moonlight if it weren't for Ta'ra, was crouched low, stalking a mouse that had emerged from a hiding place underneath one of the building stones.

The Assyrian pounced and caught the mouse beneath her claws, pinning it firmly to stop it wriggling away. A tortoiseshell tom sitting on the *chemin de ronde*, noticed her and leapt down onto the flagstones of the bailey. Not happy about the unannounced arrival, the Assyrian hissed at the tom, then carried the mouse away in her mouth.

The scene reminded me of those good times hunting mice in South Wales. I'd never been as skilled as this Assyrian, admittedly, but I still missed the joy of the hunt. Of feeling the ground vibrate through my paws as I listened for any sign of prey emerging from a hiding hole. Chasing, and chasing, until my legs became tired. Usually the mouse got away, but this was okay because a bowl of smoked salmon or some other delicious meal always lay waiting for me at home.

I stalked across the bailey, over to the keep, following the scent of snowdrop perfume upon the breeze. The doors were open, and I traced the trail to the library, where I found Seramina sitting at a desk studying a book. She didn't raise her head until I jumped up on the table beside her and rubbed my nose against her hand.

"Ben..." she said, and she pushed me away slightly so she could continue reading. But she did do her duty in stroking me after that.

"I couldn't sleep..."

"Well, you are nocturnal." Seramina's voice sounded distant. She was concentrating.

"I would have thought you'd be with Aleam... How is he?"

"There's no point watching him sleep. But he's still breathing."

I couldn't read the words in the book. Though my crystal had gifted me with the ability to speak all languages, this never included reading. But I could see the picture in ink of the pyramids, scratched out across the top of the page.

"Did you learn anything about Capitut? Have you found the pyramid that might hold the key to the Sixth Dimension?"

Seramina looked at me. Her eyelids looked heavy, and her face was a little puffy. "If I had, I would have told you, Ben. The Egyptian warlocks built thousands of these pyramids in the Calimar desert. Apparently, there are more pyramids in this world than in the Fourth Dimension."

I looked at the book again, and I sneezed. There was a reason I didn't visit the library much in Dragonsbond Academy. There was so much dust in here it was bad for my respiratory system. "Let me know if you find anything. I'll be outside, watching the cats hunt. Or maybe, I'll see if I can catch a morsel myself."

Outside, the moon was now concealed behind a heavy fluffy cloud. No more cats were in the bailey, but I caught glimpses of them stalking the *chemin de ronde*. My muscles felt heavy, and I didn't feel like doing any hunting after all. So, I went over to one of my favourite spots to be alone – underneath the stone fountain with a stone dragon holding an egg and spouting out water instead of fire into the pool.

I closed my eyes, finding some comfort in the coolness of the flagstones beneath my tummy. Perhaps I even managed to catch a few winks. Then, I heard footsteps, and I saw the heels of two pairs of shoes in front of me, rooted firmly to the ground. One pair was male, one was female. Bellari's whiny voice trickled down beneath the fountain and found its way through the dark shadows to my ears.

"Remember how we used to sit here... The clear skies... Gazing up at the stars..."

She was with Rine. I could smell his scent behind Bellari's ridiculously thick perfume. Whiskers, this was all part of her nefarious plan. She and Rine didn't belong together. Rine belonged to Ange... But Ange wasn't here right now.

I was tempted to rush out and sit on Bellari's lap, maybe even dig my claws into her thighs. She'd sneeze and complain about her allergies, and I'd be one victorious cat.

But the Council of Three was right about one thing. It takes time on a battlefield to learn about your enemies. If I stayed and listened for a while, perhaps I could learn enough about Bellari's game to work out how to stop her.

"I remember," Rine said. I could smell his pheromones, and they didn't smell good.

"I used to feel so strong in your arms... As if I could do anything. And when I sat with you, even though I knew we shouldn't be out here, time just seemed to dissolve away."

"It *was* good," Rine said, and his feet shuffled even closer towards Bellari. Their two innermost legs interlocked. "But I'm still worried about Ange."

Bellari paused. Tactfully... Deviously. "I just wanted you to know that you're special. You're a kind person underneath it all... I miss that. I miss *you*."

There was a pause. A long one that seemed to cut through the night, softened only by the rustling of leaves. In the distance, a wolf howled and an owl hooted into the void.

"I miss you too, Bellari," Rine said. "But I can't stop thinking—"

"Hush, Rine. Let's just enjoy this night for what it is. Let's just..."

Bellari's feet shifted. I heard her breath on the breeze. Whiskers,

I knew what was about to happen. They were about to kiss... Stupid, stupid Rine.

I got ready to rush out and screech and hiss at her. How dare she once again try to split Rine and Ange apart. I was meant to retire with them in a nice cottage with their dragons and Salanraja.

But just before I could skitter out from my hiding place, a bright white light filled the bailey. It was coming from the inner courtyard that led to the keep.

"What's that?" Rine said. "My crystal... It told me to go to the courtyard."

"Me too," Bellari said. She didn't sound too happy about it.

That was when my crystal also spoke in my mind in a soft Welsh-like lilting accent. *"Follow them, Dragoncat. Destiny awaits you in the inner courtyard."*

My heart pounding, I rushed out to follow the order. I sprinted past Bellari and Rine on the way, brushing past Bellari's leg in the hope that I'd at least make her sneeze. Once I was well on my way, I glanced over my shoulder to see – thank my whiskers for destiny – they weren't holding hands.

31

THE GREAT CRYSTAL
REVEALS ALL

The Inner Courtyard lay between the castle's bailey and the castle's principal building. This was the Keep Tower that housed the headquarters of the Council of Three, the library, and many of the classrooms. We gathered in the courtyard for assemblies every week, so I knew it well.

The lawn stretched across the courtyard, and beyond that a dais stood before the entrance to the keep, from where the Driars would often address students about important matters. A massive crystal hung from the ceiling above this. It emanated warm and radiant light to guide us towards it.

This was the Great Crystal. I'd learned in a recent lesson which I'd managed to stay awake in, that this was the most powerful crystal in the whole academy. I'd already seen it divine the future and the Council of Three had once used it to read my mind.

The Council of Three already stood on the dais, each a good few paces away from the crystal. They held their staffs out from their body, feeding the crystal with magical beams. Driar Yila's was red,

Driar Lonamm's was blue, and Driar Brigel's was green. The crystal seemed to suck in their power, as it let out a soft humming sound.

Rine and Bellari soon joined us, still not holding hands. Max came bounding through the archway between the bailey and the courtyard, panting away. He halted just in front of the crystal and stared up at it, as if watching a bird perched on a tree.

"The giant crystal called me!" he yipped excitedly. "It called me in my dreams."

High Prefect Lars and Prefect Asinda came rushing through the archway next, and Seramina later floated out from the keep. We stood together watching the crystal. Everyone, I was sure, was wondering what the whiskers was going on.

I took a few steps forward, but Driar Brigel snapped his head around. He bawled out so loudly that he startled me.

"Stay back," he said. "Don't get too close..." I returned to my spot beside Max and the other students.

"It's happening!" Driar Yila shouted. "The portal is opening."

"I don't think it can hold for much longer!" Driar Lonamm called.

"There's still enough power to complete the task at hand," Driar Brigel said.

"But we'll break it..." Driar Lonamm said. "It can't withstand this kind of force."

"Then that's what we'll have to do." Driar Yila turned her head to look at us. "I guess the crystals chose the six of you after all. I have no idea why."

A wind picked up from behind us, pulling as if it wanted to suck us in towards the Great Crystal. I screeched and dug into the soil with my claws. The wind howled through the courtyard, whipping up chunks of dirt. A wide vertical beam of light shot down from the crystal, illuminating the expressions of consternation painted upon the Great Driars' faces.

Presently, the glow coming out of the crystal faded. Recognisable images developed beneath its facets. Moving pictures, like I used to see on the television back in South Wales.

The crystal displayed a vista of the cracked Calimar Desert from above, rolling over dunes and sandstone buttes faster than Salanraja could fly. It kept high enough to display the vastness of the landscape stretching out into oblivion.

The beam of light coming down from the crystal expanded, pulling outwards as if two hands were tearing it apart. It formed a narrow slit, and then opened wide enough to become a portal, high above the barren plains of the Calimar desert.

As the portal stretched open, the wind coming from it became even colder, whipping back all three of the Driars cloaks and both Driar Yila's and Driar Lonamm's hair. It was night in the Calimar desert, just as it was night here. But within, I could see the first traces of sunlight emerging on the horizon. Clearly, it was far enough away to be in a different time zone.

Prefect Lars let go of Asinda's hand, so that he could cup his hand to his mouth to be heard over the din. "What would you have us do?" he shouted.

"Wait until it is time..." Driar Brigel called back.

"How will we know when?" Asinda asked.

"The crystal will give the signal," Driar Yila said. "Now just wait. We need to focus."

She let go of her staff with one hand and started waving it in the air in front of her. The other two Great Driars followed suit. Now, light wasn't just coming from their staffs, but also from their free hands which they faced towards the crystal, dancing them elaborately through the air.

I saw Max ready himself to pounce. Whiskers, the dog was so brave he was stupid. He was just about to take off when I scratched a claw along his flank. Not so hard to hurt him, but sharp enough for him to take notice.

"What did you do that for?" he whimpered. "I'm ready..."

"We'll all go together. I'll let you know when it's time to jump."

Max looked up at the Initiates and Prefects surrounding us. Everyone had their legs braced, ready to charge. Lars held Asinda's hand. Rine had Seramina's hand in one hand and Bellari's in the other. He had a smug expression on his face.

The movement of the portal over the desert had begun to slow. The wind warmed slightly and tasted dry. The portal descended towards an array of pyramids arranged in a neat lattice. It continued towards a large butte stationed on a flattened dune, then lowered itself until it looked straight at a red sandstone rockface. I recognised the craggy exterior behind it from the vision in the whirlwind back in the Sahara Desert. But there was no sign of the pyramid...

The Great Crystal began to speak, pulsing with light with each syllable. It lilted in my own crystal's voice inside my head, and with the way everyone else had their heads turned towards it, I guessed they could hear it too.

"This is Capitut's Pyramid, where the guardian warlock buried the key to the Sixth Dimension. Look behind it and the illusion will cease to be."

It took me a moment to work out what the crystal meant by this. I squinted my eyes, and the butte flickered behind the portal, then disappeared from view.

A network of crevices surrounded the pyramid, so wide that they would be impossible to cross. The pyramid itself was as tall as the Keep Tower of Dragonsbond Academy, limned at the base of all four of its wide sides by haze. It rose into a purple sky where the point pricked the fading night.

The entrance remained shut, and from the way that it had caked into the surrounding bricks, it looked as if it might never open. A familiar looking sphinx guarded the entrance. Though its eyes had no discernible pupils, it seemed to be looking straight at us.

On our side of a crevice between us and the sphinx, another character stood who we'd all come to know so well. A dragon, black and with shiny scales. It was Corralsa, meaning that Arran and Lasinta must have already arrived.

A screeching sound cut the air above us. The Great Crystal had started to vibrate in the air, like a washing machine coming to the end of its cycle.

"It's starting to break..." Driar Lonamm said.

"Just hold it," Driar Yila said. "Wait for the signal..."

Cracks appeared on the crystal, light glowing out from within. The ceiling above it also shook, and the cracks tore out across that too. If the Great Crystal exploded, the portal would vanish, and the debris from the explosion might take us with it.

But the portal was still too high above the ground, still approaching the dragon who observed us discerningly, plumes of smoke rising from her nostrils. She raised herself on her rear legs and scuffed at the ground with its foreclaw, like a horse ready to charge. Letting out a loud roar, she opened her wings as if in warning.

Suddenly, the portal stopped in its tracks, then turned towards the ground. It hurtled downwards, until all we could see was the compacted brown floor. We weren't looking onwards anymore, but through a portal suspended above the desert.

The great crystals boomed out an order for all of us to hear. "Your dragons will follow you... Go now!" It didn't sound anything like my crystal, but instead had a commanding female voice.

I was the first to charge, kicking up dust from the flagstones behind me. Really, I'd pent up so much energy from all the tension that I couldn't stop myself.

I heard the crystal shatter behind me as I leapt through the portal. The force from a heavy shockwave slammed me to the ground. Max came tumbling after me, then Asinda, Lars, Rine, Seramina, and Bellari last.

I looked up. The portal had vanished. Instead, the great black dragon hovered over us, its outstretched wings highlighted at the edges by the light from the moon.

32

THE DRAGON AND THE SPANIEL

"Defensive positions," Lars cried out, and all humans drew their staffs. A shield barrier pulsed out around us all, magicked up by Lars' staff.

We clustered within the protective sphere, looking up at Corralsa. My five dragon rider companions had their backs pressed against each other, and I wielded my staff in my mouth, safely away from them so that I wouldn't whack their knees.

Max stood at the edge of the shield, but he wasn't barking. Rather, he just stared up at the dragon, his tail wagging, his eyes wide...

Corralsa hovered over us, flapping her wide wings. Our protective shield flared brightly at the points where the downward gusts washed over it, forming flowing patterns looking a bit like iron filings in the field of a magnet. The dragon opened its mouth and let out a roar that I could hear only faintly over the buzz of the shield.

Crystals glowed above me, and I willed purple energy into my staff, trying to ignore the slight burning sensation on my tongue. The sun peeked out above the horizon, sending a warm light through the shield. It softened the angular features on Corralsa's face and cast amber highlights across her shiny scales.

Max looked at each of the glowing crystals, and then he started to bark. The dragon roared again, this time more loudly.

"Wait! Wait!" he called. "Don't attack my friend..."

I turned to him, and the light faded from my staff. "Your pwiend?" It was hard to talk with the staff in my mouth.

"I've been talking to her all this time in my mind," he whimpered. "Since we came back out of the portal from the Great Desert. She's not to blame... She's been forced to do evil things by Arran's bad magic..."

My stomach lurched. Max had been talking to Corralsa all this time... He couldn't be bonding with the dragon, could he? If so, then who were those two dwarf dragons my crystal had mentioned were on their way to Dragonsbond Academy? Who were they meant to bond with?

I stopped all magic flowing to my staff and called upon my staff bearer to remove it from my mouth. The great white hand took it, and then vanished into thin air, leaving behind a smoky scent.

"Ben, what are you doing?" Bellari screamed. "We need to get ready to attack."

"No," I said. "Stand down... Prefect Lars, could you lower the shield, please?"

"Are you crazy?"

Lars shot Bellari a stern look, then turned to me. He didn't lower the shield yet. "Ben, what's this about?"

I cocked my head towards the Sussex Spaniel. "You remember how I bonded with Salanraja... Well, I reckon the same is happening between Max and Corralsa."

"But Corralsa is already bonded with Arran," Asinda said. The light had also started to fade from her staff, as well as Seramina's. Still, Bellari's and Rine's staffs glowed bright red and blue.

"I guess she was… I don't know, maybe Arran becoming a traitor to the kingdom has diffused that bond."

Max sat on his paws, and whimpered, "Please, Ben, don't let them attack my friend."

"I'm trying," I barked back at him. Then I looked up at Lars, and said more softly in the human language, "Max tells us Corralsa is his friend. Which also makes her ours."

Lars's shoulders rose as he inhaled a deep breath. "Very well… Initiate Rine and Initiate Bellari, lower your staffs."

"But then we won't have any defences if she attacks," Bellari said. "We need to at least have Rine's ice magic at the ready. Don't you think, Rine?"

Rine didn't say anything. He was studying the dragon, as if wondering what he should do.

Lars also didn't lower his gaze from the dragon. "Corralsa is scared. I've got Camillan talking to her now…" That was one of the useful things about dragons. They could converse across great distances. I'd be asking Salanraja questions as well, if she wasn't fast asleep.

Rine sighed, and the magic winked out of his staff. Bellari's continued to shine brightly.

"Initiate Bellari, we won't tell you again," Asinda said.

Lars kept the shield up, which was wise. It would keep Bellari's magic inside and stop her from attacking Corralsa. She huffed, and lowered her staff, the light fading from it. "Fine…"

The white glow on Lars' staff faded and the shield dissipated. Corralsa roared again, and smoke came out from her nostrils. I shuddered, as the thought came to me that perhaps we'd been tricked. I closed my eyes, waiting for the fires to wash over me.

No heat came. Instead, I heard shuffling from in front of me. I opened my eyes again to see Max inching forward. Corralsa stayed hovering above, pushing herself backwards with great flaps of her wings to keep in line with the dog.

Once they were both a safe distance away from us, Corralsa landed, sending up swathes of dust around her. Max took a few more steps forward, and the dragon lowered her head towards him.

Then, something happened that caused me to lose all respect for Corralsa. I didn't mind them showing affection by pressing their noses up to each other. That, in my opinion was completely natural. But I couldn't bear to watch as Corralsa let Max roll his clumsy wet tongue right over her long snout.

From deep inside her belly, came a loud and high-pitched croon.

"Oh, so it's finally happened," Salanraja said in my mind. *"The moment we've finally been waiting for. Their first bond."*

I growled. Honestly, I don't know why. Sometimes, us cats just feel like growling. *"Salanraja... I thought you were asleep. You knew about this?"*

"Oh yes... Us dragons have been discussing it for days. You know we've always felt a bit sorry for Corralsa... She never liked Arran, and she never realised he was a traitor. He blocked her out all the time and kept far too many secrets."

"I thought you hated Corralsa?"

"Well, she was strict... She didn't have a choice in her situation. But us dragons stick together, you know?"

"So, now you're telling me that the great, mighty jet-scaled dragon has chosen a dog to be its rider?"

"And I thought you were starting to respect the Sussex Spaniel," Salanraja said.

"That doesn't change the fact that he's a dog..."

The dragon now had her chin pressed against the ground, and I half expected Max to jump on her head and start riding her just like I had done with Salanraja.

"She's not ready to be ridden again yet," Salanraja said. *"She's still getting over Arran."*

"You mean to say that she might not bond with Max after all?"

"Nobody knows..."

"Okay..." I looked over at the pyramid, impressed by its immensity. *"By the way, where are you?"*

"We're on our way over to you," Salanraja said. *"It's a long journey, but we'll get there as fast as we can."*

"How long?"

"I don't know. None of us have ever flown to the Calimar Desert before."

"Then hurry. Because I have the feeling we're going to need all the help we can get."

Seramina shuffled over to me, then glanced back at Asinda and Lars. "Ben... I know you're talking with Salanraja, but this is important."

I snapped my head up towards her. "What is it?"

"You're erm... You're the only one of us who can talk to Max. Corralsa doesn't want to talk to any of the other dragons right now."

"Oh? Why not?"

"She's ashamed. Look could you just, you know, ask him what's going on? Can Corralsa carry us over to the other side of the canyon? Because we can't see any other way to get across."

I strolled over to Max and relayed Seramina's question. I didn't like standing right underneath the hot sulphurous breath of a dragon whom, only moments ago, I'd believed was my enemy. At any time, that hot breath could become fire.

"Corralsa says that she can't carry anyone, no," Max panted. "She isn't ready to take any rider..."

"Then can't she lift us at least? We don't have to ride on her back."

"The dragon says no..." Max says. "She says this is personal. But you don't need a dragon to cross to the pyramid."

My whiskers twitched. "What do you mean? It's not as if we can turn ourselves into condors."

"Corralsa says just to walk like the warlocks did... Over the invisible bridge."

I turned to stare out at the great gaping chasm that separated us and the pyramid, and probably led into an abyss worse than death.

An invisible bridge? I didn't like the sound of that at all.

🦋 *33* 🦋

A VERY DEEP CHASM INDEED

I hadn't seen a chasm so deep since the Ghost Realm in one of the visions that it had shown us. There, the crevices had been filled with rivers of what smelled like putrid yeast extract. The chasm before me smelled just as bad – this time of rotten eggs. It emanated a ruby light from the bottom where a stream of magma flowed, clouds of ash rising upwards.

I backed away slowly, yowling as I imagined what might happen if I fell in.

"This is it," Max said as he stepped up to the edge I had just backed away from. "This is where Corralsa says the bridge is…"

"How do you know it's not a trap?" I asked.

Seramina, standing a little further away from us, laughed. "If Corralsa wanted to kill us, she would have just eaten us, don't you think?"

"I think you would have cast some dangerous magic at her first," I pointed out. "Speaking of which, couldn't we just use magic to get across? Rine could cast an ice bridge."

"Over a pool of lava?" Rine asked. "Ben, do you realise how hot it is over there?"

"See, I told you he was smart," Bellari said. "And it's probably obvious how my magic is absolutely useless. You can fight fire with fire, but not lava."

I cocked my head to think a moment. "Didn't you say shields were as light as a feather, Lars? You could use your magic to float us over on the heat currents."

"The shield must still obey the rules of gravity," Lars said. He walked over to Asinda and took hold of her hand. "It might be as light as a feather, but that doesn't mean the things within it don't have weight."

"Then we'll have to use dark magic," I said. "Asinda or Seramina could do something."

Asinda, who was standing back from all this, was shaking her head. "We're not using dark magic unless we need to... There's a reason it was outlawed by the king. Remember what Aleam said about how that stuff consumes your soul?"

"Well, I say we need to," I said, and I summoned my staff bearer. Before anyone could react, I called the staff into my mouth, and I began to cast a spell.

I'd summoned salmon once before, and it had helped us escape from the evil *Cana Dei,* a dark and mysterious force that had wanted to consume us in the Ghost Realm. I was convinced I could do it again. A massive bridge of them linked together tooth to tail. Then, when we were on the other side, we could have a grand feast roasted for us. I hadn't thought of a better idea in my entire life.

"What are you doing, Ben?" Asinda asked.

"Just one moment..."

I could do it; I knew I could. I willed the energy to my staff, magic pulsing through it, this time only lightly warming the front of my tongue. It coursed through my muscles, and every ounce of my being. My head lightened, and my shoulders felt like they'd developed wings.

I cast out the dark magic with a fizzle then a pop...

A cockroach crawled out of the glowing crystal on my staff, scuttled up the pole, and took root on my nose. I sneezed and swiped it off with my paw. Rine squashed the cockroach under his boot, leaving a puddle of purple goo and a whiff of rotten vegetable juice. My stomach fluttered as I gazed at its remains.

"Ben..." Seramina said. "Please promise you'll never do that again. You abuse dark magic, and there's no telling what it might do to you."

"Fine..." I was just glad that the cockroach hadn't bitten me.

I turned back towards the chasm. Asinda was now looking over it, holding her staff. She poked the air in front of Max with the bottom of her pole... "There's nothing there. No bridge, see?"

Max barked back at her, as if he understood. "The dragon told me! There is a bridge!"

"Here let me try," Rine said.

Bellari bristled as he stepped away from her and towards the chasm. "Rine, be careful... I don't want to lose you again."

He looked back at her and winked. Then he lifted his staff, and out from the glowing crystal, he cast a shard of ice right at the chasm. It lodged itself in mid-air right in the centre – just a little further below us than any of us could reach with our staffs.

"The bridge is below us," Lars said. "We'll have to jump onto it."

"But how do we know where it starts?" Asinda said.

"I guess we need to cast a lot more magic," Rine said. "Map our path."

Max, it seemed had run out of patience. He lifted himself on to all fours, and with no regard from the depths of the chasm or the flowing lava underneath, he took a flying leap.

"Max, no!" I barked, or maybe I said it in the human language. Whatever I said, it caused everyone to snap their heads around and watch the flying fool.

It was as if I was watching him in slow motion, his paws outstretched, as he sailed over as far as his launch would carry him, and then began to descend. His paws splayed, he started kicking air. He had misjudged and he was going to fall.

Seramina's staff began to glow, but she had no time to cast a spell before Max plummeted towards the chasm's bottom. He landed on something invisible and did a roly-poly over naked air.

He turned back to us and barked. "See... It's perfectly safe. You can feel it when you get here. You can tell where the bridge is..."

He spun back around and bounded off towards the other side of the chasm.

The hackles had shot up on my back, and I had my weight against my back paws, ready to flee. I'd assumed the same posture every time I knew that the human family back in South Wales was going on holiday. They'd take me to a place humans called the 'cattery' then, and I never wanted to go. On such days, I'd do everything in my power to stay at home, and in all honesty, I didn't know why my owners didn't let me.

It wasn't as if I didn't know how to hunt, and even if I couldn't catch anything, I'm sure one of the neighbours would have fed me. But I did know one thing for sure. I never, ever, wanted to go to the cattery. It was the worst place in the world...

Nor did I want to cross that invisible bridge.

"So, that's that, then," Rine said. "Who's going to go next?"

"Not you, Rine," Bellari said. "Surely there has to be another way."

Asinda looked back at this girl, and her eyes seemed to ask, what the whiskers does Rine see in you?

The Prefect turned back to the chasm, took a deep breath, and vaulted over on her staff. She landed almost as gracefully as a cat.

Back at the foot of the bridge, Lars let out a sigh, which I guess was one of relief. He grunted, and then he sheathed his staff on his back. He swung his arms twice, bowed his legs, and then jumped with both feet together into oblivion. He wasn't as graceful as Asinda – his landing more like an enraged gorilla's.

I turned around to Rine. "After you," I said to him.

He shook his head, his eyes wide... "Oh no, you first."

"Then Bellari..."

Bellari took hold of Rine's hand, and she didn't seem to notice my sincere sneer. "Rine and I are going to do this together, aren't we Rine?" There it was... Bellari trying to control Rine again. She seemed to do an awfully good job of it. When would he ever learn?

"So go on then," I said.

"No, no," Rine said. "Can't you see when two people need a little time alone?" He gave me a cock of the head and a wink.

I realised I couldn't win this fight. It was two against one, after all, even if both of them were idiots. With a deep growl, I took a running leap towards where I'd seen Lars plummet before. I sailed, and I soared. Then I began to fall, and I thought I'd missed my mark.

But I hit something, and I slid slightly as if I had landed on a surface of ice. I dug my claws in to brake to a halt, feeling a sudden pain in my paws.

Was this fire? I asked myself, as I scuttered along the bridge, as if walking on eggshells. But it was cold not hot. The bridge felt like a platform of ice. If I got close enough to the edge, I could feel enough heat rising from the chasm to signal me back to the centre again. Still, I kept moving, not wanting to get frostbitten paws.

I reached the other side sooner than I thought I would. "You could have warned me how cold it was!" I barked at Max.

"Wimp," he said back.

Furious, I moved as far away as I could from that smelly dog. I stumbled into a massive, sandy paw. A statue of some sort.

I looked up at the long, feline leg. Then, I had to crane my head to see its chest which was human and female with a funny headdress shaped over it. Everything was made of compacted sand.

Even further up, I saw the lifeless eyes. Even though they had no pupils, I knew they were looking straight at me. I swallowed hard, as the realisation washed over me...

It seemed that, unwittingly, I had entered a sphinx's domain.

THE SPHINX, REALLY

The ground shook so violently, that I thought that it would throw at least one of us into the lava-bottomed chasm. Only then did I turn my head to see Bellari stumbling over towards the edge of the invisible bridge – or at least where I imagined the edge to be.

Rine reached out a hand to catch her, and he pulled her back towards him. They rushed together to the other side of the chasm, Asinda and Lars both offering a hand to pull them up, before the earth shook again even more violently.

This time, I went sliding away from the sphinx. I dug my paws into the sandstone, pulling up dust before I braked to a halt.

The sphinx turned her human head towards me like no statue should be able to. Her eyes blinked, though they still seemed to have no life behind them. Her long tail wagged in the air, sending up a creaking sound as it did. She opened her mouth to speak, sand rolling off her lips as if off a crumbling sandcastle.

As it had in the Sahara Desert, the sphinx's voice sounded like sandpaper rubbing against brushed metal. Far too grating, in other words, for this poor Bengal's sensitive ears.

"Dragoncat, is it? The cat of legends... You came, just as you were destined to do. The prophecies had divined that you would be the first of your party to stumble before my feet. And so it must now be you who will complete the trial."

"What prophecies?" I asked. "What trial?"

The ground shook again. A little less violently than before, but I had already guessed that this was the sphinx's way of telling me that I'd done something to displease her.

"I shall ask the questions... Do you not know how the Trial of the Sphinx works?"

"I believe that you ask me a riddle..."

"Correct. But first I need to know, or rather I would like to know – more out of curiosity than anything, what brings you here? I've not been awoken for two thousand years. Now, you're the second visitor in the last hour."

"Does that mean Arran and Lasinta are already here? Did they bring a cat with them by any chance? A black she-cat? White diamond crest on her chest?"

This time, as the earth shook, the ground cracked underneath me. Salty dust rose upwards and made me want to sneeze. I snapped my head around to check my friends were okay. Wisely, they had pulled themselves away from the edge of the chasm.

"Didn't I say I was the one who asks the questions?" the sphinx boomed.

"But this is important."

"Just answer the question! What brings you here? And that, for the record, is not my riddle."

I growled at the sphinx. No one had told me she was so cantankerous. Whiskers, she was worse than Salanraja on her worst day.

"Isn't it obvious?" I started but was interrupted by another earthquake. This time it was less violent but rumbled so rapidly that I thought my bones might snap.

"That is a question!" the sphinx snapped. "Stop asking questions! Would you rather I just ate you and had this over with?"

I tried my hardest not to sneeze because of the sand I'd sucked up my nostrils. "Fine... To answer your second question, I would rather you didn't eat me, thank you. I don't think you'd find me all that appetising."

I paused, wondering how best to frame this. I had a feeling that if I said the wrong thing then I wouldn't last long enough to hear the riddle. I had to sound all wise, like a sagacious traveller.

"We are here to stop two evil warlocks taking the key to the Sixth Dimension and using it to destroy all the other dimensions. Is that an adequate purpose—" Remembering myself just in time, I stopped the final syllable rising so it didn't sound like a question.

It seemed to work for the sphinx.

"Interesting... Very interesting indeed... Well, you seem to already know the legend and purpose of the sphinx. My spirit was summoned from the Seventh Dimension for one purpose and one purpose only. I must pose to you a riddle."

With the utterance of the final word, time suddenly stopped around me. The sand stopped roiling and shifting underneath my feet. Heat stopped blasting up from the chasm. My friends had frozen in thin air, and the wind had lost its whistle.

It was just me and the sphinx now... The fact she'd sucked all time out of her surroundings made her voice boom even louder. "Because you are such a foolish creature, I shall give you three tries to answer the riddle. Call it a kindness of kin from feline to feline. Sound fair?"

"Yes," I said.

"Good... But be warned... If you get it wrong the third time, then I shall be forced, as legend dictates, to eat you. Now, shall I begin? Or I can also give you the option to turn back."

I didn't even hesitate. "You shall begin," I said. I stretched out my paws and held my head high. I knew what the question was going to be, as my crystal had already told me. I let the words roll over me as the sphinx grated them out...

"Who are you..." The sphinx hesitated... "Really?"

Well, I hadn't expected the extra word, but it didn't matter. Because I'd already prepared this answer ahead of time, and I hadn't even needed to think about it. It's what I'd been telling everyone all along.

"I'm Ben, a Bengal cat, descendant of the great Asian leopard cat and also the mighty George."

I waited. The air held a stillness, as time continued not to pass. The sphinx rolled her eyes... "Is that really your first answer?"

"Really!"

"Would you perhaps care to call a friend?"

"No... Wait, what do you mean?" I considered it, then decided that the sphinx was just toying with me. "Yes, that's my final answer..."

"Well..." the sphinx spoke slowly, elongating the moment. Then, she boomed out, "You're wrong! That isn't the answer to the riddle..."

The earth shook again, and in the distance a rock fell off its perch. As if the sphinx had intended the whole thing for cinematic effect, the only things to move were the earth, the rock, me, the sphinx, and the sound coursing out of her stippled lips.

"Care to try again, or would you rather I just ate you now? Because really, I've not had a good meal in two thousand years..." A very blandly coloured tongue poked through the sphinx's lips and rode its way from one side of her mouth to the other.

"I'll have another try, I think," I said. As if I had any other option.

"Very well," the sphinx said, again slowing time even more to give her voice extra power. "Who are you... Really?"

I stopped to think this time. Really... Because I guessed the sphinx didn't actually want to know who I was in my original world, but who I was in the First Dimension. I gave myself a few seconds as well to consider how to word it. After all, a creature who had the gift of all languages should know how to present things properly – especially to a legendary sphinx.

"Well?" the sphinx said, and she raised her paw, extending her claws. Clumps of sand fell from her toes – which wasn't the most pleasant of sights.

I held my head up high. "I am Dragoncat, vanquisher of the warlock Astravar. I have visited five of the seven dimensions, and I have conjured powerful dark magic. In this land, I am a hero... And I am still a cat..."

The sphinx lowered her paw and turned her head to me. "That is a very considered answer. Congratulations... *Dragoncat*."

I meowed, liking being complimented. Nowadays, it didn't seem to happen too much. "So..."

"So what?"

"Is that it? Did I get the right answer?"

"No!" the sphinx bawled, her voice shaking the crags and sending more rocks tumbling down from them. They must have crushed an awful lot of pyramids, but the sphinx didn't seem to particularly care. "That is an inadequate answer..."

Everything else around me still seemed frozen in time.

"What's wrong with it?" I asked.

"You're asking questions, again..."

"I need to so that I can complete the task at hand."

The sphinx inched towards me, sand shifting and reforming

over her body as she moved. She loomed over my head, her teeth hanging high, as if ready to eat me. Sand drizzled onto my fur, and I edged backwards as far as I could without falling into the chasm, which wasn't very far at all.

"You have one more answer left... This time, make sure it is profound enough to satisfy a creature of legends. No one wishes to die a fool..."

Now, this stupid sphinx really had me stumped. "It's not even a proper riddle," I said.

"Is that so? Then why hasn't anyone ever answered this particular riddle correctly?"

"And how many times have you asked it..."

The sphinx hesitated. "That is another question!" she rasped. "You've pushed this too far now... I'm going to consider the next thing you say your final answer. Think wise and think fast, for space is opening up inside my stomach for you and your friends."

I could feel the dryness at the back of my throat. My tummy was also rumbling. Why is it that when I get so close to death, I become ravenous?

I entered a state of panic. Thoughts spun around my head at a million miles an hour. I must have thought of a dozen things to say, none of which I said or remember, because they were too stupid. Then, something Salanraja had told me entered my head.

"You are becoming more human by the day..." My dragon had said it that way, multiple times. Or at least I think she had. Come to think of it, if I was partly human then maybe I wasn't too different from the sphinx. I guess I didn't have wings, but I did know how to fly.

I looked up at the sphinx, at her human head, and the way that it merged so well into a feline body. Her wings were folded up against its body so neatly, that they were hard to detect.

The sphinx... A cat that had become human that could fly... I didn't have any better answers.

"Come on," the sphinx said. "It's not like we have all day…"

I took a deep breath, then I rasped out, "I am you…"

"You what?" This sphinx didn't seem to have eyebrows, so instead she raised the skin – or should I say sand – that would have been underneath them.

"I am you… And you are me…" I considered if I should add anything else into the mix. Throw in a bit of surreal philosophy, perhaps. But having the gift of all languages didn't also mean I was good at metaphysics.

"And that is your final answer for your ultimate answer?"

My whiskers twitched, and I pushed away any doubt that pressed on my mind. The sphinx's teeth had moved so close to me that if I moved my head even an inch, they'd prick me.

"It is…" I waited for a long and terrifying moment.

"Profound!" the sphinx rolled back to her original position. The sand was no longer trickling between my ears. "I guess we are all the same in the universe of infinite possibilities… I will need a good thousand years to ponder on this one, I think."

I stared at the massive sandy thing, blinking. "So that's it? We're free to go? You're not going to eat me?"

"Oh, no… I don't want to do that. You could say a lot of things about me. Many travellers have… But I am *not* a cannibal."

"Well, could you please unfreeze time then? Because we really need to be saving the world."

"Certainly…" the sphinx said, and then her rasping, sandy voice faded as time swirled back into existence around me. "Since you have come with a key – and a very fine one he is too – welcome to the Sixth Dimension… Be warned that if your key ceases to be, or leaves this place, the rest of you will suffer the same fate as he. Now, if you will excuse me…"

"The Sixth Dimension?" I asked, and I looked around past the chasm. At first, I saw the same compacted and barren sandstone plateaus that stretched out before us.

But then I blinked, and all of this winked out of existence. Instead, I saw bright green hills, and golden fairies floating around, and dandelion seeds dancing on the balmy breeze. Waterfalls roared in the distance, and I could taste pollen in the air.

I blinked again, and we were surrounded by blackness. Very faintly, I saw faint blue outlines of distant shapes, and I could smell that horrible yeast extract aroma coming from somewhere.

Another blink. We were back in the Sahara Desert. Rolling sand dunes, and a camel staring at me.

I closed my eyes for longer, disbelieving. Had the sphinx eaten me after all? I opened them again, to see a rocky landscape painted in all the colours of the rainbow. Bat-buzzard creatures soared through the sky. One of them saw me, and turned towards me with a shriek, ready to dive.

Then, we were in a land of obsidian and lava, sulphur roaring out of the earth. I blinked once more, and we had returned to the original sandstone scene. Still, behind this, I imagined all the other images to exist as well.

"Where are we?" I asked the sphinx... But she was now as lifeless as a statue, looking nobly out into the distance.

"Where are we?" I asked again. Still no response.

"Ben," Seramina said, now standing beside me. "This, I believe, is the Sixth Dimension."

That was when I noticed that the sphinx had a symbol etched into its side. It was only the size of my paw, shaped like an Egyptian ankh. I'd seen that symbol before. The key to the Sixth Dimension was exactly the same shape – or at least it had been in the vision I'd seen within the Sahara Desert whirlwind.

Somehow, we had entered another dimension without a portal. To say I was confused was an understatement.

❧ *35* ❧

THE SIXTH DIMENSION

It turned out that we hadn't needed to open the door to the pyramid at all, because in the Sixth Dimension it wasn't even there. Though the landscape behind the pyramid kept flickering between dimensions, the pyramid itself and everything inside the chasm-moat seemed firmly rooted in place.

I had been so focused on the sphinx, I had failed to notice, but that same symbol I saw etched into its skin was also inset into every single brick on the pyramid walls, as well as every square metre of the floor beneath my feet. I caught a whiff upon the air of rotten vegetable juice, and from beyond the door I could make out a faint purple glow.

"What do you mean we're in the Sixth Dimension?" I asked Seramina. "And how do you know, anyway?"

"Remember that book I was reading in the library?" Seramina said. "I learned a lot about the Sixth Dimension then..."

"But we didn't pass through a portal."

"No," Seramina said with a slow shake of the head. "That's not how the Sixth Dimension works..."

"Then how does it work?" I'd had enough of mystical nonsense with the sphinx's ridiculous riddle.

Seramina wiped the crystal on her staff with her shirt. "It's a bridge," she said. "The Sixth Dimension unites all the dimensions. Anything that exists in the Sixth, exists in them all. The crystals, for example, reside here..."

Now this was a headache to understand. "What? How's that possible? And how do you know, anyway?"

"I found a book... A very old one at the bottom of the library. The librarian told me that nobody had read it for decades."

"But that means... This pyramid... It exists in all the dimensions. Which means we must as well. That means I can find a way to get back home?"

Seramina shook her head and pointed to the bridge we had used to cross. I could see it spanning the chasm now – it wasn't invisible anymore. Rather it let out a blue glow that highlighted the walls of the chasm.

"If everything the book said is true, that bridge will lead us back to the dimension from which we came. Unless we have the second key... We can use that to stay in the Sixth Dimension..."

"So how do we do that?" I asked.

"I don't know," Seramina said. "The book had pages missing."

"Lasinta or Arran must have taken them... Whiskers, if they can walk between all the dimensions, there's no telling what they might do... We have to stop them fast."

I looked back towards the doorway, trying to ignore the horrible smell coming from it. The other four students now stood on either side of it. Bellari and Rine took the left side, their staffs drawn, ready to charge inside. Asinda and Lars had the right. Rine and Lars kept peering around the entranceway, reporting in whispers what they saw inside.

They didn't have much to look at, admittedly, as the door looked into a corridor that led to the right. I bounded up to Max, who was gaping at the flickering landscape beyond the chasm.

"It's beautiful," he said. "Is this magic?"

"Not quite…" I told him, making sure to speak in whispers. We didn't want to alert Lasinta and Arran to our presence. Not yet anyway.

"So what's next?" he asked.

"We're going in… You coming?"

Max barked his approval, and we bounded together towards the door.

"Ben, wait," Seramina called. "There could be traps…"

"You forget that I'm a cat," I said back over my shoulder. "My feet are less likely to trip a wire than a clumsy human's."

"And what about the dog?" Rine whispered, a sly grin on his face. I was now close enough to talk to them.

"Stay behind me," I told the dog. "When I say freeze, you freeze. Understand?"

Max barked, "yes!" far too loudly.

"Shut up," I hissed, and my instructions were accompanied by loud shushes from the five students. Max turned sheepishly away and lowered himself onto his paws.

Before anyone had a chance to stop me, I entered the pyramid, followed the corridor to the right and stalked into the first chamber, taking note of the purple light reflecting off the walls. I kept my whiskers poised as I did so, testing the air and surroundings for anything that might feel out of place.

But what I saw when I went inside the first chamber shocked me even more. All the traps had been sprung. The arrow slits were empty of their arrows, the trip ropes had split, and spikes already stuck out of the walls and floors. I could smell rotten vegetable juice all around me. Lifeless crystals lay strewn across the dusty floor – empty spirits of golems and Manipulators no doubt.

A narrow corridor ahead of me led to the next chamber, where I could see shadows dancing about. Murmurs were coming from the end of it – the ambience of the corridor creating an echo chamber. Something meowed in the room beyond. My heart skipped in my chest when I realised who it was. Ta'ra...

Max padded up next to me.

"Don't you dare bark," I warned him... "Don't even whimper."

"Yes, Dragoncat boss," he panted, as quietly as a dog could pant.

"They're in there..." I whispered. "At the end of the corridor..."

I heard more footfalls coming from behind me. Asinda and Lars came into the room first, followed by Rine, Bellari, and Seramina.

"The traps have been sprung," Bellari whispered.

"You don't say," I said.

"Any ideas?" Rine whispered... "I'm guessing they're going to have plenty more golems where these came from."

No one had a chance to answer, because the wall of the pyramid in front of us suddenly turned bright blue, as a glowing purple mist rose from the floor. A female cackle of laughter came from no determinate direction, then in the mist two yellow glowing eyes and a wrinkled face began to form. Soon after, we were looking right into the wispy visage of Lasinta, staring down with a piercing gaze.

"They're here," she said... She wasn't talking to us yet. Behind her I could see Arran's silhouette, standing aside Capitut's sarcophagus.

"I thought you said that Aleam would dispose of them, grand-mother," Arran said.

"Do not worry, I've prepared for this eventuality..."

Arran put his hands on his hips. "That's it? You've prepared? When exactly did you intend to let me know about your plans?"

"When I can trust you," Lasinta croaked. "Now shut up and observe, boy..."

There was something about the glow in Lasinta's eyes that drew you towards them. Fire seemed to dance behind her gaze, just like I'd seen with Seramina so many times.

Presently, all the crystals strewn across the room glowed. The floor heated up, and tendrils of mist seeped out of the crystals, reaching upwards.

"What the..." Bellari said.

"It's a trap," Lars said. "Brace yourselves. Gather inwards."

The students all bunched together, but Max and I stayed standing where we were. Prefect Lars was the fastest out of all of us to draw his staff. The crystal glowed white on it, and the trace of a shield started to form around my companions. But at the same time, several tendrils of mist formed quickly into what looked like a hand, that closed over his crystal, snuffing it out like a candle. This developed into a cloying cloud that completely blocked Lars' chances of casting any magic.

The same happened to every other staff in the room, making me glad I hadn't summoned my staff bearer. The last thing I wanted was a cloud of rotten vegetable odour floating just inches away from my face.

"What is this sorcery?" Rine asked.

"It's much more than sorcery, young man," Lasinta said, delight in her voice...

"What are you up to, Lasinta?" Asinda asked through clenched teeth. "You cannot get away with this."

"It isn't your place, young lady, to tell me what I can and cannot do," Lasinta snapped back.

In the image on the wall, I saw her raise her hand, her forearm blocking off the view of Arran. She snapped her fingers, and the crystals on the floor of our chamber lifted themselves up in sync.

"Magical wargs!" Max barked, growling as he said it. "Evil, flying, magical wargs!"

Whiskers, I needed to show him what a warg really was. I also had my back arched and was hissing out foul words in the cat language. As I did, I followed the path of the crystals that hovered, vibrating in the air, like wasps seeking a target.

"Now!" Lasinta screamed. "Feel my power!"

As one, the crystals shot forward in all kinds of confusing directions. Some went straight for my head, but I used my superior Bengal agility to swipe them out of the air. They fell back to the floor like stunned flies.

Max, somehow managed to crouch his head underneath them at the last minute, and they zipped past him and crashed onto the floor.

The humans though weren't so lucky. Each of them tried to use their staffs to knock the crystals out of the way. But they didn't have the instinct of animals, and so only managed to hit one or two each.

Not long after, the crystals were spinning around their heads, whizzing so fast they looked like purple glowing haloes.

"What is this?" Asinda called out... She was struggling to free her own crystal from the purple cloud. The offending crystals as they whirled around her and my other companions, made this hideous buzzing sound. Meanwhile, the crystals that Max and I had knocked down vibrated on the floor as if they were getting ready to come back to life.

"I'm teaching you the value of silence," Lasinta said, and her eyes glared bright amber. She clicked her fingers again, and the crystals shot inwards and buried themselves in the five students' heads.

How they managed to get through the skin, I don't know, because they showed no traces of entering. Straight after, everyone's eyes went glazed, and the muscles on their faces slackened. Everyone that was except me, Max, and whoever was in the chamber beyond.

"Evil magical wargs!" Max continued to bark over and over. "Stop the evil, magical wargs!"

Lasinta turned her eyes down towards him. Her lips curled in distaste. She snapped her fingers one more time.

But I knew what I had to do. I whispered, hoping that she wouldn't hear me over the buzzing sound of the crystals remaining on the floor, which had started to glow again. "Max... Freeze right now, and don't argue why. They need to believe we're under their control."

I did exactly the same. I froze and pretended I was a taxidermy. I stared into the distance to make my eyes look glazed. But Max wouldn't stop barking...

More crystals came up from the floor, whirling abuzz in the air. They spun towards Max's head, and this time he wasn't quick enough to stop them assuming their orbit.

"Magic won't work on the dog, grandmother," Arran said smugly. "We tried it before."

"No..." Lasinta said. "But it also doesn't seem to go right through him, which means he won't go through it either. Gravity is gravity after all."

With another click of her fingers, the halo gained an extra dimension turning into a hemisphere that surrounded Max. The warlock clicked her fingers again, and the structure became a solid purple glowing cage. One more click, and the cage lifted upwards, taking Max with it as it transformed into a floating sphere of criss-crossing magical bars.

Max went silent, seeming to know when he'd been defeated. I guess he knew that complaining might make things worse. I stayed stock still as well, hoping that Lasinta couldn't hear my pounding heart...

"Well, well, this is a better state of things," Lasinta said. "Come now into the next chamber, my children. Where I can keep an eye on you."

This time, she beckoned us forward with a sweep of her hand. The students traipsed mournfully onwards and the cage with Max inside floated after them. I mirrored their steps as rigidly as I could into Capitut's burial chamber.

36

THE KEY PROPER

It took all my will to fool the warlocks that I was under their control. I had to march to the rhythm of my comrades – Max floating silently in his spherical cage alongside them – through the long corridor that connected to the burial chamber.

This was smaller than the first chamber. But then it didn't need to house the one thousand traps that Lasinta and Arran had triggered using their magical creations. It was large enough, however, to house the sarcophagus, and a raised dais at the centre of the room with an altar in the middle. On top of this, a large crystal floated, aglow.

On the walls, every single brick was marked with that same ankh symbol. Except in here, the symbols glowed red. I squinted my eyes to see faint tendrils of light feeding into each of them from the crystal.

Arran and Lasinta stood between the crystal and the sarcophagus, Arran slightly to the left and Lasinta slightly to the right. They each had their staff held out in both hands, magicking cold and smelly energy into the crystal.

Another narrower beam led out from the crystal to the key in the sarcophagus' hands. This wasn't the multicoloured, beautifully gemmed thing I'd imagined from the vision in the Sahara Desert. Rather, it looked as lifeless and colourless as hard rock. Where the beam struck, the gems on the treasure seemed to be gaining their natural colours and the dusty look was being replaced by the ankh's natural gold. The effect was creeping outwards, and it didn't take a genius to work out what the warlocks were up to.

The key needed magic to restore it to a usable form. Once they'd done that, there was no telling what the warlocks might do.

Maybe they would summon demon dragons from the Seventh Dimension or use the key to turn into those scary hippopotamuses.

A hook secured a magical spherical cage, just like Max's, to the ceiling just behind the crystal. Much to my horror, Ta'ra lay inside that cage, groaning in her sleep.

Be warned that if your key ceases to be or leaves this place, the rest of you will suffer the same fate. I recalled the sphinx's words. They had to keep Ta'ra alive, but that didn't mean they couldn't sedate her.

I wanted to sprint forward, turn into a chimera, and try to save her. Fortunately, common sense kept me rooted to the spot.

I couldn't let them know that I wasn't under Lasinta's control. If I tried to do anything, she'd just conjure another one of those cages. Since getting locked in Astravar's tower, I'd come to hate cages.

Fortunately, Lasinta seemed convinced by my ruse. Magic alone couldn't unmask the marvellous acting abilities innate to cats that we use time and time again to get fed.

"Welcome to the chamber of the future," Lasinta said, addressing us all. "I am honoured that such esteemed and talented individuals have come to witness the inevitable transformation of the worlds..."

She paused, and turned her ear towards us, cupping a hand over it.

"What's that? Did one of you want to say something? Oh, that's right, none of you can speak." She let out a wicked cackle. Whiskers, what was it with warlocks and their terrible sense of humour?

"What exactly do you want them for, grandmother?" Arran asked. "Do you plan to feed them to Apopis once we're done?"

Apopis... I recalled the name with a shudder... The overlord of overlords that Aleam had talked about... The giant snake demon. From the way that the two warlocks talked about it, I counted myself lucky that it wasn't here in Capitut's burial chamber with us. I'd never liked snakes, particularly those nasty adders that hid in the long grass in the hills of South Wales.

"No," Lasinta said. "We shall keep them as our slaves, and maybe later use them as bargaining chips. Or maybe they could launch the first attack on their precious academy before the demons rain chaos across the realms..."

"You've still not explained to me how exactly you plan to get them to do that. You must know you can't trust a demon."

"That's because I hoped you'd have worked it out by now. Have you not at least found a book somewhere that explains how the Sixth Dimension actually works?"

Arran shook his head. "No, grandmother. From what I remember, warlocks know very little about the Fifth and the Sixth Dimensions..."

"That's what we say, yes... It's easier to keep a secret that no one believes worth unveiling. But it's all buried deep within the literature somewhere. Where men like you and the rest of the population are too lazy to search for it." She gave Arran an assessing look.

Arran put his hands on his hips and huffed. "I'm not lazy. I've just been too busy manipulating fairies and locating Capitut's tomb to be reading books."

Lasinta let out a croaky sigh. "That is your problem, young man. You understand so little about the nature of knowledge. You should always make time to learn. That is how you become successful."

"So, are you going to tell me, or what?"

"No..." Lasinta said. "Instead, I'm going to ask you to use your eyes for once. What do you see on every single stone, brick, and device in this pyramid?"

"The ankh symbol..."

"Which is?"

Arran put his hand to his chin. "The same shape as the key," he said. "It's the same size, in fact..."

"Exactly... So maybe now you understand?"

Arran shook his head slowly. I didn't blame him for not getting it, because I hadn't yet worked it out either.

"And you wonder why you aren't as powerful as a warlock yet," Lasinta said. "Why you haven't yet gained your carrion eater form. You will need to become smarter to get there, young man."

"So maybe you can just explain it to me," Arran said.

"Fine... That symbol that you can see everywhere in this chamber... Glowing on the bricks and flagstones and everything else here is Capitut's Brand. Any item marked with it exists in all dimensions at once. I've never worked out how Capitut did it, but he imparted the key with the ability of the crystals to exist across all dimensions. But not just that, he gave the key the ability to transfer this property to anything material."

Arran put his hand to his chin. "So every single brick and flagstone in this pyramid belongs to the Sixth Dimension because of the symbol upon it? Because of Capitut's Brand?"

"Exactly..." Lasinta said. "It's remarkable magic. If only we could learn how to recreate it. Just think of the potential."

"But that doesn't make sense," Arran said. "How come we're in the Sixth Dimension? We've not been branded with the key..."

"Because the sphinx transferred us into the Sixth Dimension when I answered its trite riddle. And it will transfer us back again as soon as we cross the chasm. Unless..." She trailed off, waiting for Arran to complete the sentence.

"Unless we use the key to transfer the symbol onto ourselves..."

"The ancient textbooks actually surmise that Capitut's Brand," Lasinta said, "the symbol itself with all its intricacies, is the true key to the Sixth Dimension. Think what will happen if we transfer this brand to demon dragons... They will exist in them all and will unleash havoc on all the dimensions at once. They can no longer be banished back to the Seventh Dimension, because Capitut's Brand will hold them in the Sixth. We will rule the dimensions, with Apopis as our right hand, and an army of demon dragons at our mercy. Can you imagine the power that we warlocks would hold?"

Whiskers, I wasn't liking this at all. Plus, it was awfully dusty in this room, and I could feel a sneeze building up inside me. I let it go, as quietly as I could. Arran snapped his head around towards me.

"Did you hear that? The cat sneezed."

Uh oh... The last thing I wanted to do was attract attention to myself. I made sure my eyes stayed glazed and unblinking, focusing on the most distant point in the room. Arran shifted over to me, continuing to feed energy into the crystal. He tapped me with a sharp steel toecap.

"It's the one they call Dragoncat," he said. "The one who vanquished Astravar..." He pulled back his foot as if ready to kick me.

"Don't be a fool, Arran," Lasinta said. "Their bodily functions are still going to work, even if they're under our control. Otherwise, they'd just stop breathing, wouldn't they?"

Arran lowered his foot. "I guess..." He looked back at the crystal, then at the ankh that had almost fully gained its natural colour in the sarcophagus' hands. "There's just one thing I don't understand…"

"You do ask a lot of questions, don't you… Do you have trust issues, Arran?"

"No… It's just, if anything were to happen to you. I need to know what the situation is at hand."

Lasinta shook her head. "Nothing is going to happen to me. I've seen my fate in the crystals. I know exactly how I die. All the possibilities lead to the same place."

"Then just answer my question for my own peace of mind. Because I don't understand how you can trust a demon overlord."

"We can't," Lasinta said.

"But you're going to work with him anyway…"

"Because he is a fool. All demons are."

"Please explain…"

Lasinta studied her grandson, and Arran turned his head back to her. I took the opportunity to shift a little – it hurt where Arran had tapped me with his toe.

"Why do you think that Apopis never steps out of the portal? You must know what happens when a demon leaves the Seventh Dimension."

"It becomes a servant of whoever brought it out of that dimension," Arran said. "But they won't have left the Seventh Dimension as they exist in them all…"

"I am not contradicting myself," Lasinta said. "You are just seeing things too analytically, and I'm telling you how exactly they are going to be…"

Arran shook his head. Really, every time I'd seen him, he'd been bossing everyone else about. Now, I was finally seeing how he behaved with someone above his station. He was just a puppet at the end of the day. A coward who wasn't in charge of his own destiny at all.

"So, our condition for handing Apopis the key," Lasinta said, "is that I'll use Capitut's Brand on him, thus transferring him from the Seventh to Sixth dimension. Having left the Seventh Dimension, he'll become my servant, and I'll have all the demon dragons under my thrall with new abilities."

"But will he have even left the Sixth Dimension?" Arran put a hand to his chin. "I suppose by a certain debatable definition, he will. In the world of magical contracts that's enough, right?"

Lasinta nodded. "Do you see the power of this thing now?"

Arran took a deep breath, and his eyes went glazed. "I do..." he said, his voice filled with awe. "I do..."

37

COURAGE FROM WITHIN

I hated to admit it, but Lasinta was a better teacher than any of the Driars in Dragonsbond Academy. This was the first magical lesson, in fact, that I'd understood perfectly...

Ta'ra let out a weak mewl from her cage, and she opened her brilliant green eyes, glowing over the white crest on her otherwise black chest. She must have seen me then, and she blinked as if confused. Her gaze passed over the other students standing stock still, and finally settled on Max floating in his cage next to the crystal.

I considered how I could get her out of there. I could probably jump from the dais on top of that cage, and then perhaps I could knock it off the hook. Would it break when it fell to the floor? If so, Ta'ra and I could work together to take Arran and Lasinta down...

Not that she'd be much use in a fight. When I'd met her, Ta'ra had been a Cat Sidhe, with the ability to turn from a cat into a fairy, and also to increase or decrease her size. But she'd lost all these abilities when she had completed her final transformation and become a regular cat.

My plans were interrupted by a sudden shout coming from Lasinta.

"It is done," she said, and she cut off the power from the beam.

Arran did exactly the same, and both warlocks turned to face the ankh in Capitut's hands. Ta'ra continued to squirm in her cage, meowing softly.

"Someone will find and stop you," she said, watching me as she said it.

That was when I saw it in Ta'ra's eyes. She knew that I was here and conscious and that I had a plan.

Maybe she'd heard them talking about me when her eyes were closed. Unlike Arran and Lasinta, Ta'ra knew me well enough to know when I was faking something. She knew, in other words, that this was all an act.

She must have believed that I had the power to stop them. She must have still thought of me as the mighty Bengal who had defeated Astravar – a hero. But I didn't have any power, really. I was a fraud...

I'm sorry I can't help you yet, Ta'ra, I thought. *I'm not powerful enough.*

"This is it," Arran said, and he stepped forward and reached out for the key. He snatched it up with his hand, which began to glow as a grin stretched across his face. His expression registered a sense of victory, as if it was he alone that was about to conquer the dimensions.

"Oh no you don't," Lasinta said, and she batted his hand with her staff.

Arran dropped the key back into the sarcophagus' hands.

"It is I who shall control the key," Lasinta said. "Your place has never been at the top, Arran, and it never will be..."

She reached out slowly and carefully for the ankh. I could only see the back of her head now, the light from the massive crystal highlighting her knotted grey hair. Now that Arran and Lasinta were focused on the key, Ta'ra watched me intently. I moved my head to look at her, and I lowered it, then looked up.

"*Please,*" she mouthed to me silently, and I understood as if she were speaking within my mind. "*Ben, you have to do something...*"

"*I can't...*" I mouthed back, and I really believed it for a moment.

Ta'ra's eyes went wide, and I saw how weak and helpless she was in the cage. Seeing her like that caused the memories to flood back to me...

Ta'ra flying into Astravar's beam as a fairy wisp, buying me time to defeat him...

Ta'ra fluttering to the ground, until her golden glow became lost to the sky...

Then seeing Ta'ra lying in her fairy form dead in the grass, her face helpless and pale.

All this happened before she lost her final Cat Sidhe life and became a true cat... I remembered the emotion... I remembered what I had to lose.

I remembered who I was as well... I was Dragoncat, the creature of legends who had defeated Astravar. I had the power to turn into a chimera, and to stop these evil warlocks in their tracks. I was the only cat in the whole of the seven dimensions, who could speak every single language known to living creatures. Salanraja was right. I was a cat, but I was also partly human...

But my identity didn't matter. Not really... What mattered was that I was the cat who fought, and that was how I wanted to be remembered, whatever happened.

Lasinta had snatched the key and she examined it in the palm of her hand. I watched in horror as she slowly closed her fingers around the ankh, an expression of awe filling the features between her wrinkles.

My heart was beating like a thousand snare drums in my chest. I couldn't let this happen... My crystal had told me in the Sahara Desert that I needed to protect that key...

"Oh no you don't," I shouted.

I turned into a chimera so fast that I didn't even feel the pain. At the same time, my staff bearer appeared and shot towards me, and I clamped my mouth around my staff. I let out a beam of purple energy at Lasinta.

Before the key had a chance to glow, as it had when Arran had picked it up, Lasinta yowled and dropped it, sending it spinning across the floor...

❧ 38 ❧

GOLEMS OF SAND

The force of the blow didn't just cause Lasinta to drop the key. It also sent her stumbling back against the sarcophagus. She tripped and fell to the floor.

"What in the Seventh Dimension?" Lasinta said. "Stop him, Arran!"

Arran lowered his staff and turned it towards me, hate on his lips and in his eyes. But I was already charging on my rear goat hoofs and swiping out at him with my lion paw.

Calling upon the strength of three lions, I knocked him across the room.

A shot of energy came from behind me... A purple beam grazed the side of my goat's head, singed the hairs on my lion's mane, then sizzled against the wall. I snapped my snake's head around, urging it to hiss as I focused on the vividly coloured image I saw through its eyes.

Lasinta had her staff drawn, a beam of magic shooting out of it. That horrible sharp odour of rotten vegetable juice filled the air.

I rolled to the side, as she tried to bring her magic around to cut me in two. I still had the staff within my mouth, and I shot a beam to meet hers, buying me a little time. I ran underneath her magic, and I hit her hand hard with the butt of my staff, causing Lasinta to drop hers.

At my rear, through my snake head's eyes, I could see Arran sitting up and swinging his staff around towards me. Soon, he'd cast some more magic at me. One warlock was enough, but I couldn't take on two of them. I knew I needed help, so I directed a beam of magic at the hook that secured Ta'ra's cage. It fell to the floor, and each wall of the cage fizzled out, allowing room for Ta'ra to leap out.

She was immediately on all fours, sprinting towards Arran, just as a beam of magic came out of his staff. Ta'ra climbed up Arran's chest, leaped onto his shoulder, scrambled down his arm, and bit at the hand holding his staff.

"Ow!" he said as he dropped the staff. "Stupid cat..."

He swiped at Ta'ra with an open palm, but she was already sprinting out of the way towards Arran's staff. She grasped it firmly in her mouth and carried it across the room.

Arran went chasing after her. At the same time, I watched Lasinta with my snake eyes, trying to work out what to do next. Her gaze was on the staff, lying right underneath the key. She reached out slowly for her weapon, and I readied myself to pounce.

I failed to notice the motion of her other hand that had reached into the pouch attached to the belt on her hip. She lobbed four dark magic crystals towards the crystal at the centre of the chamber. They landed between me and her.

"Sand golems, lend us your might!" she shouted.

Fearing the worst, I turned and leaped towards her, but four sharp eddies blew out of the ground and blocked my path. They started small, ripping out the flagstones from the floor, which crumbled as they entered their embrace.

As the whirlwinds grew in power, they pulled me towards them.

I dug my massive claws into the ground beneath. But this was quickly crumbling, and it wouldn't hold my position for long.

As the sand golems whirled, they made a groaning howling sound that reverberated off the walls of the chamber. The bricks themselves were straining, starting to get ripped away from whatever mortar held them together.

"Grandmother," Arran said. "You'll bring down the pyramid."

"Then get your staff back so you can protect yourself," she called back.

These sand golems behaved like another golem I'd encountered in the past. Forest golems also sucked in their surroundings and used it to build up an almost impervious skin of wood and other bits of forest materials.

But the sand golems didn't seem to want to create armour out of what they sucked in. Rather they ground it down into sand. Enough of them could turn any land into a desert.

Growling, I tried shooting magic into the whirling monsters. But my purple beam just vanished into their depths. At the same time, the sand underneath my feet had started to whirl. It picked up speed, and I saw a hole forming at the centre of the emerging pit. I was already starting to lose my balance. It didn't matter how strong a chimera I was – I didn't have a chance on this terrain.

The sand golems moved aside a little, so I could see Lasinta between them. At first it looked like she was floating on a column of air. But then I saw how the sand had lifted her up, much like it was trying to pull me down.

She stood on a dust cloud, a column of it billowing upwards underneath this to support her. Not far from her, the ankh hovered on a similar, but smaller, cloud.

Lasinta once again had her staff and she lifted this above her head.

"Behold the power of a mighty warlock!" she screamed. A fountain of light erupted from her staff, thousands of beams arcing towards the ground. More eddies sprung up out of the sand at the contact points, again becoming great swirling whirlwinds of dust. There must have been dozens of them by this point, and I couldn't work out where the golems containing the crystals were.

Whiskers, these were the most dangerous golems I'd ever encountered.

The whirlpool of sand had become massive, spinning around the centre of the chamber. The crystal that Lasinta and Arran had used to revive the key hovered high above this, safe from the sand golems' magic.

I caught glimpses of Ta'ra, Arran, and all of my friends except Max, whirling around the central point. Instead, Max hovered in his cage above the swirling pit of sand.

The pyramid had completely crumbled now, leaving only the sarcophagus that also spun around in the whirlpool. I went around slowly enough, that I could make out the depth of the chasm beyond, for we were now outside. Except the terrain we stood on was no longer compacted sandstone, but a mass of sand spilling down into the chasm.

Whiskers, Lasinta had destroyed it all...

"Ta'ra, come closer ..." I swam towards her, trying to stop her tumbling down to the centre. But my efforts seemed to bring me closer to my doom as well.

"I can't hold on," she said... "Ben, is this the end?"

"No," I said. "We must survive this." *Would they let her die?* I wondered. Maybe now they had Max, they could lose the key that had brought them here.

I tried to shoot another beam out of my staff at Lasinta to knock her off her perch. But it spun around aimlessly and didn't hit anything.

I was so close to the hole now... Turned out that me being the heaviest out of all of us, the sand had pulled me down first... I caught a glimpse of the hole that sank so far into the darkness that I couldn't see the bottom of it. My head throbbed. My ears rang. My throat felt dry.

Whiskers, I was doomed... Or at least I thought I was...

"Hang on... All of you..." A voice... A female one... Familiar.

"Who is that?" I called.

"Ben? Ben, is that you? It's Ange. Hold on!"

And I thought I had to be hallucinating, because I could swear that in front of me a desert cheetah sprinted across the whirling sand.

39

AN ALLY RETURNS

I went around and around the sand pit, spinning so fast now I was close to the vortex's centre. On each rotation, I sighted the desert cheetah in different positions. I saw it pouncing up towards the cloud Lasinta was on. One more spin, and it leapt high at Lasinta. Alas, not high enough to hit her, instead sailing through the cloud the warlock floated on.

Another spin, and I thought Lasinta was falling. I heard a screech and saw a cloud of purple mist develop underneath her. Another turn, and a massive condor lifted off from the dissipating dust cloud into the sky.

The cheetah had moved so fast that I guess she'd taken Lasinta by surprise. Fortunately for us, the elderly warlock wouldn't be able to cast magic while she was in her condor form. We only needed to keep her at bay.

"Ben, hold on..." Ange called. Her voice sounded so distant now with the amount of sand I had in my ears.

But it was too late. I slipped past the threshold into the hole at the centre of the sand whirlpool, and I prepared to fall.

Instead, a carpet of vines stretching across the hole caught me. They spread out in all directions, buoying my companions up above the whirlpool. I looked up to see Ange standing on a platform of vines herself. She looked different than she had before. More confident... Her eyes glowed green as a lacework of patterns spread from her staff. A safety net to keep us all safe from the sand.

My comrades now lay down with their eyes closed, but they were still possessed by Lasinta's magic. Arran had rolled along the carpet and positioned himself far away from us.

The cheetah tightroped her way across the vines back to Ange. It was the same cheetah that I'd faced in the Saharan Desert. I recognised the set of her amber eyes, and the markings that stretched across her fur.

I strolled up to the cheetah, as Ange petted her on the head. The cheetah made a high-pitched chirping sound in appreciation.

"So, the legends are true, Dragoncat. You really can take a mighty form."

I growled from my lion's head to emphasize my mightiness. "I didn't expect you to cross dimensions. I thought that our last meeting would be our last..."

"I told you I'd see you again..."

Of course... It made perfect sense now.

"After you met the Lady of the Vines, I remember," I said. Ange's crystal must have opened a portal and transported her and the cheetah here. The same had happened to me in the Seventh Dimension once...

I wanted to say more, but my attention snapped back to the key, still floating on that tiny cloud of sand, the condor angling herself high in the sky above it. Lasinta, I could see, was readying herself to snatch it up in her talons.

40

REBOUND ATTACK

Lasinta grunted, and she entered her dive with her talons poised. She swooped down. Ange shot out a spiny tumble-weed that grazed the condor's belly and knocked her slightly off kilter. Lasinta lifted herself back up with heavy flaps of her wings, her grab for the key unsuccessful.

"Wake the others up," Ange said, squinting at Arran who had deftly jumped onto his feet and grabbed his staff. "I can't take them both alone."

"We need to get the key," I said.

Arran had the same idea, and he sidled slowly towards it, the crystal glowing on his staff. "The key is ours..." he said. "Respect that, and you can leave unharmed."

"Never," I said, and I fancied myself ready to fight Arran. He wasn't as mighty as Astravar after all, and certainly not as mighty as a chimera.

I focused my beam at Seramina who was lying on the carpet of vines. It hit her right on the forehead, and her eyes snapped open.

I'd never seen the young teenager react so quickly. In another life, perhaps she could have been a cat. She coiled herself up, and then sprung onto her feet, drawing her staff from her back in one smooth motion.

Arran shot a beam out of his staff, and I smelled burning where it singed my mane. Seramina met the beam with one from her own staff and pushed Arran's magic back towards him.

A battle of light and magic ensued, both Seramina's and Arran's faces tightened in consternation and rage. For a moment, it looked as if it would never end. But the balance had already started to tip in our favour. From beside me, Ange shot out a vine at Arran's shoulder, and he lost his concentration. He yelped and ducked underneath Seramina's magic before it could destroy him.

I went bounding after Arran, and I pinned him to the floor. He looked up at me in terror, and I roared into his face, making sure he received the full extent of my putrid lion's breath. His body went limp, and he closed his eyes.

I could feel Arran's heart beating against my paw, and I knew that he was playing dead. But I was a cat, not a stone-cold killer. I kept him pinned as I observed my surroundings. Somehow, I knew that the battle wasn't over yet.

Seramina took the opportunity to cast some mind magic on Rine, Bellari, Lars, and Asinda, waking them from their slumbers. She broke Max's cage last, who fell to the carpet of vines, whimpering.

Up in the sky, Lasinta grunted again. She wasn't going to give up on that key. Both Seramina and Ange tracked the condor. This time though, Lasinta wasn't positioning herself for another dive. Instead, I saw magic working around her, a cloud of purple glowing mist developing there.

Her human body emerged from the mist, and I caught sight of her face and a wicked grin set on it, as she kept her arms stretched out to her side, falling from up high. She still had her staff in one hand, and from it she cast a beam of light out towards the massive floating crystal.

The magic hit the crystal, and sparks of light erupted out of it, hitting points beneath vines. Dozens of tiny purple crystals floated up from above the vines, and a Manipulator blossomed out of each of these, spectral white staffs stretching out from their wavering forms.

41

ALL POWERFUL WARLOCK

Just before Lasinta hit the carpet of vines, she transformed back into a condor, and effortlessly soared back up on the currents created by the magic swirling around us.

The Manipulators also sprang into action. Within seconds, they used their staffs to summon bone dragons above them. Purple mist and the stench of rotten vegetable juice enveloped us all. Next thing I knew, a bone dragon came swooping down, knocking me away from Arran, and sending me tumbling across the vines.

Arran stood up… "Grandmother, you're a genius," he said, with a hefty laugh. His legs wobbled as he went, but he made his way surely towards the key all the same. He wove his way around the Manipulators with nothing to stop him.

I tried to follow, but the bone dragon that had butted me off him blocked my path. Now on the ground, it snapped its jaws at me. I ducked out of the way and knocked its face to the side with my mighty lion paw. Then, I gave it a taste of its own medicine by lowering my goat's head and ramming it in the ribcage on its side.

The blow would have been enough to splinter its bones, had its host Manipulator not been right next to it, repairing it with its magic. Still, I knocked the bone dragon to the floor, and I spun around to look for a Manipulator I might be able to destroy. I had my staff in my mouth, and I shot a purple beam right at the heart of one feeding a bone dragon that was harassing Max.

The crystal dropped out of the Manipulator and, now lifeless, fell beneath the net of vines into the sand that still whirled towards that empty hole.

"Thanks, Dragoncat!" Max barked, and he pushed towards the key.

But another bone dragon manoeuvred into his path, its ribcage blocking Max. This time though, it wasn't attacking us. Instead, it lunged at the barrier Lars held to protect him, Asinda, Rine, Ange, Ange's cheetah, and Bellari. Several bone dragons kept pecking at the barrier, and I knew it wouldn't hold forever. Ta'ra was in there too, staring out at me with wide and terrified eyes.

The shield flickered out in calculated intervals to allow the party to cast fire, ice, and leaf magic back out at the bone dragons. Still, they could do no damage with the bone dragons blocking any view of the Manipulators providing the healing magic.

We were losing, and Lasinta had poised herself delicately in the air, ready to dive down once again and grab the key.

"Enough!"

The call was one of rage, coming from a powerful feminine voice. It didn't belong to Lasinta this time, and it thundered so loudly across the battlefield that it sent everything trembling in its path.

"This has to end now!"

Whiskers, it was Seramina shouting out at the top of her voice. She'd always been so softly spoken. But now her voice held might and authority and danger. Indeed, she was about to show everyone the true extent of her raw power.

A blinding white light emerged just metres away from me. It seared its way through the tangle of bones and vines. From the centre of the radius, Seramina lifted into the air, glowing alabaster and looking even more magnificent than a Manipulator.

I recognised the fire in her eyes. It burned whenever she lost control.

Max was also staring up at her, barking loudly. "Dangerous magic!" he said. "Dangerous magic!" This time, he didn't even dare imply Seramina was a warg.

Where Seramina hovered, I could see her teetering, the magic building in her staff like air builds in a balloon. She was going to blow, and if we didn't get protection, she'd take us with her.

Lars beckoned me towards the shield. He was shouting something, but I couldn't hear it from behind his buzzing barrier. Static pulled on my skin, and Seramina seemed to suck all the purple mist into herself, drawing power from everything around her. Destroying Manipulators, bone dragons, sand golems, and vines.

The crystal hovering in the air shrunk as an immaterial sphere grew around Seramina's staff, brimming with sparks. The air lost its texture, and for a moment it didn't smell of anything. Just emptiness.

"Max," I said. "Get under the shield, or you're dead!"

He looked in the direction of the key... I caught a glimpse of Arran, still making his way towards it. Moving, slowly, as if his blood had suddenly filled with thick honey.

"No..." he barked. "The whirlwind sphinx gave me a mission."

"Don't do as I say, and you won't live to fulfil it." I realised that Lasinta had said Max was immune to magic, but I doubted he'd be able to withstand this.

The explosion lashed out from Seramina's staff, and I sprinted as fast as I could. Max bounded after me, panting as he went. I felt a tugging on my fur, and a searing heat washed over me, slowing me slightly.

Lars let the shield open for a split second, and Max and I tumbled inside just in time. Then bright light filled the scene, Lars' shield guttering so violently that for a moment I doubted it would protect us. I transformed back into a normal Bengal again to conserve valuable oxygen, and I completed the transformation smoothly, this time without much pain.

In cat form, I waited, listening to the heavy heartbeats in everyone's chests. The light reached its brightest, and my head throbbed. Someone next to me screamed. I gasped for breath, thinking I was about to suffocate.

I'm sure I wasn't the only one who thought I was about to die.

THE FATE OF THE KEY

The light faded.

The crystal had gone. All the Manipulators, bone dragons, and sand golems had been magicked away into oblivion. No crystals remained other than those on everyone's staffs. The carpet of vines had been obliterated, except for a small section that still stood strong underneath Lars' shield.

Arran had completely vanished, no doubt destroyed by Seramina's magic. There was no pyramid anymore – the warlock magic had ripped that apart. Instead, as with my crystal in the Fourth Dimension, it had been reduced to thousands upon thousands of grains of sand, which formed the cooling carpet on which we stood. This sand trickled down into the chasm as if the whole scene was part of a gigantic hourglass.

I guess it would fill the chasm in all the dimensions, burying whatever was underneath it in each one. The pyramid would eventually settle at the bottom of this chasm until perhaps another civilisation entered the Sixth Dimension and decided they wanted to build it all again.

Around us, beyond the chasm that separated the Sixth Dimension from the others, reality flickered from dimension to dimension. I caught whiffs of all of them. A cocktail of dry saltiness, pollen, agave, sulphur, charcoal, and yeast extract. Suffice to say, there wasn't a trace of rotten vegetable juice left.

Seramina still floated in the air by Lars' shield. The glow had left her skin, and she stared straight ahead, her eyes glazed. I knew what she was thinking. She had lost control, had found the source of her power to cast her magic. But she had killed someone in the process...

She had killed Prince Arran.

The condor, Lasinta, wheeled overhead. She had been wise enough to keep her distance from the explosion. I saw movement... Something shiny sailing upwards... The key... Tossed up by Seramina's ultimate spell. Of course, it couldn't be destroyed, even by the most powerful magic I'd ever seen.

Just as it reached its apex, Lasinta began to dive. I watched the key, trying to judge where it would land.

Max had noticed it long before me. He stayed close to the edge of Lars' shield, also tracking it. A moment later, Lars let the shield down, and Max sprinted out, his gaze fixed on the ankh as it spun through the sky.

Whiskers, what was he planning to do, knock the bird out of the sky before it caught it?

The key was coming so close to him, and the condor close to the key. She was going to catch it... I knew she was... Or at least I thought she would, until a beam of purple light shot out of Asinda's staff, grazing the condor on the wing. Lasinta hissed and wheeled sideways in a spiral, completely missing the key.

At the same time, and much to my astonishment, Max turned his snout upwards and opened his mouth. The key glowed brightly, and Max caught it as if he was catching a bone. He closed his mouth, and in one deft motion he swallowed the key whole.

All went silent for a short but long moment.

"I did it!" Max barked eventually. "I completed my mission! I completed my mission!"

I blinked at him, astonished. He began to glow red, just like a demon dog. But the glow didn't last for long, or rather it shrank to cover an area on his side. The fur there changed from liver golden to ash black, then it wilted leaving a brand in the shape of an ankh.

Capitut's Brand... Which meant Max had received the power to walk across all the dimensions. My crystal back in the Sahara Desert had instructed him to do this, but why?

Ta'ra seemed to detect my frustration, and she came up to me and nuzzled against me.

I purred loudly, the happiest cat in all seven dimensions. "Ta'ra... So many times, I thought I'd never see you again... But we always seem to find our way back to each other."

"We do," she replied. "Let's just enjoy the moment."

And I did. For a good half a minute, all I knew as we lay down in the sand – which had stopped whirling – was the warmth of her body against mine. Max also lay down, looking particularly pleased with himself. Rine and Ange chatted. Bellari stood a distance away from them, watching with her arms crossed. Lars and Asinda held hands, as they also spoke in hushed and loving tones.

Seramina continued to gaze into the distance. I didn't doubt that she was remembering her vision in the Ghost Realm we'd seen all those months ago. Destiny had dictated that she would fight a battle against the warlocks, causing the destruction of the lands. Now, she had demonstrated this raw, unbridled power, killing Arran in the process. How far, if she lost control, would she go?

I was just about to go over and comfort her when our moment was rudely interrupted.

The condor, Lasinta, who had been watching us from high

above, wheezed loudly. She wheeled around Max in a narrow perimeter, as if considering attacking him. But she eventually seemed to think it a bad idea. Instead, she flapped her wings, and sailed over the chasm, back into the dimension from which she had come.

❧ 43 ❧

PROVISIONS

We safely crossed back over the invisible bridge. There was no sphinx left to see us off, and I wondered if she too had been destroyed in the blast.

We emerged on the cracked desert landscape of the Calimar Desert in the First Dimension. I looked over my shoulder, hoping to see at least some ruins. But instead, the towering sandstone butte that had previously glamoured the pyramid stood tall, shimmering in the desert heat.

We were in raw daylight now, and the sun beat down from up high. I touched the butte with a paw. It wasn't a glamour. It was as real as any rock in this desert, as if nothing had ever lain behind it. *Yowch,* it was hot.

"So," Bellari said. "We emerge into the raging heat without a dragon in sight. Within moments we'll be dead. Or has anyone got a plan?"

Max barked, seeming much more confident ... "This way! This way!"

He led us around the butte into the shade where Corralsa

waited for us. We must have looked like such a motley bunch to her – six young adults, a cat, a dog, and a desert cheetah. But it was the dog that Corralsa seemed pleased to see the most of all.

She lowered her head towards Max, who licked her with his clumsy and slimy tongue. Whiskers, I don't know how she put up with it... Dragons were strange creatures.

It was awfully hot, even in the shade, and our other dragons weren't anywhere to be seen. I looked up into Corralsa's eyes, wondering if she could carry us all back to Dragonsbond Academy. She growled as if understanding my intention.

Having nothing better to do, I reached out to Salanraja, who I could sense was flying over some sea somewhere.

"Please tell us you'll be here soon," I said to her.

"Still some distance yet..." Salanraja said. *"But we're going to get there as fast as we can..."*

"And how long will that be?"

"You're going to have to spend the night there. We'll hopefully make it for the morning, but no promises..."

"The night?"

"There's nothing we can do, Bengie..."

I didn't bother to correct her this time. Somehow, after my run in with the sphinx, I didn't care so much about my identity. Of course, that didn't mean I wouldn't tell people that I was a Bengal, descendant of the great Asian leopard cat, when I met them though. Greetings like that were important for posterity's sake.

"You know, I was worried when you went to the Sixth Dimension," Salanraja said. *"Part of me wanted to be angry about you leaving me again. But it was only instinct."*

"I needed to go," I told her.

"I know you did. I'm just glad you're back..."

Salanraja and I talked for as long as the mistress back in South

Wales used to talk to her friends when she picked up that strange device called a telephone.

I told her about the battle against Lasinta, how I'd turned into a chimera and almost saved the day, until Ange arrived with a cheetah, and then we woke Seramina up, who ultimately was the one who saved the day. I saved the riddle of the sphinx until last, because that was the part I was most proud of. I really had beaten the sphinx at her own game.

"I told you, you were becoming more human," Salanraja said. *"Maybe you're right. Maybe you will turn into a sphinx after a while."*

"Or maybe, it's just that everyone around me is becoming more feline," I said. *"I also have a lot to teach them..."*

"I'm sure you do..." Salanraja said. *"I'm sure you do..."*

I was interrupted by a loud raucous laugh that came from nearby Corralsa. I lifted my head to see Rine standing next to the dragon's open panniers, a massive roll of mutton sausages in his hand.

"We may have a wait ahead of us," he said. "But we can still have our traditional feast this evening..."

He handed the sausages to Lars, then he reached into Corralsa's panniers again and produced a bundle of firewood. Corralsa didn't seem to mind.

The sun set, and the cold desert night fell. Corralsa had provided us with enough firewood to light us a nice warm fire using her breath. We feasted on sausages for a long time, and there was plenty of food to go around. I finished with that wonderful herby taste on my tongue, mixed with a different kind of dragonfire than I was used to. I had been ravenous about an hour ago, and now my tummy felt comfortably full.

I sat next to Ta'ra, really happy that I hadn't lost her. I could feel the beating of her heart against my hip, and she had fallen asleep.

She had warmed to Max instantly, and the dog also lay asleep on the other side of her, his tail wagging as he breathed softly in the way that dogs do. He had that tiny ankh brand burned into his fur, but he hadn't yet tried to walk between the dimensions. Or at least I didn't think he had.

Asinda and Lars kept to themselves on the other side of the fire. Asinda rested her head on Lars' shoulder where they both sat cross legged on the sand. Ange sat not far away from us, stroking the cheetah who rested her chin on her lap.

I was a little jealous, admittedly. When I'd imagined my retirement with Ange, Rine, and Ta'ra, I'd never imagined a cheetah would join our family, let alone a dog. Soon, they might want to find a zoo instead of a cottage, but then a zoo would remind me too much of the cattery. So, we'd have to live in a mansion instead.

Rine sat with his arm, around Bellari, who was also asleep, her head propped right up against Rine's chest. Once again, Bellari was a threat to my plans of settling down with Ange and Rine, and now it seemed she was back to strike again.

Ange looked at them, and I don't think Rine saw the distaste at the corner of her lips, but I certainly did. She wiped this expression from her face before she spoke to him.

"So, are you and Bellari together again?" she asked. "Really, I'm happy for you..."

Rine looked down at Bellari, then turned back to Ange and shook his head slowly. He cupped his free hand to his mouth and whispered, "we're not serious, Ange..."

Bellari was immediately up out of his arms, standing up and spinning around at him. "What do you mean we're not serious?"

"I—" Rine looked up at her his eyes wide. "I just meant—"

"You're pathetic, Rine, you know that? Well, this is no good, I'm not going to be played by some imbecile who thinks he's the best creature women have ever seen."

She left Rine with his jaw agape as she stormed to sit by herself on the other side of the fire. Ange shook her head, and she turned away. Much to my dismay, she didn't look impressed.

Next to me, Ta'ra opened her eyes and looked at Bellari. "Poor girl," she said.

"Yes," I said, sarcastically. "Poor girl indeed."

Bellari may have been upset, and I could hear her sobbing under her breath. But I was content that we'd had a good meal and we'd saved the world.

Feeling ever so slightly satisfied, I closed my eyes and went to sleep. It had definitely been a long day.

EPILOGUE

I'm sure that reports of my death have been widely exaggerated by now. Because I fooled them all. My grandmother, and those stupid students, that cat, and I guess that dog too...Well, woe be to them.

In all honesty, I doubted anyone felt any woe. Because no one ever cared about Arran. They always thought I was too snobby, too stuck up, too pompous. All because I dared to demand a little respect. I was a prince after all...

A prince who deserved to be on the throne. I was much more suited to the position than that cur, King Garmin, and the short selection of royals in line between me and him... Grandmother was meant to help me dispose of them...

But not yet Arran... Not until you are older. Not until you have proven yourself worthy. It didn't matter anymore. Because I didn't need her... I didn't need the warlocks. They had failed after all.

I also didn't need my dragon, Corralsa, who had never understood me anyway. It had been hard to keep my secrets from that one. But like everyone else, she had completely underestimated me.

Now, she would never have the pleasure of talking to me again.

Mind you, I'd also completely underestimated that witch, Astravar's daughter. She was the only one who showed potential. Maybe, one day, I'd recruit her as my ally. She was meant to destroy the warlocks, after all.

I sprinted along the pathways between the worlds. One moment, I was running the ridges of Crystal Pass in the First Dimension, another I was in the Ghost Realm surrounded by echoes of *Cana Dei,* another I was in one of those steel cities in the Fourth Dimension, passing along one of those strange striped crossings which stop those devices they call cars. The wind was hot, then it was cold, then it was clammy, then it was dry.

This is what it meant to experience all the dimensions. To travel without portals. It truly was a beautiful thing.

What an idiot my grandmother had been to assume I didn't read books. Did she really think I could have full access to the King's Library, and not be tempted to study its ancient tomes? I probably learned about Capitut's Brand long before her.

I also knew that you didn't make a deal with the Overlord of Overlords in the Seventh Dimension lightly. Lasinta had promised the demon snake something she couldn't deliver, and now there would be a debt to be paid.

The heat of the Seventh Dimension kissed at my skin. Black towers of obsidian rose into the sky around me. Beyond them, magma painted the landscape red. The air smelled rich with sulphur and a power I'd never have thought reachable, until now.

Usually, I wouldn't have been able to survive more than half an hour in this place. But I brought in enough of the other dimensions to give me good air to breathe and cool the latent heat.

I found the place where two obsidian cliffs clashed together, with a large archway leading between them. The skin tingled on the palm of my hand, and I felt my staff rubbing against my back. I had everything I needed here.

The archway led to a ledge — a perfect circle that hung over the lava sea. Its power pulled at the hairs on my skin. This, apparently, was the most powerful place in the Seventh Dimension.

A black pentagram was inlaid into the rocky ground of the ledge. Its centre was large enough to house four stone golems. I felt insignificant standing within it, until I reminded myself of the power I held within my hand.

I took a deep and rich breath.

"Apopis!" I called out, and I waited. There was no answer from the lava beyond. "Apopis! Emperor of Chaos, Overlord of Overlords. It is I, Prince Arran of the First Dimension, seventh in line to the throne of Illumine Kingdom, and grandson of the warlock, Lasinta..."

My voice reached out into the distance, and for a while I thought I wouldn't have an answer. But soon enough, the lava started to boil below, and a whirlpool developed in the raging liquids.

Apopis rose from the sea of magma. A snake fifty times as long as a man. He was made from obsidian, glowing underneath the cracks woven in a diamond pattern along the length of his body. He towered higher than the tallest castle, supporting his great weight as if through magic. Lava dripped from his lips back into the sea, as he looked down at me with glowing red eyes.

He didn't open his mouth to speak, but instead his voice hissed and sizzled in the sea itself, as if from every direction at once.

"WARLOCK!" he cried. "WHERE IS MY KEY!"

"I do not have it," I called back. I was afraid – who wouldn't be? But I didn't show it. "Lasinta lost it..."

"THEN YOU HAVE FAILED," Apopis leant forward, and his sulphurous breath washed over my scalp.

"No... My grandmother has failed. But I no longer lay claim to my heritage. It is she who must pay her rightful debt to you, Apopis."

Suddenly, what must have been a hundred geysers shot out of the sea. They came down at once, and the demon overlord's voice boomed out even louder. "Then why have you come? Why do you dare disturb one as powerful as I?"

"Because I can save you the effort of having to chase that debt," I said. "I can bring the warlocks to you, to do with them as you please... I can get the key for you... All I need is your loyalty... Your promise that you will aid me in bringing down my enemies."

Silence fell for a moment. Then, out of the depths of the lava came a laugh that sounded like a thousand hissing snakes. "You? What does a measly human like you have over the power of six infamous warlocks?"

I swallowed my pride. I could have summoned *Cana Dei* straight from the Ghost Realm and ended Apopis right there. But instead, I needed him for my plans.

"I have something that they don't have... Something that changes everything."

The giant snake demon cocked his head. "Really? And what is that?"

The power now burned inside my hand, as if knowing it was ready to reveal itself. I opened my palm in front of me and looked down at the brown symbol of the ankh burned into the skin. Then, I turned the palm towards Apopis, and with a flourish and a smile, I showed him Capitut's Brand.

ACKNOWLEDGMENTS

Thank you to everyone who has helped along the way in the journey of publishing this novel.

Special thanks to Wayne M. Scace for his editing work, and Carol Brandon for the proofreading.

I would also like to thank my family, particularly my wife Ola who does an incredible amount of work to help bring these novels into fruition. Thank you also to my mother and father for the continuing support you have given through my writing career.

I'd also like to thank my ARC team, and I would like to express my gratitude for readers for everything that you do to help grow both the indie publishing community and the world of literature at large.

THANK YOU FOR READING *"A Cat's Guide to Questing for Treasure"*. I hope that you enjoyed it and that it added value for you in your every day life.

I have written a prequel novelette to this novel entitled *"A Cat's Guide to Serving a Warlock"*, which you can download for free by signing up to my newsletter at https://chrisbehrsin.com/servingawarlock.

I send bi-monthly emails with promos, giveaways, information about new releases and news about what's going on in my life in general.

The key to open worlds is inside the belly of a dog ...

Since Max, the dog, swallowed the key to enter every dimension, the worlds are no longer safe.

Firstly, the warlocks themselves will do everything in their power to get hold of that key. That's a problem because they're both awfully powerful and awfully evil.

But they're not the only ones who want the key. A mysterious new contender has entered the realm, and if he or his lackeys get hold of the key every single one of the seven dimensions are doomed.

Which means it's once again down to Ben the Dragoncat, his dragon, and his dragon rider companions to save the day. This time, though, they have a whole load of unicorns to help out, as well as a feline cat goddess from an ancient time, not to mention the oldest and wisest fairy of them all ...

"A Cat's Guide to Travelling Through Portals" is the second book in the second Dragoncat trilogy – a series of fun and kid-friendly dragon riding adventures where not only humans befriend dragons, but cats (and a dog) too.

AVAILABLE AT MAJOR RETAILERS

www.ingramcontent.com/pod-product-compliance
Lightning Source LLC
Chambersburg PA
CBHW020752190726
48285CB00006B/1988